# To The Far Shore

À Madame
Monica Maries
en amical hommage
Négovan Pasic

Trois-Rivières
15 janvier 2010

# To The Far Shore
## Négovan Rajic

Translated by Nora Alleyn

Cormorant Books

Copyright © Négovan Rajic 2007
This edition copyright © Cormorant Books Inc. 2007

All rights reserved. No part of this publication may be reproduced, stored in a retrieval system or transmitted, in any for or by any means, without the prior written consent of the publisher or a licence from The Canadian Copyright Licensing Agency (Access Copyright). For an Access Copyright licence, visit www.accesscopyright.ca or call toll free 1.800.893.5777.

Canada Council for the Arts    Conseil des Arts du Canada

ONTARIO ARTS COUNCIL
CONSEIL DES ARTS DE L'ONTARIO

The publisher gratefully acknowledges the support of the Canada Council for the Arts and the Ontario Arts Council for its publishing program. We acknowledge the financial support of the Government of Canada through the Book Publishing Industry Development Program (BPIDP) for our publishing activities.

Printed and bound in Canada

LIBRARY AND ARCHIVES CANADA CATALOGUING IN PUBLICATION

Rajic, Négovan
[Vers l'autre rive. English]
To the far shore/Négovan Rajic; translated by Nora Alleyn.

Translation of: Vers l'autre rive.
ISBN 1-896951-82-1

1. Alleyn, Nora  II. Title.  III. Title: Vers l'autre rive. English.

PS8585.A359V4713 2007    C843'.54    C2006-901866-9

Cover design and cover photograph: Angel Guerra/Archetype
Text design: Tannice Goddard/Soul Oasis Networking
Printer: AGMV MARQUIS

CORMORANT BOOKS INC.
215 SPADINA AVENUE, STUDIO 230, TORONTO, ON CANADA M5T 2C7
www.cormorantbooks.com

*This book would not have been possible, at least not in its present form, without the kind assistance of my friends Madeleine Laval and Clément Marchand who were willing to read the manuscript of a perpetual student of the French language. I wish to convey to them my deepest appreciation for their generosity.*

*To Milenko and all the other
freedom-loving pilgrims*

## Contents

I    A Summer With No Clouds   1
Or a Farewell to Arms

II    The Return to Belgrade   37

III    A Bleak Autumn   59

IV    The Abyss   103

V    The Die Is Cast   131

VI    Pilgrimage to Prizren   163

VII    The Round of Farewells   181

VIII    Yesteryear's Landscapes   197

IX    Adieu Belgrade   229

X    The Border   255

*Who will revive the past? Who will defend its martyrs, felled by bullets? Is this not why we are here?*

—VLADIMIR JANKÉLÉVITCH

# A Summer With No Clouds or A Farewell to Arms

*Time, beyond recall, has fled.*
*The hour is drawing to a close.*
— PAUL-JEAN TOULET

*A garrison is a dull place in peacetime.*
— CARSON McCULLERS

MY LAST MONTHS in Niš — I was still in the army — were the worst since I had joined up in October 1944. That autumn, through a string of extraordinary circumstances, I joined the Partisans under the command of Captain Boško. We were stationed near Užice, a town in the mountains of Western Serbia, and the birthplace of my father.

The army was hardly a summer camp, but as long as we were ready to die without a whimper, discipline in the garrison was minimal. Both the officers and non-commissioned officers turned a blind eye to our peccadilloes. The rough lodgings and plain food forced us to improvise to make the overcrowded conditions more tolerable. For us, the 1945 Armistice marked the end of an adventurous, almost bohemian existence. Garrison life, by contrast, turned out to be excruciatingly boring. The army became a machine for churning out mindless regulations and endless drills. I can still hear the drill-sergeant barking out his commands: *right, left ... right, left ... right, left ...* Worse yet, life was returning to normal and we were being left out of it.

Shreds of memory survive from that time, but the chronology of events grows foggier and foggier, in the same way that faces fade in old photos. Still, certain images persist and remain amazingly sharp.

The summer of 1945 remained cloudless for days on end. Then a sudden downpour would freshen the air temporarily. For an hour or two, the barracks courtyard turned to mud and the Nišava River swirled by, silt-laden. When the sun broke through again, the paved streets of Niš dried out in patches. Two days later, the clay along the riverbanks would crack into spidery patterns.

The hours limped along, filled with rounds of fatigue duties and dull ideological indoctrination sessions held in a classroom with desperately blank walls. Our minds and our bodies would succumb to the sweltering heat. The blank-faced commissar would drone on, reading aloud the latest speech by the Grand Master of the Keys, known to a small group of insiders as Tito — a troublemaker and an unprincipled nabob who had emerged as the strongman from the murky events of the Second World War.

The speeches, meant to be edifying, invariably started with: *Comrades, I think ...* Was he about to say: *therefore I am?* No. This boor had never even heard of Descartes. So what was he going on about? Mostly he expatiated on the past and the future, rarely on the present: On how, before the war, our country was so poor, and then the Germans invaded and destroyed what little we had. As for the future, he said it beckoned like an enchanted land. Tomorrow, the Tower of Babel, built by our worthy people, would reach into the heavens. The only snag: the enemies of the people. They had to be flushed out and crushed like vermin.

We were often subjected to theories hatched more than a century before by a pedantic German philosopher living in exile in London. Our poor commissar. He had to wrestle with these badly digested concepts, which made him look like the demon thrashing around in holy water. History was reduced to its simplest terms: after primitive communism, slavery, feudalism and capitalism, humanity was edging towards the magic Land of Plenty, towards an era of geometric Justice. And that was how History would end.

During these lectures the soldiers — poor devils, yanked out of their fields by the war — would yawn till their jaws nearly came unhinged. Had the commissar announced the Apocalypse for tomorrow, they would have continued to stare at him vacant-eyed.

One day, a large irreverent housefly disrupted the scene. Buzzing and circling around our instructor, the fly afforded a welcome distraction. I couldn't help smiling — and was severely reprimanded. Slowly but surely the army was turning us into morons.

༄

I had lived through so much since that dark, moonless night of October 2, 1944 when I crawled along a muddy riverbank to escape from the besieged city of Užice. During that fateful year, when the destiny of so many European countries was sucked into the maelstrom of History, the war was drawing to a close. The Third Reich was in its death throes, but the Great Paranoiac, hiding in his wolf's lair, his *Wolfsschanze* in Eastern Prussia, was high on Wagner's *Götterdämmerung*. He kept hoping that his secret weapons would save him, just as Empress

Elisabeth Petrovna's death saved Frederic the Great from the Russian invasion of 1762.

It was game over in the Balkans by autumn 1944. The last German divisions were pulling out of Greece. In Serbia, the Allies followed some obscure geo-political strategy: they abandoned the Nationalist Resistance forces to support the Grand Master of the Keys and his Partisans. Night after night, airplanes would parachute arms and munitions to his troops, enabling him eventually to seize power.

In the end, everyone pursued their own agenda. Some were running after glory while others believed in the justice of their cause. As for myself, I can't explain why I joined the Grand Master's Partisans who were fighting around Užice. I knew I wanted to be a part of the history that was unfolding around me. Was it vanity on my part? Or a spirit of adventure? Death-wish, or a desire to feel truly alive? To see clearly into one's soul is not easy.

An old slight also pushed me to join the Partisans. An elderly woman had once remarked to me: "Your grandmother Jelena was lucky. Her three sons wore glasses. They all came back from the war while my only son was killed during the battle of Cer." Her words rankled for a long time. So I belonged to a family that refused to spill its blood? Was I being overly sensitive? The only way I could rid myself of guilt was by enlisting.

We all had to choose sides in this triangular war between the guerilla troops of the Nationalist Resistance led by General Mihajlović, the Partisans led by the Grand Master of the Keys, and the German army. Each side wanted to see the other two bleed to death. The Nationalist Resistance Movement, with its slogan "For King and country," had a theatrical ring to it whereas the Partisans were convinced they possessed the truth.

In these troubled times, the future was very unpredictable. If I hesitated, I would miss the war.

So I made the leap and found myself in a detachment of Partisans commanded by Captain Boško. However, in my heart of hearts, I swore I would never fire on General Mihajlović's troops even if it meant being killed. The only time my company engaged in a skirmish with them, I slipped away, claiming I had a slight wound to my left leg.

In several clashes with the German occupying forces, I managed to cheat death. I was convinced that some unknown force was protecting me. Whenever we attacked an enemy position, I would run, not from the Germans but from my own cowardice. Sometimes the coward rises up against his own cowardice. My superiors saw this as devotion to the Master Design. They suggested I join the Party. An inner voice whispered to me to avoid those in power, so I refused.

My brief war experience ended the night of December 18, 1944. That day, the Second Company of the Second Battalion entered the liberated town of Užice. One week earlier, the Allies had rained bombs down on the city. Charred beams like broad strokes of charcoal lay amidst the snowy ruins of the town.

We marched into a sleepy neighbourhood in single file. With our mismatched uniforms, we looked more like an army in flight than the victors. People opened their windows and doors to greet us and ask about their loved ones. Ten minutes later, I found myself standing in front of my family's house. I was stunned. A bomb had blown away the facade, and you could see the furniture in the room. The building looked like a doll house with its Lilliputian furniture.

I climbed to the first floor and found my Aunt Elisabeth and the faithful Klara safe and sound. The apartment no longer had a living room. When I opened the door, I found myself staring into space. The wall on the street side no longer existed. Nor did the floor. Snow was falling softly onto the debris of beams and parquet. Luckily, the other rooms were habitable. The bathroom was also intact. When I entered its steamy atmosphere, I appreciated the cult of the *hammam*, the Turkish steam bath. Divesting myself of my flea-infested clothes, I plunged into my first bath after three months of exhausting marches and sleeping on straw pallets. My stomach and legs were covered with tiny red bites. I wanted to spend the rest of my life luxuriating in the tub. Such bliss to slip into clean sheets and pyjamas. It was a strange night. Beech logs crackled in the great tile stove and a soft warmth permeated the room. Nothing seemed to have changed, yet all I had to do was open the livingroom door to feel December's bite and see the snow falling on Ljubica Street.

In the hallway stood the old cupboard with the curious painted face. During my childhood this piece of furniture had been in our country house, and it used to keep me awake at night. Glimpsed in the faint light of the bedroom, the bearded face would make me feel anxious — and compassionate. My imagination identified the face as that of Judas, condemned to expiate his betrayal of Christ until Judgment Day. In the morning, when the light returned, I would pluck up my courage and peek into the cupboard. Inside, there was only my grandmother Jelena's Sunday outfit. She had died just a few weeks before I was born.

Before falling asleep, I let my thoughts wander. The next day was the Orthodox feast day of St. Nicholas, my family's guardian since time immemorial. Centuries ago, one of my ancestors converted to Christianity and adopted St. Nicholas as his patron saint. Before the war, when my mother was still alive, we would celebrate his feast day with friends.

My thoughts strayed to my father. I had had little news of him except that the Gestapo had released him, in poor health, just before the German army's retreat from Belgium. He probably knew nothing about what was going on in my life.

⌇

During this winter of war, a brief love affair left me with a bittersweet aftertaste.

At the beginning of December, I took advantage of a short leave from the Second Division, temporarily stationed in the village of Varda. The gently rolling countryside slept under its blanket of snow. It was almost midnight. With my rifle slung over my shoulder and my kit on my back, I set out under a full moon, and walked along a little path that followed the meandering of a frozen river. On either side, trees stretched out their gaunt branches. The cold was starting to penetrate my bones. The long trek from Varda was almost over.

A warm fire, a roof, and maybe a dish of polenta were awaiting me in a large villa that rose up like a Scottish castle on its promontory, with the little river at its feet. Before the war, this luxurious dwelling had belonged to a wealthy lawyer. Looted and plundered by successive waves of transients, it now sheltered a merry band of young artists. They performed in a nearby market town. They sang, danced and put on plays for the soldiers, who, on returning from the front, were anxious to rid themselves of fleas and grab a few days' respite. At one time I also had been a member of the troupe, but had left in a fit of temper.

Suddenly, I became aware of strange noises coming from a small hill above the road. Bang! ... Bang! ... Bang! ... Someone was hammering on an empty barrel. At least that was what it sounded like, but why at this hour of the night? Without knowing why, I started to climb the path running up the hillside and found fresh tracks left by mysterious night visitors. Gradually, the mystery was revealed. At the top of the rise was a small abandoned-looking cemetery with dilapidated fences and leaning headstones. A scattering of pines stood guard. Four men, their faces lit by a storm lantern, were standing near a pile of freshly turned earth. Bang! ... Bang! ... Bang! ... A fifth man, down on one knee, was hammering nails into a coffin. After he finished, the men lowered it into the grave. You could hear the rope rubbing against the wooden sides, followed by the dull thud of clumps of frozen earth. I quickly retraced my steps, having no wish to meet these nocturnal gravediggers. Nevertheless, I was intrigued by the death of this unknown person. Was it an enemy of the people, a deserter, or one of our soldiers killed at the front? And if it was a soldier, why had they not fired a salute?

These questions continued to haunt me as I crossed the threshold of the villa, the solitary structure in the landscape. The warm air inside filled me with an animal happiness. In the empty rooms stripped of furniture, the boys and girls of the troupe were fast asleep on straw pallets. In the great hall, a young teacher, a recent graduate, was waiting for me by the fireplace where a good fire was burning. The firelight played on her pure fresh face framed by ash-blonde hair. Moved by this dreamlike vision, I launched into a lengthy and lyrical flight of fancy, expounding on love and the brevity of human existence. She and I were soon re-inventing the world.

A mere two hours by foot from this solitary villa, in No Man's Land, shivering sentries busily scanned the wintry horizon. At times, a rocket would shoot up and slowly descend, shedding a sinister green light over the snow. The staccato bark of a machine gun would disrupt the silence, and then all would be still again. Thanatos, disguised as a hoary old man, was lurking nearby, invisible, and hard at work.

Is that why we felt so transported by Eros during this night stolen from war and death? I tried, with the magic of words, to create the sense that we were sailing towards some imaginary Cythera, far from the villa and the mysterious gravesite on the hillside. The embers were dying when our brief idyll was sealed by a kiss. It left me with the bittersweet taste of an unfinished dream.

Early the next morning, I set off for Varda to rejoin the Second Company of the Second Battalion. The intense cold and bruising shoulder straps soon snapped me out of my lovesickness. As I passed the hill with the abandoned cemetery, I thought about the strange night-time burial and the five mysterious gravediggers. Who were they and how many more anonymous graves were salted away in our countryside?

The two months following my return to Užice passed in a surreal atmosphere. Neither soldier nor civilian, I slept at the house and went skiing on my Aunt Elisabeth's property with a rifle on my shoulder. This left me plenty of time to go courting. Inevitably, the memory of that romantic night by the fireside slowly faded. In any case, the young teacher had set her heart on a tall blond fellow, a hero of the Resistance. At a dinner dance one evening, she reproached me for inviting her to spin to a waltz because I was keeping her from the arms of her great blond lover. Ah, Love was not the cosmic adventure I had thought it was.

I was making rapid progress in my understanding of life. Or was this simply the delusion of a philosopher — or that of a prig? I didn't doubt that the future was about to project me into new adventures of mind and body.

I continued to stride down the streets of Užice with my Browning Automatic in its black holster. Some people must have thought I was still in the army. In the general confusion, nobody knew whether I still belonged to the Second Company or if Captain Boško had given me leave. My situation began to feel somewhat precarious. The fighting continued to rage on the Syrmian Plain and in Bosnia. It no longer felt right to be having a good time when young people were coming back crippled or not at all.

In February 1945, Providence sent me my distant cousin, Efrem Popovič. He was now a lieutenant colonel and political commissar of the 47th Division stationed not far from the little town of Ćuprija. He suggested to my cousin Dimitri and me that we enlist in his division, a ragtag band of soldiers as we soon discovered. From February to April 1945, we lived in Ćuprija and Jagodina, two small towns in Serbia. When his division was disbanded, we were sent to the front.

Life and death were strictly a matter of chance. By a stroke of luck, my cousin and I were able to ride out the war. Many students from Belgrade were not so fortunate. In October 1944, when the fate of our country was hanging by a thread, they were dispatched to a bloodbath on the Syrmian front two hundred kilometres west of Belgrade. Many were mowed down by German machine guns. The Third Reich was nearing defeat but a mortally wounded beast can still attack.

Had the Party deliberately used the children of the bourgeoisie as cannon fodder, as some claimed? We will probably never know, but true or not, the officers sent to the Pannonian Plain had been trained as guerillas in the mountains and lacked any experience of trench warfare.

In the spring of 1945, when we received the order to join

the 21st Serbian shock troops, the end of the conflict was only weeks, or days, away. The front was moving like wildfire towards Zagreb, capital of the short-lived independent Croatian state. For us, these famous shock troops were like a figment of someone's imagination. We tried in vain to catch up with them. By the time we arrived by train from Jagodina to Vinkovci, they were already moving across Slavonia; by the time we finally found ourselves marching under the blazing sun on the dusty roads of this picturesque province, they were already near the Austrian border in trucks captured from the *Wehrmacht*.

On the evening of May 8, 1945, we stopped trying to catch up with them. The Second World War was over. It had begun to the sound of band music on September 1, 1939 with a *sondermeldung*, a special message announcing Hitler's attack on Poland. In Belgrade, we had paid scant attention, as if this attack were happening on another planet. Race cars were backfiring around the old fortress of Kalemegdan. Our jubilant capital was proud to be holding its first car race. To commemorate the event, the Yugoslav post office had printed a series of stamps. Two thousand and seventy-five days later, the Third Reich, supposed to last a thousand years, was no more. This is a fitting subject for meditation on the impermanence of empires and the vanity of their founders.

The news of the Armistice caught up with us in a little Slavonian town, after having completed a full day's march. We were exhausted. The railway network had been destroyed. As they retreated, the German army had hitched a huge ploughshare to a locomotive and dragged it over the railway tracks, splintering the ties like matchsticks. Their destructive genius was commensurate with their creative genius.

On May 8, 1945, the head of our column entered Djhakovica, a small medieval town. The dark mass of its cathedral towered above the peaked roofs of the houses, a startling sight in this market town. Its soaring steeple mirrored in stone the crazy dream of a nineteenth-century Croatian bishop who had wanted to unite all the Slavs of the south into a single state. The scene resembled an antique etching of the sun setting fire to the Western sky.

Suddenly, we heard shots coming from town. Was it an ambush? Soldiers were running up to meet us, gesticulating and shouting: "The war is over ... the war is over!" Overcome with emotion, we too started shooting into the air, hooting and shouting and hugging one another. All over Europe the same gesture was repeated.

Behind us, on the Syrmian Plain, bodies were piled into the common graves of Kragujevaùc, Bajica, Krčagovo. Men, women, the elderly and children had had their throats slit in the Orthodox church of Glina. Many who survived the war would die soon after, their bodies mangled, their lips chapped with thirst.

Those of us who had survived rejoiced because we still had our legs, our arms, our eyes. We could walk and shake hands. We could see the streets and the forests. For us, tomorrow had meaning again. In a few weeks or months, we would shuck off our rags and guns and sleep in clean beds. Once again I would go dancing in Zlatibor. The waltzes and tangos would ring out in the streets of Užice to the annoyance of our neighbours. What did we care? We would take back the night. I would twirl with a beautiful girl in my arms under the soft light of the lanterns. The next morning, she and I would walk among the trees of the Great Park and we would embrace to our hearts' content.

One day in July, I boarded an old train that rattled its way out of the town of Niš. The hot air came rushing in through the windows and the filthy curtains fluttered in the breeze. By two in the afternoon, the heat was as oppressive on the plain we were jolting across as it had been on the city pavement. The sun had scorched the orchards and the stubbled fields. In the distance, grapes were ripening in the vineyards. At times we would pass a house with its shutters closed. The residents were probably having a siesta. Lucky people. I unbuttoned the collar of my woolen tunic — regulations be damned — and watched the landscape go by. Despite the heat, I was content to escape the dreariness of the barracks.

I had been granted special leave to visit the infamous Tower of Skulls. From the time we were in grade school, teachers had been dinning stories into our heads about this monument. In 1804, a ragged army of Serbian peasants and beggars had rebelled against the Turkish sultan's troops over the humiliations inflicted on them. After an initial success, the uprising ground to a halt in the spring of 1809. A detachment of this motley crew had besieged the Turkish garrison in Niš but had overestimated their strength. On the last day of May, the Ottoman troops streamed out of the fortress and hacked their attackers to pieces. Stevan Sindjelić, commander of the Serbian army, seeing that the battle was lost, allowed the enemy soldiers to approach the powder magazine which he then ignited. The explosion and fire had killed defenders and besiegers alike.

The Turks erected a macabre tower made of the severed heads of the rebels on the side of the road to Istanbul. The tower was intended to serve as a warning to the *roumis* (Christians) should they be tempted to rise up again against the Sublime Porte, the government of the Ottoman Empire. But the Serbs, thirsting for freedom, had not yet learned their lesson, and six years later, the *raïa,* or guerilla troops, rebelled anew. Fighting with rusty old guns and cannons made from the trunks of cherry trees, they succeeded in wresting some measure of independence from the Turks.

Getting off the train, I saw a monument topped by a chapel-like structure but without a cross. The interior was in ruins. A deathlike silence reigned. The bones and plaster gave off an acrid odour. What many of us had imagined as a powerful dungeon turned out to be a small square tower barely four metres high. Originally, there had been 952 scalped heads, but some of the cavities were now empty. Women would come, from far and near, to scrape the plaster and the skulls in order to concoct a fertility potion, in the belief that the bones of their dead heroes could engender new life.

I was the only visitor. I walked around the strange ruin and discovered a black stone commemorating the visit of Alphonse de Lamartine. The inscription, in French and Serbian, read thus:

> "... may this monument endure! It will teach children the value of independence by showing them the awful price paid by their forefathers."
>
> — LAMARTINE, JULY 1833

Standing there, I tried to picture the poet's stagecoach coming to a standstill in a cloud of dust in front of the Tower of Skulls and the traveller from France alighting to examine the tragic structure. In his *Voyage en Orient*, he referred to it as the "cornerstone of Serbian independence."

What curious people these Serbs are. Instead of destroying this sinister tower, it was preserved so they could mortify themselves in perpetuity. The French would never consider inscribing the names of Bérézina or Waterloo inside their Arc de Triomphe.

Why had the people of Serbia chosen to commemorate their dead so conspicuously and morbidly? A Wuthering Heights of history. At least they could have moved the tower to a more isolated spot. Frederic Barbarossa's crusades had passed by here on their way to the Holy Land, and the Ottomans used the route on their way north to lay siege to Vienna.

I might have stayed longer, reflecting on our people's destiny in front of these skulls with their empty eye sockets, but I had to be back at the barracks, located inside the very fortress that the Serbs had attacked so many years ago, before five o'clock.

The train rattled its way back to Niš. Alphonse de Lamartine had awakened memories of my stay in Paris during the 1937 World's Fair. On July 1 of that year, I had disembarked from the train at Lyon Station where I was met by Madame Laval and her daughter Madeleine, a lovely blonde who had just passed her exam to become a German teacher. We descended into the bowels of the subway: long tiled corridors, trains thundering in and out of the tunnels, and crowds hurrying towards unknown destinations — I was stunned by all of the bustle. The city was an immense hive of activity. In comparison, Belgrade seemed like a small provincial town.

My father had sent me to France to learn the language. He secretly hoped that I would choose a diplomatic career. In any case, French would always be useful. While boarding at Madame Levi's on Rue Monbel, I enjoyed walking around the pavilions of the World's Fair and visiting the museums. A veritable passion to explore every corner of the capital took hold of me: I would leave the house after breakfast and only come home for supper. A fascinating world had opened up around me. Along the grand boulevards, the street vendors with their sales pitches for ties and cheap fountain pens intrigued me.

The French spoke with incredible eloquence. Two or three times they cheated me, but eventually I discovered their secret by watching the shills who pretended to buy a necktie or a pen in order to encourage the onlookers to do the same. In a cutlery shop on the Boulevard des Italiens, opposite the Gaumont Theatre, the world's greatest movie house, a man pretending to be a robot mesmerized me. At the end of two months, I returned to Belgrade, convinced that one day I would go back to Paris to continue my education.

I woke from my reverie as the train reached the city. I got off in front of the officers' club and headed for the citadel. The gunners' barracks seemed more mournful than usual.

On the street between the citadel and the main street stood an old palace. Its marble ornaments bore witness to more prosperous times, but it was now falling into ruin: its steps cracked, the walls flaking, and the huge windows bare. The building had a sinister aura. The shabby building housed the Youth Corps, boys still all in their teens, most of them war orphans. At times, they would go on a pub-crawl in Niš. Their laughter made my blood run cold. Rumour had it that they had helped execute prisoners. This did not seem far-fetched for some of their faces revealed the cruelty of seasoned soldiers.

A sentry armed with a submachine gun stood guard. He had a striking face. During the war, I had learned to spot those who had killed defenseless men. The signs were unmistakable: shifty eyes, vacant minds, a glint of pain in their eyes. They often appeared to be conversing with ghosts. Were they seeing the spirits of those they had murdered? Despite their youth, they resembled mature men wearing apprentice executioners' masks to cover their oftentimes still beardless faces.

Who was responsible for them? Was it the fault of the men beholden to the Grand Master's Master Design for Yugoslavia who were inciting these youngsters to crime, enforcing obedience to the new order through bloodshed?

It was around this time that the idea of living in a divided world came to me. One part was visible, and consisted of professional revolutionaries, heroes of the Serbian National Resistance, who were the first wave of guerilla fighters. Then came the Partisans and all the others: generals weighted down by medals, puppet representatives of the people, unilingual diplomats, journalists who claimed the right over life and death, janitors who watched over every building and who in turn were spied on by other informants, and the list went on. Every day we were bombarded with well-meaning and edifying speeches intended to teach us about our imperfections.

But beyond this visible world lurked a secret and subterranean one and from time to time, fissures opened up allowing us to catch a glimpse of it.

After seeing these prematurely old faces of the Youth Corps, my suspicions were confirmed by the arrival in Niš in August 1945 of Slobodan Penezić, head of the powerful secret police.

I first met Slobodan Penezić back in 1941. War had just broken out in Russia and North Africa, and in Serbia, where an insurrection against the occupying army had resulted in a bloodbath. The flag of an undefined Red Republic was raised in Užice, recently liberated by the Nationalist Resistance fighters. On November 22, at two in the afternoon, the city and the surrounding hills shook with a dull explosion. An underground arms factory had just been bombed. From my Aunt Elisabeth's house, we could see a thick black cloud slowly rising in the cold autumn air. I ran like someone demented and found myself fifteen minutes later at the underground factory. I joined a group of young people taking turns activating an archaic hand pump, which would have made a lovely collector's piece in a firemen's museum. It served no real purpose. Everyone in the factory's tunnels was killed.

I first saw Slobodan Penezić as he was aiming an automatic pistol at the crowd. His faded-blue eyes feverishly scanned the people who had started to assemble. Some of the workers' wives were already crying. The man with the pistol looked at them, and then at the thick black smoke gushing out of the tunnel. The throng was growing by the minute. Was there a spy or a saboteur among them? Tall, thin, with the pallor of a consumptive, and wrapped in his long officer's cape, Slobodan Penezić resembled a caricature of a Russian revolutionary from the 1800s.

The circumstances of our meeting in Niš were less dramatic, almost friendly. He had come to the city to attend a meeting of the secret police. He had also expressed the wish to visit the surrounding area. One August afternoon, several of us were ordered to the hall of the officers' mess. Towards two o'clock, a door opened and Slobodan entered, as thin and pale as ever. Through the half-opened door, we could see the officers, their collars unbuttoned, chatting over their fruit and cheese.

We had a cordial talk with Slobodan. After a lunch not lacking in alcohol, he was in an excellent mood. We exchanged pleasantries, and mentioned people we knew in common in Užice. Occasionally, he would peer at us as if trying to read our deepest thoughts. It gave me the shivers. Standing before this guardian of revolutionary rectitude, few of us felt above suspicion. Luckily, we were small fry. Despite our forced smiles, the man probably had no illusions. No one liked him. The solitude of an exterminating angel must be immense. Was he hopeful that one day the whole world would finally be delivered from evil, so that the survivors could love one another like brothers? After ten minutes of fitful conversation, Slobodan Penezić dismissed us, as one would dismiss a servant, and returned to his official meeting. His expression sent a shudder down my spine; for once the heat outside felt quite bearable.

༄

Why pretend? My sense of living in a dual world stemmed from an inability to fall into step with what was happening all around me. Had I been a member of the Communist Party, I may have had a more optimistic outlook on life. Twice my friends gave me the opportunity to join the inner circle of the initiated, and twice I had the impertinence to refuse.

The first opportunity came in Užice on a dull November day in 1944. Evening was darkening into night and a grey sky was threatening snow. The war was only twenty kilometres away, the room was cozy with a good fire crackling in the cast-iron stove. *Carpe diem* — sieze the day, seize the moment. We had learned how to do this.

"If you become a member of the Party, you could take over the political training of my dispatch riders and remain at division headquarters. Why risk being killed when the war is almost over?" asked Captain Boško.

His concern was touching, but his offer caught me unawares.

"But I believe in God!"

"Ah!"

To brandish one's belief in God to avoid joining the Party was tantamount to blasphemy. The captain looked at me as if I were the last living specimen of a race on the road to extinction.

"You might keep that to yourself," he said.

The era of the catacombs was back. We had to keep God buried in the galleries of our conscience.

Our conversation ended there, rather awkwardly. With hindsight, I realise that the captain had just betrayed the Party.

The situation was quite different in Niš. I was approached by one of those creeps who, once the war was over, suddenly discovered their vocation as revolutionaries. With a conspiratorial look, he asked me to meet him in the basement of the First Army's headquarters. I knew what was coming, and even the phrasing he would use to approach the subject.

"Comrade, you're an honest man. Your place is in the Party!"

I almost burst out laughing, and was on the verge of replying: "No, comrade, I'm not an honest man, I am deceitful and wicked and, anyhow, the honest men are all in prison." Apparently, the Party needed a few innocent suckers to regain a sheen of some respectability. Instead I answered: "No, comrade, I can't become a member. I don't agree with some of Marx's theories."

I had probably never voiced such a foolish argument in my whole life. The sergeant, stunned by the enormity of my comments, was struck dumb. A simple grunt in the signals battalion had dared to disagree with "God." And I didn't even know what I was talking about. In high school I had tried hard to read *Das Kapital*, but had given up. Marx's arguments were just too tedious and abstruse.

The sergeant didn't insist. Instead of saying goodbye, his last words were: "You asked for it, comrade!"

So far, they had nothing against me, but they could keep me in the army long enough for me to miss registration at the university. I lost sleep at the thought of spending a whole winter doing fatigue duty in the gunners' barracks.

My fate as a rebel and a nomad was probably sealed on that day.

༄

The sudden appearance of Milenko, my old school friend, broke the monotony of those cloudless summer days, and lifted my morale. We had met in the autumn of 1934 at the beginning of the school year, and since then our shared interests and tastes had made us close friends. He arrived in Niš with the staff of the First Army. Working as a radio repair technician, he enjoyed prestige and privileges that he would not otherwise have been entitled to as a lowly private. All because of his expertise in electronics, which had been his passion since the age of thirteen. It had started when he built a crystal set. With his endless patience and curiosity, he had accumulated enough knowledge to repair the clandestine transmitters of the Resistance. This highly dangerous activity might have cost him his life, for the Gestapo did not deal lightly with people like Milenko.

He became head repairman in the First Army's workshop. Since the autumn of 1944, Milenko had been living like a pasha. In Niš I found him installed in a plush villa overlooking the city. From his room he could walk out into a vineyard lush with lovely amber grapes. Compared to my workshop-dormitory where five of us were crammed into small quarters, he lived in indecent luxury.

We enjoyed chatting about all kinds of things, but especially about our dreams of going to university. He told me, with a certain justifiable pride, that the army had offered him a scholarship to study at Lomonosov University in Moscow. Unfortunately, he had made the mistake of expressing his preference for an American university, and as a result, he never received any scholarship, not even for Belgrade University. The intrinsic value of a human being no longer had value: only the Master Design counted.

Much to my regret, Milenko did not stay long in Niš. He was demobilized just three weeks after our reunion.

⁂

Ten days later, my cousin Dimitri was also demobilized, and more than happy to get back to Belgrade. Since Ćuprija, we had always been in the same division, and his departure now deepened my sense of isolation. Like the other students who were serving in the army, I was champing at the bit, anxious to recover my freedom and to resume my studies. During the German Occupation, all institutions of higher learning were shut down. We Serbs were not allowed to receive an education. In Belgrade, I couldn't bear to walk by the imposing building that formerly housed the School of Engineering, now transformed into the *Kriegslazarett*, the German military hospital, without feeling enormous frustration. The sight of the sentry going back and forth in front of the hospital's sharp-tipped fence filled me with hatred for this soldier, as if the poor devil were personally trying to prevent me from entering the faculty.

The air was rife with demobilisation rumours. Priority would be given to those whose studies had been interrupted by the war. At other times, priority shifted to those who had been the first to enlist. By the end of August a new rumour was making the rounds; those who were temporarily unfit for active duty would be the first to be demobilized. The wording was vague. Why "temporarily?" If one eventually recovered and was considered fit would one be recalled? The news triggered an epidemic of maladies more or less imaginary: allergies became full-blown, eczema flowered, ankles hurt and flat feet multiplied. As for myself, I was myopic. For once, this disability might come in handy. Unwisely, I rushed to see my commanding officer.

"Comrade Commissar, as someone suffering from myopia, I am unfit for duty, therefore eligible for demobilisation."

The comrade commissar smiled in a friendly fashion. "Wait a minute, comrade! Not so fast! Who will give me my French lessons?"

I had totally forgotten. I might be useless in an army during peacetime, but I was useful as a tutor for our brave commissar. A shoemaker by trade, he was taking courses to earn his baccalaureate. The army not only distributed promotions, but also diplomas. These French lessons were my revenge for the insipid ideological courses I was forced to take, for when I sat beside the commissar and read: "Here is a pencil ... this pencil is red," I became his superior. Eventually he must have realised that learning a language was a more serious matter than reciting the Grand Master's nonsense.

"But, Comrade Commissar, let's suppose that during battle I break my glasses, how will I aim?"

"Don't be a smart aleck! You know as well as I do there won't be a war, at least not for another ten or fifteen years. By then, you'll be demobilized and if there is another war you'll be able to guard the bridges."

The commissar said this laughingly, happy to have countered my argument. I could choose to take his comments lightly. But the prospect of being forgotten in the army worried me. I left determined to reiterate my request.

The next day, I registered for an eye exam. With my myopia and astigmatism, the thing was in the bag. At first, everything went well. In the darkness of the ophthalmologist's office, the brightly lit letters flipped by: K, Z, M ... The doctor kept changing the lenses. After the exam, he handed me a prescription for a new pair of glasses. And that is when I bungled.

"Am I temporarily unfit?"

"Oh no! Your vision is now 100%. You are totally fit."

To avoid any ambiguity, he asked me for the prescription and wrote: "Complete correction, fit for active duty."

What a fool I was! I called myself by all sorts of names, but of course that would change absolutely nothing. How could I have made such a stupid remark?

Two days later, coming into the barracks and feeling somewhat depressed, I ran into Bazil, a medical student and an old acquaintance from high school days. He was also in the army, in the sanitary services according to the label on his uniform jacket. We exchanged pleasantries and I told him about my aborted attempt to be discharged.

"You should have spoken to me first, old bean! You have to have a different approach, but don't worry, I'll fix it for you."

"How?"

"Let two weeks go by, just long enough for the doctor to forget your face, and then go back for another eye examination. And bring me the medical certificate afterwards. And don't say anything to anybody. I'll take care of the rest."

I was hopeful, but the two weeks seemed endless, like a long day without water. Finally one afternoon I climbed the staircase of the First Army's ophthalmology clinic. Would the commander remember me? Would he suspect some kind of trickery?

When it was my turn, he invited me to sit on the stool as if there were nothing unusual. In the darkness, the letters followed one another and shrunk in descending lines. These were decisive minutes. Could the doctor hear my heart beat? I recited the letters one by one, and suddenly the idea came to me to appear more nearsighted than I actually was. I made so bold as to say that I could no longer distinguish the letters when, in actual fact, I could read them perfectly. At the fourth line, I began to stutter.

I cheated, but my conscience was easy. My years at war had taught me how to be crafty, only, I must not have been doing a very good job because the doctor played with the corrective lenses, and perhaps caught on to my game. I became confused, no longer sure whether I should be reading the lines on the board with the lenses he held up to me. I've always been a poor liar.

Speaking in neutral tones, he said: "And do you see better this way? And now, try to read the fifth line."

When the light came back on, he looked at me straight in the eye. I was wearing gold-rimmed glasses. To have the appearance of an intellectual was a serious defect in those days. Did he sense my desire to quit the army? He wrote down my dioptre: oculus dexter less four, oculus sinister less four and a half. I had gained one dioptre for each eye. I can still see the doctor's thin face and swarthy complexion. His eyes looked right through me, as if to say: *Young man, I am not fooled by your trick, but* ... He handed me the paper.

I went down the stairs two by two and ran straight to the Medsanbat. Bazil was my last chance. I repeated like a mantra: *To the Medsanbat ... to the Medsanbat ...* and strangely, for the first time since I had joined the 21st Division, I realised the meaning of this abbreviation: medical and sanitary battalion. What a strange world. Ideas and thoughts shrunk into slogans. The names of institutions had all become acronyms. The Department of Propaganda had become Agitprop, the Central Committee the CC, the Political Bureau the Politburo and so on.

Bazil reassured me. With a little luck, everything would be fine. According to him, in a few days time I would be called up before the medical commission who would probably proclaim me "provisionally unfit." I hung onto this idea with a mixture of hope and despair. I was increasingly alone since the end of August, and time felt oppressive. Every day I would hear of so-and-so being demobilized. The faces of the Belgrade students were disappearing one by one. My cousin Dimitri's departure made my solitude in Niš even more painful. The thought of spending the winter sweeping out the workshop, firing up the cast-iron stove, and serving as the factotum of the technicians who were secretly delighted to have a university graduate under their orders, exasperated me to no end.

On September 15, the schools re-opened, a sign that summer had ended. The first rains of autumn moved in. There were fewer people along the *corso* and the *café* owners brought in their tables and chairs. There was nothing for me to do but bide my time, sing the blues, and wait for the commission to call me in.

Finally, on September 27, I received a summons to present myself the following day at ten o'clock at the Medsanbat. I asked to see the Commissar so he would sign my leave. He scolded me for not following the normal channels, but as he didn't want to seem nasty, he signed my leave. At this juncture, the smallest *faux pas* could wreck my plans.

The following morning, at a quarter to ten, I showed up promptly at the Medsanbat, an old one-storey building probably requisitioned from an enemy of the people. My nerves were frayed. I couldn't stay put so I walked up and down the grey-tiled corridor, alternately sitting on a bench and then pacing. The commission was sitting behind a great white door. Bazil, in his capacity as secretary, kept coming out to call up the next person. When he saw me, he reassured me that the doctor was on our side. As for the other two officers, there was nothing to worry about. They were not very bright. However, despite his reassurances, I was still very anxious. It can be tricky dealing with such people.

To control my nervousness, I tried to occupy my mind with something else. Seated opposite me was a soldier in his thirties. His whole head was nothing but a festering wound. He was in very bad shape. His eyes had such a look of resignation, of suffering and animal sadness. It was obvious that he had no more expectations. Seeing him made me ashamed of my little scheme to get myself demobilized. But at the same time I was angry. Why had this man not been demobilized a long time ago, or at the very least sent to a hospital? Did the people's army need to hold onto such human wrecks?

Finally, the big white door opened. My turn had come. Bazil reminded me to speak as little as possible. I entered the large and almost empty room and gave a weak salute. The commission was in session behind a table covered with a white cloth. There were four men: two officers, a young doctor, and Bazil, who was taking notes.

Was this the tribunal that would seal my fate, or was it simply *avant-garde* theatre? It all seemed the same in the end. "Myopia oculus dexter less four and oculus sinister less four and a half." The doctor turned towards the officers and said:

"Provisionally unfit."

The two comrades did not seem to appreciate this diagnosis. If everyone is demobilized, who would remain to serve?

"Comrade Doctor, must we demobilize him?"

"Comrade Captain, the regulation is categorical. If an accident occurs due to myopia, we are held responsible."

"Well, in that case, we'll sign."

Phew! It was over. It was obvious that the comrade officers didn't want any problems. I left the room. Bazil joined me in the corridor.

"In two or three days, a demobilisation order will be sent down to the office of the signals battalion."

I thanked him profusely, but Bazil had little time for such effusions, he was already calling the next name. As I left the Medsanbat, I was tempted to throw my cap in the air, to dance, and to hug the first person who came along, but I managed to maintain self-control. War, and my last few months in the army, had made me careful and cunning. What if, in the end, the commissar turned out to be opposed to my demobilisation, dug his heels in, and ordered a new evaluation? You never can tell with a chain of command. It is as mysterious as the Lord's ways. Better not to think about it.

To hell with it. To celebrate my first step towards freedom, I bought myself a big piece of *burek*, a puff pastry stuffed with meat, and a bunch of grapes. Delighted with my provisions, I sat down by the Nišava River and had myself a picnic.

The muddy river flowed by lazily. Soon, it would swell with the autumn rains, but in our army camp, everything would go on as usual. Reveille would sound the beginning of the day's terrible routine: the undrinkable *ersatz* coffee made from chicory, the reports, the reading of the latest speech by Number One or Number Two, the floor sweeping and potato-peeling fatigue duty ... Poor sods! I felt for those left behind. Fortunately, I would be safely removed from the commissar's blather, unless ... unless ...

The days passed, and still my demobilisation order hadn't arrived. I walked by the company's clerk hoping that he would stop and give me the good news. September 30. Nothing. In theory, registration at the university would be over in ten days. On October 1, the daily routine dragged on, but on October 2, just as I was washing out my mess tin after the noonday meal, the company's pen-pusher approached me with a knowing smile and asked me to report to the comrade commissar's office at three o'clock. After that, everything went very quickly.

My case was proceeding well, but I had to watch myself and not speak out of turn. At ten to three, I was already waiting outside the commissar's office. He was coming back from the mess hall, apparently in high spirits. And why wouldn't he be? The food and wine were excellent, and the waiters wore white jackets and bow ties. Our comrade captain had come a long way since the days of repairing worn-out shoes in a wretched shoemaker's hole in the wall!

"Pray come in, comrade, and please take a seat."

Well, well. The commissar was being very polite. Did that mean that I was no longer under his authority?

"So, it looks as if you'll be leaving us!"

I pretended not to understand him.

"Come now ... you know perfectly well that your demobilisation order has just arrived!"

"I had nothing to do with it. It was the medical commission's decision: 'provisionally unfit.'"

This ambiguous expression, provisionally unfit, made me very nervous, but at the same time I found it pretty amusing.

"What do you mean? Stop pulling my leg," he said.

"I want to continue my education. Four long years lost because of the Occupation is a long time."

"So! You're leaving us because you want to study or because you're provisionally unfit. Let's get this straight!"

I grew confused and kicked myself for having spoken out. Luckily, the commissar had decided to be a good guy.

"It's alright, comrade, I understand. I also wanted to go to high school, but we didn't have the money. You're lucky, you'll become an engineer or a doctor, whereas I ... Well, I won't stand in your way. Your demobilisation form is already signed."

He handed me a small piece of paper and a train ticket, the army's going-away present, along with the uniform I was wearing. The only things I had to hand in were my belt and my rifle.

"One last word, comrade, I have here in my drawer your evaluation, and you must know how important it is for your future. According to the information we have received from Užice, you showed courage in battle, which is to your honour ... It's a pity that during peacetime, you have not been more disciplined, more ambitious. You could have quit the army with a sergeant's rank. That is all I have to say. You're free to go. I suppose you'll be off to Belgrade?"

"Yes, Comrade Commissar, I'm taking the night train this evening."

"Ah! So you can't wait to get away from us ... In any case, you're free to do as you wish. Have a good trip, comrade, and don't think too badly of us."

I left the office in a hurry. I wasn't particularly proud of myself. He wasn't a bad sort. He had started from nothing and ended up a captain, so how could he not swear allegiance to the new masters of the country? He had fought for the revolution and the revolution had made him what he was. A cog in the huge machine that was the Master Design, he was like so many others, trying to promote the ideology that eventually would crush us all.

But who had thought up this confounded machine? Who had the idea of building a new Tower of Babel? Was it the little man with the goatee resting in his sinister mausoleum in Red Square? Or was it the pedantic German philosopher, living in exile in London, filling entire notebooks with his fine Gothic handwriting, the one who declared that owning property was an act of theft. And what if it were Adam, chased out of Paradise by the wrath of God, who swore one day to build a tower so high that it would give him access to the Garden of Eden? In any case, all this was of little importance now. Soon I would be out from under the Master Design and I would resume my studies.

Before leaving town, I wanted to say goodbye to Fani, a girl I met during my stay in Niš, but she too had left for Belgrade to study French literature at the university. She could have chosen to go to Athens or Paris, or anywhere else in the world for that matter. Her family had Greek citizenship and she was free to leave Yugoslavia legally, an extraordinary privilege at a time when the entire country was trapped inside a cage. There was a charm and innocence about Fani that lingered in her wake as if she were a creature from another sphere. I still smile when I recall the crazy circumstances of our meeting.

Before the army issued me with a thick woolen uniform, I would wear the white anorak of an alpine fighter. The long sleeves covered my hands and at certain angles, it looked as if I had no hands. One hot July evening when I was wearing the anorak, I noticed Fani on the promenade amidst a milling crowd of young men and women. Each time our paths crossed, I would stare at her. Finally, she caught on to my interest. Since the anorak covered up my left hand, she thought I was disabled and had said to her sister: "Poor guy, he must have lost his hand in the war."

A week later, just as we were about to pass each other once again, she saw me gesticulating with both hands. Thanks to a miracle worker, my hand had grown back. After being introduced, we went on a few innocent walks along the streets of Niš. Fani even invited me to her home, where her mother received me in a large drawing room dominated by a grand piano. There was a quaint bourgeois charm about the room, which was very appealing to a young man living in a gunners' barracks.

I also wanted to bid farewell to a young peasant woman from Užice. During my months in Niš, she had often welcomed

Dimitri and me in her family home. Dimitri had met her father in the sinister Zemun concentration camp. Her father had been arrested as a member of the underground resistance network and beaten to death. The SS caught him cheering at the sight of the first American B-52s flying overhead on their way to the oil fields of Romania. Dimitri always kept the circumstances of her father's death to himself.

I hurried over to say goodbye to this young woman and to pick up my Browning, which I had hidden in her home. Afterwards, as I still had a few hours to kill before the train, I treated myself to a dish of grilled meat at a rotisserie near the station.

At eleven o'clock, I boarded the night train for Belgrade, which was scheduled to arrive early next morning. My excitement at seeing the city and my friends after long gloomy months was tempered by the extreme nervous fatigue of the last few days. As soon as the train started to move, the monotonous clickety-clack of the wheels sent me into a deep sleep.

When I woke up, the train was stopped in a station. The locomotive was wheezing in the silent night. On the deserted platform, an employee wearing a red cap was walking alongside the train. The big clock indicated three a.m. Still half asleep, I read the name of the town: Ćuprija — a small place lost in the Balkans. A milky light spilled down from the lamps. After four years of living in blacked-out cities, it was wonderful to see the lights back on again. The war was definitely over.

As the train rolled through the outskirts of town, I thought I recognised the lights of the hydroelectric plant. Not far from the red-brick building on the other side of the tracks, I glimpsed the corn fields and the copses where we had trained in February and March of 1945 while waiting to leave for the front. Much had happened since those days when we played war games in that bucolic setting. Everything seemed so long ago, so childish.

The train picked up speed. A few lights glimmered here and there in the night, and reminded me of how desolate the countryside could be. Settled into my corner, I listened to the monotonous clicking of the wheels hammering out: *to Belgrade ... to Belgrade ...*

And after Belgrade? Who knows, maybe further still.

## II

# The Return to Belgrade

*It is not the years that weigh heaviest,*
*but what was left unsaid,*
*what I didn't say or simply hid.*
— TAHAR BEN JELLOUN

I AWOKE WITH the dawn. We were nearing Belgrade. The passengers were struggling with their luggage and preparing to leave the train. Outside, the dappled forests of autumn could be glimpsed through wisps of smoke. We passed no end of thatched cottages, stubbled fields and pastures. At times a whitewashed house by a grove would appear suddenly, only to fade back into the bucolic scene.

So much hardship was hiding beneath these Roman-tiled roofs, in these low-ceilinged hovels with their smoking oil lamps. Barely released from the long Ottoman night, poor Serbia was already dreaming of joining Europe. Europe — the name kept cropping up, obsessively, in my father's letters to his parents when he was studying in Moscow. At times, the wretched poverty of our people throbbed like a dull pain, but there was little I could do. You cannot negate your pain without negating yourself.

I knew this countryside well. During the Occupation, famine — that shameful sickness — ravaged the towns of Serbia. In the streets of Belgrade, old men floated inside their shabby suits. They resembled ambulant scarecrows. Citizens sold off their furniture and household objects at ridiculous prices just to be able to eat. Others would go into the countryside and barter entire wardrobes for a sack of flour or potatoes.

Three years before, in August 1942, I had embarked on a similar hunt for food for my Aunt Lou. I got off at Obrenovac Station and spent the day walking up and down dusty roads, trying to exchange three kilos of nails for one kilo of lard. People looked at me as if I were a beggar that dogs bark at. The light was fading fast. Exhausted and miserable, having abandoned all hope of finding a farmer who would agree to the barter, I was making my way back to the station when I came upon a house under construction. The frame was already up, the beams forming squares and diagonals. The unkempt carpenters ignored me and kept right on working. Nobody paid attention anymore to the starving people tramping the roads in search of a little food.

I offered my nails to the one who looked like the owner of the house. While we bartered, the women and children brought food and drink to the workers. At first, the man eyed me rather disdainfully but his attitude softened somewhat during our discussion. He seemed disconcerted by my wooden clogs, my jute pants and my gold-rimmed glasses. Finally, he accepted the swap. Out of pity perhaps? I swallowed my pride because I didn't want to return to Belgrade empty-handed. The urbanites' disdain of peasants had evolved into the peasants' new disdain for us. We deserved it.

As I was handing over the bag of nails, I felt as if I was outside of time, adrift in the history of my country with its countless wars and famines, ruined villages and occupied cities, towns ravaged by soldiers and mounds of bodies massacred by sword and gun. In the midst of all this chaos, little islands of peace still survived, like the one I had just discovered. Here, men still built houses and brought up children as if they didn't know that tomorrow their houses could be burnt, their wives raped, and their children impaled on fences. Those who had known the Thirty Years War were more fortunate than we were. In our country, we had never known a war to begin or to end. How many centuries had I been wandering these dusty roads in a state of exhaustion?

The train pulled into Obrenovac Station. Its strident whistle yanked me back into the present, as cruel a time as any my ancestors had lived through. The night express flew by, ignoring the small station. Civil servants waited on the platform for the commuter train into Belgrade. My Aunt Lou had once lived here in the house of Martha Bartos, an office colleague.

As we entered Belgrade, memories flitted in and out of my mind, as fleeting as the landscape. We passed the airplane factory and off in the distance, I saw the White Palace, the former residence of Prince Paul. At the train crossing, near Gunners' Park, a young woman with a bike was waiting for the barrier to lift: my first glimpse of a Belgrade woman since before the war. Beyond the hippodrome, we skirted the walls of the Mint, the Seven Poplars Public Baths and the Vapa Paper Factory with its Masonic-style inscription: LIVE AND HELP OTHERS LIVE. Finally, the brakes started to squeal; the train was entering the station with its glass canopy. Finally, Belgrade. Finally, home.

After four years of war, I was returning to the capital for good. I could hardly believe it. From time to time during the Occupation, I had come home dragging heavy bags of potatoes, flour and other foodstuffs, always apprehensive of the plainclothes police posted at the exit who were eager to confiscate provisions under pretext of fighting the black-marketeers. Near the freight station, men and women would line up, a mournful grey wall, patiently awaiting their ration of coal. After curfew, Belgrade would sink into a cataleptic sleep. The dark, deserted streets belonged to the patrolling *Feldpolizei*.

Towards the end of the Occupation, during my brief sojourns in the capital, the sinister sound of sirens would awaken us in the night. Formations of B-52s would fly over the city. The dull humming of the engines would blend with the detonations of bombs and the crackling of the air-raid defense. People didn't know whether they should rejoice at this demonstration of the Allies' strength, or curse the planes that unloaded their cargo of bombs on us. Aunt Lou would beg me to join her in the cellar at night, but I was too lazy. Relying on my luck, I stayed in bed. I could hear the explosions off in the distance followed by the all-clear signal. Reassured, the city would go back to sleep.

Now I could stroll all night in the brightly lit streets of Belgrade. But mixed with my joy at being back was a certain anxiety. After an absence of four years, was this still my city? Threading my way through the crowd of civilians and military, I emerged onto President Wilson Square. In front of the station, travellers were rushing to board the streetcars, or discussing fares with the drivers of rickety *calèches*. The restaurants and *cafés* were opening for the early-morning clientele. Belgrade was slowly coming to life.

My eyes automatically searched out a window on the third floor of a building across from the station. For years now, it had exercised a fascination over me. Behind this window had lived a young woman who worked in a government department. In her off-hours, she was a fortune-teller. We met when my aunt moved into an apartment on the same floor. One day, when my aunt was away, the woman invited me in to read my cards. The table was very narrow. Our knees touched, and instead of pulling back, we pressed up against each other rather indecently. The tarot cards — and my undisclosed future — were forgotten, and we gave in to a carnal passion that was as sudden as it was violent. After that, every time I arrived at Belgrade Station, I instinctively looked up at this window. But our tryst was long over. The fortune-teller had married and moved away.

Despite spending the night on the train, I felt quite invigorated. I was tempted to tell the first passerby how the army had chased me from its ranks, and how happy I was to be back. Long live the army! I had been declared provisionally unfit for active duty. These words rang in my ears like an academic distinction, a sort of *summa cum laude*. In discharging me, the army had relieved me of my gun and the political indoctrination sessions which had bored us all to death. To think that at this very moment my comrades were probably marching in the courtyard of the barracks, to the barked commands of the sergeant instructor: *"Left, right! ... left, right! ... left, right!"* Poor sods, how they must yearn to be back in their villages with their young wives and children.

In the meantime, I needed to reclaim Belgrade, to stroll down the paths of the botanical gardens, to tread on the soft carpet of leaves in the shady square opposite the venerable old Church of the Assumption near Queen Natalija Street where we used to live at one time, and where my mother had taught chemistry at the school for young girls. I wanted to walk along the ramparts of the old Kalemegdan Fortress, inhale the odour of barley hops from the Bajlon Brewery, and the hot axle grease of the streetcars. So many places to revisit, so many friends to see again. Who knows? Maybe my real life was just beginning.

That morning, the walk up from the station to my aunt's house on Ilija Street felt marvelously new to me even though I had done it many times in my life. Even the Transport Ministry, housed in a dark, massive, granite building topped by a little Greek temple, looked almost charming to me. My aunt, a patient woman, had spent her working life within its walls as the bookkeeper for the railway ties department.

On Prince Illiterate Street, the remains of the old Military Academy, flattened by bombs, had not yet been cleared away. Only the rubble had been carted away from the foundations, which now resembled an archaeological dig. At last I came to Ilija Street. The street was littered with yellow leaves.

It was October 3, 1945. I felt as if my life was starting after being struck a paralyzing blow on April 6, 1941, when the sirens had shrilled the arrival of the first Luftwaffe bombers over Belgrade.

How can we forget all the horrors we have endured since that time? How can we forget that day on April 12, 1941, when a panzer intercepted a train full of soldiers on the crossing near the Gymnasts' Palace in Užice. The bullet-riddled cattle cars were heaped with the bodies of the wounded and the dead, their waxen faces covered with a fine dust. We worked for hours to extricate the survivors. It was a beautiful spring day, and from the nearby dispensary came the sweetish smell of blood and ether. Hardly a month later, I beheld through my binoculars the bodies of the first prisoners who had been shot, lying in a ragged heap. I was horrified. Many other shootings were to take place on the hill behind the cemetery. Now it was time to close the door on such Goyaesque scenes and concentrate on life and my future studies, as if there had never been a war. Such memories nevertheless cast a shadow over my joy at being back in Belgrade.

It was barely seven in the morning when I rang Aunt Lou's doorbell. She lived in a bachelor apartment at 42 Ilija Street opposite the Swiss Embassy. She was retired and led a quiet life, going about her daily chores, seeing friends and feeding the pigeons on her tiny balcony shaded by the foliage of a great chestnut tree.

It was understood that I would live with her while I was at Belgrade University. In fact, where else could I have lived? I had been without a real home for a long time. My mother had died in 1930. I lived with my father for four years and then in the autumn of 1934 I was sent as a boarder to Alexander I School. Three years later, my father entered the religious orders and left Belgrade to run an Orthodox diocese in Hungary at the foot of the Carpathian Mountains. After the war, he was appointed bishop of Prizren in Kosovo Province. Once my father entered the priesthood, I was bounced around between boarding school, my aunt's place and a *pied-à-terre* we kept in Užice.

Aunt Lou had been expecting me; nevertheless, she was surprised to see me so early in the morning. Her kiss, which had a peachy taste, revived fond memories. She was so happy to see me. After four long years of war and uncertainty, I was going to resume a more or less normal life once again.

We had last seen each other during the final days of May when the shock troops of the 21st Division had just returned from the front. The capital was festooned with flags and banners. We were expected to parade in the streets of Belgrade, but our hearts weren't in it. There were few onlookers and the cheers were few and far between. Everyone was happy that the war was over, but the shadow of the Grand Master of the Keys loomed over the country, and peace seemed a dubious proposition.

Our Division had started off at the Save Bridge and stretched over two or three kilometres. The elite units marched up front in martial order. The rest of us took up the rear, in joyous disorder. As we had only joined the division ten days earlier, we hadn't earned the right to share in the glory enjoyed by the veterans of the unit. We marched like imposters, but in any case we were pretty indifferent to the glory. Four of us, all friends, marched in the last rank of the last company. We looked untidy and disheveled, as if we were out on a spree. As we came into Slavija Square, my Aunt Lou saw me and came to hand me a new shirt. My comrades thought it was a gift from a stranger.

Dear Aunt Lou. When I was a child, I used to call her a globe-trotter because she had taken a few trips abroad. She had been a part of my world for as long as I could remember.

❧

As soon as I finished breakfast, I left the house. My aunt looked a little disappointed to see me go off so soon, but she understood how anxious I was to see Milenko. We had so much to catch up on, so many impressions to exchange, and, of course, so many plans to make.

It was a beautiful October day. On Ilija Street, the trees still had most of their leaves. A streetcar coming from the station turned to go up Hartvig Street. I looked at these ordinary sights with new eyes. Those who take freedom for granted will never experience the exhilaration of freedom recovered. Were the best years of our lives about to begin?

Ten minutes later, I was on Grandmother Griotte Street and then on to 31 Galsworthy where Milenko lived in an old house with yellow walls. I smiled when I saw the curtains still drawn on the ground floor. Monsieur was still sound asleep. He hadn't changed. Since leaving boarding school, my friend had developed the habit of going to bed late, often around two or three o'clock. While the city slept, the young man indulged his passion for electromagnetic waves. In the quiet of the night, he would sit and reflect in front of a radio, trying to figure out why it didn't work, methodically applying the process of elimination. Every success added to his store of knowledge, which made him really happy. The radio lamps glowed like the smoldering tips of cigarettes. His room smelled of tobacco, coffee, and the paste he used for soldering.

That morning I took pleasure in awakening him rather roughly, but he didn't hold it against me. We had so many things to talk about. Milenko told me how he had severed his ties with the Communist Party. When he quit the army in Niš and returned to Belgrade, he had orders to present himself at a confidential address to renew contact with the Party, a visit he kept postponing. One morning when he was on Crown Street, he found himself in front of the building in question. There was a constant stream of people going in and out, like bees in a hive. They were probably Party members, activists, and agitators, coming to submit their reports and receive instructions. At that point Milenko had a flash of insight: these people were busy just moving air around. The atmosphere of false conspiracy surrounding the Party was absurd. Furthermore, to stand in front of some smart-alecky kid and ask to be re-integrated into a cell was just too childish. He felt like laughing and decided not to cross the threshold of this grey two-storied building.

Turning down the scholarship to study in Moscow isolated him even further from the society that was emerging, a society increasingly intolerant of individuals with minds of their own. Without a scholarship he had to rely on repairing radios to support himself and his mother. All this in the name of freedom. It might seem ridiculous to someone not trapped in this kind of world, but to us freedom was paramount.

I told him how I had sidestepped the Party and bluffed my way out of the army, thanks to Bazil. It was no mere coincidence that we shared the same way of thinking. During our school years together, we would discuss, far into the night, a variety of topics, and little by little we built up a community of ideas and viewpoints that sometimes surprised us. We had both signed up with the Partisans to fight the occupiers. We were never the least bit tempted to serve the Grand Master of the Keys, or to become involved in the drive for power, where loyalty to the Party took precedence over everything: including courage, friendship, and intelligence.

For a long time, I had been living under a dangerous misconception. One day in February of 1945, I had declared to Saša Božičković, a painter and a friend of mine, that the Party needed me more than I needed the Party. He said I was pretentious, and he was probably right. I was convinced that by specialising in a profession, I could gain a sort of ideological extraterritoriality. A grave mistake. The Party needed no one, not even the geniuses — and even less a lunatic like myself.

During my reunion with Milenko, something strange happened. After a while, we fell silent as if we had run out of subjects to talk about, something which happened very rarely with us. Only the ticking of an old alarm clock — a sound that always reminded me of a one-legged person walking — could be heard.

Suddenly, one of us, I can't remember which one, broke the silence and said that our only choice was exile. Agreement was immediate and total, as if the idea of leaving the country had been slowly germinating in our minds, and our reunion had brought it to flower. It was like a summer storm that unleashes itself suddenly and without warning. That day, the idea of living in a free country crystallised. The rest was lost in a haze of questions and ideas: where to go? ... when? ... France ... the West ... the United States ... One thing was sure: we wanted to be far away from the Grand Master.

The idea of living elsewhere, particularly in France, first had come to me when I visited the Tower of Skulls. Lamartine's words had released a flood of memories. That night, in Niš, lying on my pallet in the gunners' barracks, I dreamed of my stay in France in 1937.

I was in a boat, motionless, on a pond near La Ferté-sous-Jouarre. Fernand Mayer, professor of physics and Madame Lévi's brother-in-law, had invited me to go fishing. Under the cloudless sky of the Île-de-France, time stood as still as our boat. The calm water of the pond reflected the rushes, dried out by the sun. The birds were chirruping in the nearby woods. From time to time the silver flash of a carp broke the surface. The professor was teasing the minnows, and firing questions at me at the same time, obliging me to speak in my broken French. Professor Mayer was determined to teach the language of Molière to a young savage hailing from distant Serbia. We returned to La Ferté for dinner. My head was buzzing, too full of French words.

With its beautiful summer skies that had obsessed so many impressionist painters, its landscapes smoothed by man's labour, its striped barges gliding down the Seine, its *châteaux*, and its parks created by the famed Le Nôtre, France now seemed so far away, inaccessible to people like myself, and yet ... I had not renounced the idea of seeing France again one day.

༄

The news of friends and acquaintances clouded my excitement at being back in Belgrade, and at first I kept any feelings at bay because I didn't want anything to spoil my first day back home. During our long-awaited reunion, Milenko and I talked at length about what had happened to some of our classmates. The time had come for a sombre reckoning.

The years spent at boarding school had created among our fellow students enduring quasi-brotherly relationships, much stronger than those usually found among the day pupils. We never would have been so close without Kosta, our headmaster, whose inner passion had driven him to inculcate in us a strong collective soul which transcended national, religious, and economic differences.

A strange man, this Professor Kosta: divorced, according to some, for wanting to sleep with his bedroom window closed while his wife preferred it open. His throat was delicate and the slightest draft would affect his lovely tenor voice. Two or three times a year he would sing at High Mass at the Orthodox Monastery of the Transfiguration that adjoined our boarding school.

As Kosta never had children of his own, he adopted us, his students. His mission in life was to turn us into exceptional beings. We were his project. During those eight years, he molded us — sometimes roughly, with slaps to the face and threats of depriving us of our Sunday outing. But he also opened up new horizons in history, philosophy and literature for which he had a real passion.

Sometimes, he would fuss over those of us who remained at school during the Christmas and Easter holidays because we couldn't afford the train fare for the long trip home. He organised excursions to Zemun, a little town on the other side of the Save River. We would go down to the port and climb aboard paddlewheel boats. When we arrived on the other side, we would treat ourselves to delicious Viennese pastries and coffee with whipped cream, or go to the movies in an old-fashioned cinema. We would return in the evening when the city lights transformed Belgrade into an immense cruise ship sailing up to the juncture of the Save and Danube Rivers.

Above all, Kosta taught us to believe in new beginnings. Every Saturday or Sunday, before our outings, he would announce a new and ambitious plan to improve our performance in class. This was when he showed himself to be a real leader. He had worked out all the details — how the weak students in composition would be coached by the strong ones, how we would master new subjects, and so forth. After three or four days, the plan would prove too ambitious and would fall apart, but Kosta was never discouraged. He would acknowledge the failure and then add: "Never mind for this week. On Monday we'll start all over."

The following week, the same scenario would repeat itself. These repeated beginnings shaped me. Today, despite life's inevitable failures, I still have the impression that my life begins anew on Monday.

Kosta belonged to that species of lone wolves who live with the memory of a personal tragedy buried deep inside them, a wound that never heals. Vague rumours circulated about a great and impossible love he once had for a student, who happened to be the principal's daughter. It took place a long time ago in a regional school at a time when women still wore long dresses and large soft hats over their chignons. But this story might also have been dreamt up by some romantic soul. Was it to soothe this mysterious wound, and give meaning to his existence, that Kosta joined his destiny to that of a group of teenagers, as if their young sap could return to him some of his own youth? A solitary and tragic being, he hid his inner pain behind the tenderness he lavished on us.

His Pygmalion scheme was scheduled to peak in June 1941, at the traditional banquet given by new graduates in honour of their professors. But, on April 6, the sinister wailing of sirens and the Luftwaffe's first bombs cut short our dreams. The destroyed buildings in Belgrade and the smell of putrefying bodies trapped beneath the rubble confronted us with a cruel reality. In comparison, our school worries and Wertheresque yearnings appeared trifling — like mere scratches. The Occupation was just starting when we finished our baccalaureate that June. The class dispersed to the four corners of the old Yugoslavia, and beyond. However, our collective soul had been so solidly forged by Kosta that it survived the break-up of the country and the ravages of time. Perhaps when the last of Kosta's students die, the group soul will also perish, but who can say? It might even live on, sustained by the magic of his words.

War fragmented our class and mangled our futures. Several of my classmates had been killed, others had disappeared without a trace, but the majority survived. We could consider ourselves lucky. Our schoolmates at Kragujevac High School had been less fortunate. Machine guns had wiped out entire classes, along with their professors. The principal, spared from conscription because of his age, had chosen of his own accord to accompany them on their voyage of no return.

Our comrade Ivan Korunić had succumbed to typhus somewhere in the rocky mountains of Dalmatia. He was political commissar of a battalion of Partisans and his dream was a just society for all. His unshakeable moral rectitude predestined him to be a Savonarola, or a commissar. The revolution and the civil war turned him into a priest of a godless religion. What other occupation could there have been for the son of a humble shoemaker tormented by hunger since his childhood on the arid island of Korčula? He must have felt miserable and excluded, looking at the privileged young ladies whirl around the dance floor at the sparkling balls of Alexander I High School.

Stanislav S. was killed in action in a muddy field reeking of manure. It became the battlefield and burial ground of many young people from Belgrade. The unfortunate boy took a bullet in the neck in circumstances that remain obscure. Never very polished, always a bit rough around the edges, Stanislav was nevertheless a good chap.

As for Boško Popovič, son of an Orthodox priest from Mladenovac, his fate was unusual and tragic. One day, during the Occupation, he was in the office of one of the youth work sites when a picture of King Peter II fell off the wall and the glass shattered. The oracles had delivered their sinister omen. An onlooker quipped: "One king less. Now what?" The disrespectful young man who said this was later denounced for the crime of *lèse-majesté*. He was arrested outright, deported to Mauthausen, and never came back. At the end of the war, an informer pointed to Boško, as having ordered the young man's deportation. Boško protested vehemently, but Ozna, the secret police, harassed and overworked, did not want to bother with endless verifications. One morning at dawn in October 1944 my schoolmate was led away to be shot.

The only one who saw the depressing cortege go by was the baker, already up and kneading his dough. Boško knew what was about to happen. He struggled and protested his innocence, but in vain. The baker's assistant rushed off to alert Boško's brother. The brother came running until he ran out of breath. He caught up with the deathly procession just as the machine gun rat-tat-tatted. He saw his brother crumple at the foot of an old oak tree, his shirt torn and bloodied. The whole scene resembled something out of a film, but, unlike in cinema, our friend was not even given the honour of a real firing squad. After all, this was serious stuff. It was a revolution. Thus died our friend Boško, whose Cossack ancestors had fought on the Don Plain.

As for Bogdan, an outstanding athlete, his end remains a mystery. All we know is that he left his home near the Hay Market, one day in October 1944, the same month that saw our nation shaken to its foundations. He left for Bosnia with his ski boots and a few gold pieces sewn inside his jacket. Many young people from Belgrade headed off in the same direction and were never heard from again. What did they think they would find in those inhospitable mountains? Nobody knew exactly, but many hoped the Allies would break off their alliance with the Grand Master and come to the assistance of the Nationalist Resistance.

It was hoped that the powerful Allied armies would join General Mihajlović's ragged troops and change the course of Yugoslavia's civil war. But this hope turned out to be pie in the sky, despite the desperate need for small nations to find an ally for protection. In the West, powerful generals had other fish to fry. Churchill had decided that the Partisans of the Grand Master would deliver more German corpses than General Mihajlović's troops. In this cruel game of alliances, it was strictly a matter of numbers.

Nothing was known of Dušan Drobnjak. My memory of those days is somewhat vague. On one of my unplanned trips to Belgrade during the German Occupation, I ran into him in front of the Theatre of the Performing Arts. With his high-collared overcoat, black suit, white silk scarf and derby, he resembled a magician ready to pull a pigeon out of a top hat, or a Parisian denizen in a story by Guy de Maupassant. He noticed my sombre expression, and smiled in a friendly, if somewhat condescending, fashion. Dušan liked to play the dandy, a provocation that was annoying in light of the hardships and food shortages we were suffering.

"What kind of a get-up is this?" I asked him.

"What get-up?"

He enjoyed making fun of me.

"Stop joking! Tell me how you've been," I said.

Smiling mysteriously, he looked at me with his jet-black eyes as if he wanted to hypnotise me.

"My friend, I'm studying what is most important. I'm studying life! Can you even imagine what life means at a time like this?"

His comment had a theatrical ring to it. A kind of flippancy.

A year later, during the summer of 1943, our paths crossed again on a worksite for young people. This time he was wearing a monk's habit and his head was shaved like a Buddhist's. He told me he was living the life of an ascetic — body and soul. He was dedicated to a great cause: saving the Serbian people. Nothing less.

We met for the last time in August 1944. Leaning against the wrought-iron gate of Užice Station, thin and dressed in rags, he resembled one of those poor wretches who hire themselves out as day labourers in the villages — a strange metamorphosis for an ex-dandy. And yet it was the same man. He was waiting for a train, maybe the last one in these uncertain times, as the German troops were beginning their withdrawal from the Balkans. The sun was beating down, and the railway ties gave off an odour of creosote.

We talked briefly. He had been hired to work as a liaison in General Mihajlović's Nationalist Resistance movement, which explained his strange outfit. As we were about to take leave of each other, he put his hand on my shoulder and, staring straight at me, declared in a serious voice: "If I fail, I shall become a Bolshevik." Did he have doubts about his present engagement? Did he have a premonition that his life would be cut short? I'll never know. One thing is certain, though. He belonged to that race of people who thirst after the absolute, and are ready to ride out their passions until the ultimate sacrifice. In the autumn, he left for Bosnia with General Mihajlović's soldiers, who, hunted down like animals, walked day and night in single file along mountain ridges, snow-whipped and harassed by the Grand Master's Partisans.

Years later, Sava Bosnić, a mutual friend and survivor of this death march across Bosnia, told me about their last meeting. Dušan had survived ambushes, exhausting walks in ferocious weather along mountain peaks, and even typhoid fever. On March 19, 1945, less than two months before the end of the war, he was dragging himself, half starved and toothless, towards Slovenia. A sergeant hit him in the face over a loaf of bread. Exhausted, Dušan went to sleep on the side of the road, the loaf still under his arm. Seeing him emaciated and helpless, soldiers took advantage of the situation and stole the bread from him. No one ever saw our friend again. Sometimes, I picture his grave by a mill at the foot of a mountain, with the waterfall singing him a lullaby. I know this is naïve, but I can't help it.

Years later, when I was living in Paris in the Hotel du Château, Dušan came to me in a dream. He entered my fourth-floor room noiselessly, and sat down on a chair in the middle of the room. He stared at me with his black eyes as he had that time we met at the station of Užice. I woke up with a start and lay motionless. A pale light fell over the cupboard mirror, the sink, and a small table in the middle of the room. The only chair was empty. But I could feel his presence, tenuous and invisible.

A metronome was beating painfully in my throat. I got up to fetch a glass of water and approached the window. It was snowing outside. In the deserted street, I could see a set of footprints wandering off into the distance.

*III*

# *A Bleak Autumn*

*Beyond the world we live in,
way beyond, lies another world...*
— SØREN KIERKEGAARD

EVER SINCE CHILDHOOD, the changing seasons have always delighted me. I have the sense of witnessing a mysterious transformation of the earth and the sky, which reflects back into my own life and renews it. I always await the coming season with eagerness and impatience. This attitude springs from a rather naïve side of my nature that I can't seem to shake, but must accept, just as others have to accept their shortcomings.

As a student, autumn would fill me with feelings of plenitude — classes resuming, friendships renewed, new professors and books with their smell of fresh ink. The school library, with its thousands of books, was a treasure house of adventure and travel. The thought of long evenings of reading while the wind and rain raged outside always delighted me. In October, we would take advantage of the beautiful weather to walk in the park, trampling underfoot the large yellow leaves that whispered to us and gave off a musty odour. The crack of tennis balls would ring out on the nearby court. Sometimes, at suppertime, they would serve red grape juice that gave off a delicious resinous aroma. Our youthful imaginations, always searching for the eternal feminine, were excited by the approach of the first dance. I can still see Beli, Gavrilo, Biba, and Ivan in our dormitory, shining up our shoes, putting on clean shirts, and smoothing down our hair with brilliantine before we set out for the ballroom. By the time we got there, the first of the young ladies were arriving, and the musicians of the Štule Orchestra were busy tuning up their instruments, getting ready to fill the hall with jazz, tangos, and waltzes.

Time would pass almost imperceptibly, and soon it would be the season for snow and the Christmas holidays. Each season would chase away the preceding one, bursting on the scene like a promise.

෴

Was it because of all these sad memories that the autumn of 1945 felt particularly bleak, filled with shadowy uncertainty? Again, I had the vague sense of living in two separate realities, as if the city and its inhabitants concealed another city, subterranean and frightening, the existence of which I only suspected, and which was slowly taking shape like a tree emerging from the mist.

The morning after my arrival in Belgrade, in the course of a conversation with Aunt Lou, I learned the strange circumstances surrounding the death of Professor Branko Popovič, or Uncle Branko as I used to call this childhood friend of my father's.

"They shot him last November, probably on Gypsy Island," said my aunt.

"Who?" I asked.

"They did!"

"Who are they! Who are these mysterious men that no one dares to name clearly?"

The only answer was my aunt's stricken expression. She looked at me as if I were too young to understand.

"And for what reason?" I asked.

"We don't know. No one knows. *Politika* simply ran on the front page a list of the 105 names of the men condemned to death as collaborators."

"But Uncle Branko was not a collaborator. He was profoundly pro-Western and had no sympathy for the Nazis," I said.

"I know that. But they accused him, nevertheless, of having denounced his students."

I was dumbfounded. My aunt searched the small library for a crumpled newspaper clipping which she handed to me. *The tribunal of the First Army condemned the following persons to death...* Most of the names on the list were unknown to me.

"They concocted a cocktail of names of a few real collaborators along with innocent people. They always do that. You didn't hear about this list? In Belgrade, people were terribly upset and angry, but no one dared protest," she said.

"Last autumn I was in the army, and my company rarely stayed more than two days in the same village. And we never saw the Belgrade newspapers."

I hadn't known this immensely cultured man very well. He had been a boyhood friend of my father's in Užice. As children, they fished together in the millpond opposite my grandparents' house. Life had separated them early on. At eleven, my father and my Uncle Branko's twin brother left for boarding school in Odessa. The two childhood friends didn't meet again until the early 1900s in Belgrade as university graduates, sporting fashionable boaters. In the meantime, Uncle Branko had picked up a degree from the Munich Academy of Fine Arts where he studied architecture and hung out at painters' studios. After the First World War, he was named to the art history chair at the University of Belgrade.

One very hot July day in 1940, my father and I were crossing National Theatre Square when we saw Uncle Branko coming towards us. It was a sad meeting, just around the time when France had capitulated to Germany. The German panzers were still sweeping the Atlantic coast but in the forest of Compiègne, French politicians had already signed the capitulation papers. On the Champs-Élysées, German soldiers were being photographed in front of the Arc de Triomphe. Uncle Branko and my father bitterly regretted France's humiliation, but their indignation was of little importance. France was far away and life in Belgrade continued as usual. The streetcars kept on circling the equestrian statue of Prince Michael, the asphalt continued softening in the heat, and nearby at Pelivan's, the big oriental pastry shop, people were refreshing themselves with *boza*, a delicious Turkish drink.

"But who denounced Uncle Branko?" I asked.

"No one knows. But one thing is certain, the painter Andrejević has already moved his furniture into his apartment on Prince Michael Street, while his widow, Divna Popovič, has been forced upstairs into the attic with her three sons. Andrejević Kun, a faithful supporter of the Grand Master, has been put in charge of artistic affairs." He had tracked down the professor's paintings, and given orders that they be used as canvases for young artists. Luckily, Branko's friends were quick enough to lay their hands on them and hide them. Divna Popovič called upon Moša Pijade, president of the National Assembly, to demand an explanation. The two men had been friends from their days together in Munich. Pijade had not even heard about the execution. Visibly embarrassed, he regretted his ignorance of Popovič's arrest. Had he known, he might have been able to prevent his friend's fate. Too late. Nothing could bring him back among the living.

A first settling of accounts after the Liberation had resulted in a number of remarkable people being done away with. A month later, they might have been saved, or at least condemned to life imprisonment. Rumour had it that during an interrogation, the professor had fiercely resisted his interrogator who then proceeded to kill him in a fit of rage. But that was just a rumour; his death still remains a mystery.

I was absolutely stunned by my aunt's story. My mind refused to accept this violent death. Before the war, Uncle Branko had lived in a lovely home on the little square facing the National Library. While I was at boarding school, Mrs. Popovič often invited me to spend Sundays with their family. The large dining room exuded an air of comfort and refinement. At table, in the presence of a French governess, conversation sometimes was carried on in the language of Molière. A servant waited on table with impeccable style. In the Louis XVI-style drawing room, I was particularly in awe of a certain ornament that turned out to be the hand of a mummy. Uncle Branko had brought it back from a trip to Egypt. Brick-coloured, it looked like a sandalwood sculpture.

On April 6, 1941, a phosphorus bomb had transformed the house into a blazing inferno. The flames devoured this beautiful home with its elegant drawing room, red chairs and mummified hand. A writer of fantasy stories might have read into the fire the ultimate revenge of the mummy snatched from its ancient tomb. Four and a half years later, all the time spent there already seemed so long ago and hazy.

Other news, also not very cheerful, awaited me that same day. I planned to visit the sister of Dušan, my old classmate. I did not yet know what Sava Bosnić would tell me years later about his last meeting with Dušan, shortly before the Armistice.

Unaware of his fate, I went to visit Dušan's sister near Slavija Square, hoping for good news. Sometimes, miracles do happen. The families of the young people who left for Bosnia in the autumn of 1944 were often without news for months, or sometimes a year before receiving a card from Italy or France or even Australia. That could have been the case with Dušan.

Nervously, I knocked on the door of an apartment at the back of a tiny, filthy courtyard. The door opened and suddenly everything became clear. Dušan's sister, a young woman in her thirties, wan, with dark circles under her eyes, stared at me as if I were an intruder. Behind her stood an old woman who resembled a marble *Pietà*, like those on the work site of the Bertoto Brothers, makers of funeral monuments. I was tempted to turn around and run.

The mother and sister had no knowledge of Dušan or his father. Both had fled on that long dangerous road to Bosnia, which was now strewn with anonymous graves. Had the father want to protect his son, or did he fear the people's vindictiveness in Ripanje, a large town near Belgrade where, as a rich man, he was a suspect in the eyes of the populace? Driven from their home, the two women now lived like recluses in Belgrade.

After we exchanged a few words, there was nothing more to say. Mother and sister looked at me suspiciously; after all, I might have been one of the Party's henchman come to gather information on the whereabouts of Dušan and his father. The secret police were tracking down those in exile, even beyond the Yugoslav borders. Refugees were kidnapped in Klagenfurt, in Cracow, and even as far away as Paris. During all this time, we continued to live as though nothing were happening, as if the thugs and the informers were not pursuing the living and the dead, destroying their paintings and their books, desecrating their tombs.

After a while, the silence became intolerable. Whether or not these women suspected me of being an informer, they probably couldn't forgive me for being alive while their Dušan hovered in a world between life and death. With their sunken eyes, the two women showed me the door. Before escaping, I muttered a few polite platitudes. The putrid smell of the courtyard made me nauseous as I hurried across. Back out in the street, I finally breathed deeply.

Many people in our country were living in fear; many others hid this fear even from themselves. How had we arrived at this state of affairs? What had we done? Who was the guilty party? Was it the mummified body lying in state in Red Square in the centre of Moscow? Or was it all of us for having abdicated in the face of those who claimed to possess the truth, to possess the philosopher's stone and the keys of History? Or was our destiny sealed at Yalta when two aged men in poor health, in the company of a crafty Georgian, carved up Europe like a big birthday cake?

At Slavija Square, without thinking, I boarded the first streetcar that arrived. I wanted to continue making the rounds to all my friends whose fate remained uncertain.

༄

In 1942, the Gestapo had arrested Tihomir Jakšić, the older brother of my childhood friend Djordje Jakšić, who was headed for a career in music. At the end of the war, a few survivors returned from Mauthausen, Buchenwald, Dora, and other infamous concentration camps, but Tihomir was still missing.

Milenko and I both greatly admired our friend. He had been a student at the School of Engineering in Belgrade. An experienced ham radio operator, a few years before the war he had built a shortwave transmitter that allowed him to communicate with operators around the world. Milenko dreamt one day of doing the same.

Tihomir's parents lived on a quiet little street near the Botanical Gardens, an enchanted place for me as a child. Getting off the streetcar near Vuk Karadžić, my primary school, I took Takovo Street, which brought me directly to their house. Once again, his mother's drawn expression told me everything about her son. She kissed me affectionately. In the old days, she would do this with compassion for an orphan. Today, she did it remembering the old days.

No, Djordje and his mother knew nothing of what had happened to Tihomir. Oh, of course, there were rumours — those poisonous plants proliferating in the swamps of our angst. Apparently, he had been spotted chained to the bottom of a barge transporting deportees towards Vienna. He was also seen at Mauthausen, in a *sonderkommando*, a special unit in charge of burning the corpses from the gas chambers. In Norway, he was rumoured to have picked up a frozen cabbage left by charitable peasants on the deportees' road.

Tihomir's whereabouts were traced back to the archives of Banjica concentration camp near Belgrade. Someone had written anonymously next to his name: "Volunteer with the SS troops." The note had an air of slander, as this young man, prematurely aged by delicate health, never would have committed such an offense.

As soon as decency permitted, I bid Tihomir's mother goodbye. Djordje accompanied me out, and in the street he confided: "Mother is still hoping, but my father knows that we will never see him again."

"Why did the Gestapo arrest him?" I asked.

"Nobody knows."

"Was it because of his shortwave transmitter? Your brother must have belonged to a resistance network."

"Perhaps."

Djordje remained evasive. Obviously, he didn't want to talk about it. He invited me to listen to music at his friends' house. Without knowing why, I accepted. There was a strange atmosphere at Djordje's friends' place. In a big, almost empty apartment, two brothers were playing old classical music records. Absorbed by a Bach string concerto, they looked at me suspiciously, or was it my imagination? In any case, my presence did not suit them and after a few minutes, feeling most unwelcome, I left. Djordje and his enigmatic music-loving friends barely said goodbye. Belgrade obviously had its secrets. It felt as if the city didn't exist anymore, or at least not the city I had known before that fateful day the first Stukas descended upon the capital like birds of prey.

As I walked by the imposing gate of the Botanical Gardens, I was tempted to go in and stroll down its paths, for old time's sake. There were few people. The sand crunched under my feet. I used to hang around here after school with Igor and Mihaijlo, our book bags still on our backs. At the edge of the small water lily pond, everything looked the same. Seated on a bench, I inhaled the green smell of the vegetation, and listened to the city humming in the distance. Little white metal plaques stuck inside the flowerbeds indicating the Latin names of the plants.

At the beginning of the century, my mother must have walked here while studying for an exam in botany. Studious and proud to be among the first generation of women admitted to university, she probably wore a long dress of beige cotton — at least that is how I pictured her from an old photograph. Written on the back of the photo were the words: "Leopold König, Photographer by Appointment to His Majesty Peter I of Serbia." Dreamily, I gazed down the path as if she might appear carrying her herbarium under her arm.

What a morning. All these friends, vanished without a trace, and then a monstrous lie about my comrade enlisting as an ss volunteer. Suddenly, an old memory came back, shedding some light on this mystery.

On a Sunday afternoon during the last autumn before the outbreak of the war, my Uncle Branko drove his sons and me to the military stadium of Banjica. He wanted to give a driving lesson to his eldest son, Simeon. It was a sunny October day. The car did figure eights on the field where usually the troops paraded. Suddenly, several military vehicles appeared on the scene, their antennae bristling. To my amazement, on the running board of one of these cars, I saw Tihomir. I would have been less surprised to see a Martian. What was he, a civilian, doing riding in an army car? Just as our Nash was passing his car, I waved to him. He waved back, but looked very annoyed. His companions peered at us suspiciously. "Secret-service men," was my first thought.

That evening back at the boarding school, I told Milenko what had happened. He suggested a fairly plausible explanation: Perhaps Tihomir was collaborating with the counter-espionage services who wanted to set up a detection system for clandestine transmitters that could be mounted on a moving vehicle and thus difficult to detect.

His explanation dovetailed with what we knew about this secretive man's life. Well before the war, he had had a run-in with the counter-espionage services because of his shortwave transmitter. The services had located his transmitter and warned him not to broadcast without a license. But because of his passion for perfecting his transmitter, and his desire to communicate with ham operators around the world, he had gone and done it again. The secret services, impressed by the technical quality of his programs, had finally granted him a license, provided he worked with them in locating underground transmitters. After the start of the Occupation, the older members of the services had probably rebuilt a network service for the Resistance, and Tihomir was likely part of it. Perhaps the goniometric detection system of the German army spotted him and he was arrested as he was transmitting a coded message to Malta, or another Allied base. All that was known was that the agents of the *Abwehr* — the counter-espionage service of the German army — had knocked on his door at three in the morning and taken him away. The rest was conjecture...

However, one point remained unclear. Why had some malevolent hand felt the need to inscribe the following disparaging remark by his name: "Volunteer with the ss?" The only explanation lay in the fanaticism of the secret police serving the Grand Master whose agents had probably tacked it on after the Liberation in order to discredit the Nationalist Resistance Movement. The Partisans, claiming they had been the only freedom fighters, could not admit the existence of other freedom fighters hunted down by the Gestapo.

The first version of history is always written by the winners. Djordje probably knew why his brother had been arrested, but didn't dare admit it. It could compromise him if he were to acknowledge that one of his brothers had belonged to General

Mihajlović's resistance movement. As for the empty apartment and his two music-loving friends, I didn't know what to make of it. The enigma was unveiled to me several months later when Milenko and I were camping in the pine forest of Iessi, a small Italian town on the other side of the Adriatic.

I left the small lily pond and walked by Vul Karadžić Primary School. I went up Palmotićeva Street feeling a twinge of sadness. Mihaijlo Celegin, my childhood friend, had lived on this street. During our first years at grade school, we spent many hours playing in the huge studio of the sculptor Petar Palavčini, father of Igor, the third member of our tightly knit and lively little group. Milhaijlo lost his life on the Syrmian Front during the terrible winter of 1944–45 when the Grand Master threw thousands of inexperienced young people from Belgrade up against the hardened veterans of the *Wehrmacht*. That same winter, General Peko had declared to a contingent of Belgrade youth in the antiaircraft artillery: "I am capable of shooting all of you like dogs, and then going for breakfast as if nothing had happened!" Whether this was a simple joke or the truth, the young men had felt shivers going up their spines.

Passing by Mihaijlo's parents' house, I was tempted to ring their doorbell, but I lacked the courage, or else was stopped by a modicum of decency. I had never seen a more devoted couple, the father a handsome man from Dalmatia and the mother a lovely Belgrader from an old family. They were such a happy family before malevolent forces, jealous of so much happiness, banded together to tear them apart. Sick at heart, I continued on my way. After Dušan Drobnjak and Tihomir Jakšić, Belgrade was gradually filling up with ghosts.

At noon, feeling weary, I turned onto Poincaré Street and headed towards the offices of the *Politika* newspaper. Next door was a restaurant where I indulged my taste for a delicious pancake. When I was at school, I would sometimes sneak out at recreation to eat one of these little delicacies.

As I approached the National Theatre, the crowds grew denser. People were walking by me, hurrying and jostling. I was obsessed by the idea that behind the usual rush of crowds another city was hiding, packed with unmarked graves, living people presumed dead, and dead people presumed living; people who had been despoiled, humiliated, and insulted; the outcasts, the expulsed, along with the intruders, profiteers, opportunists; the voiceless and those whose voices pierced our eardrums; humble people, the *nouveau riche*, old money fallen into poverty; pushers of penicillin, bogus judges, informants, and henchmen spying on henchmen; the terrified, brave youth dreaming of escape ... and I don't know what other kinds of people!

∽

The long-awaited deadline for registering at the School of Engineering was the following week. During the Occupation, grey-clad sentries and a spiked gate had guarded the faculty building, which had been transformed into a German military hospital. They had vanished like the actors and stage props of a play. During the war years, the colleges had continued to turn out new graduates, but under the Occupation, the institutions of higher learning were forced to shut down. We could consider ourselves lucky. The Poles were only allowed to attend grade school, while French and Belgian students were allowed to continue their studies as before. On the scale of sub-human, the Nazis reserved an intermediate place for us Serbs.

That autumn, baccalaureate candidates from four different years jostled with one another in front of the narrow door of Belgrade University. The Grand Master of the Keys and his henchmen could easily have opened the university after the capital was liberated in October 1944, but motivated by an unprofessed, tenacious hatred of intellectuals, they preferred to pack us off to the front. Professionals and engineers, able to build machines, bridges and railways, were considered acceptable provided they stuck to their area of expertise.

On this memorable day in October, Milenko and I found ourselves in a long queue of men and women awaiting registration. It was cool, and a fine drizzle was falling. The endless lineup shuffled along in front of the grey stone facade, struggled up the monumental steps, penetrated into the vast hall, turned into the right-hand corridor and inched its way to the counter of the admissions secretariat. We were a lengthy boa of survivors filled with hope and fear.

Many could not hide their anxiety. Not every one would be admitted. The university had established strict admission criteria. Veterans were first in line. The year of graduation also mattered. Milenko and I were eligible on all counts: we had just been demobilized, and we belonged to the group that had lost all four precious years of study. Our only worry was the less tangible evaluations. These could play against us but the hour of reckoning had not yet arrived for the undesirable elements of society.

How poor we looked in our worn clothes and army pants, shoes many times resoled, and with our pale faces — many of us never ate our fill — but we hoped that a degree would help us to a new life — our real life. Strangely, my friends' difficulties always struck me as greater than my own.

One question never ceased to obsess me. Why did this nation, every twenty or thirty years, have to rebuild bridges, railway stations, roads, and burned-out libraries and schools? Why had our ancestors chosen to build their homes in the middle of a route used by the Crusaders heading south to Jerusalem, and by the Ottomans pushing north to the heart of Europe?

We were all keen to take up our studies again, not just to acquire a decent standard of living, but to recover our dignity. In a muted way we were also waging a battle against time and against the Party. The sooner we became engineers, physicians, or professors, the sooner we would gain a certain ideological extraterritoriality. We believed that those who rebuilt the country and helped make the machinery of state function would be exempt from brainwashing. Without being aware of it, many of the young already were trying to escape the Master Design. And so a curious social symbiosis was taking shape, between the strongmen and the mole-men. The first, under pretext of building a new world, had the power and enjoyed the privileges. The mole-men, specialists of all kinds, wanted only to do their work without being bothered by ideological claptrap.

Who could blame them? We were all impatient to settle into cozy lives. Close our eyes, block our ears, and concentrate on our studies. Who among us was not tempted by this easy path?

If I could not accept this swap — a small sphere of individual freedom in exchange for serving the strongmen with my skills — it was due more to my propensity for always seeing the big picture rather than concentrating on the details. As a jack-of-all-trades, I was incapable of integrating myself into a rigid and unchanging order; however, this became clear to me only much later in life.

☙

That autumn, the instinct for self-preservation weakened many a conscience, slowly and inexorably. *Primum vivere, dedne philosophari* (first life, then philosophy) never felt as real as after four years of curfew, ration books, deportations, and cattle cars filled with miserable wretches moving through the bleak countryside.

When I think of the Occupation, a terrible image comes to mind. In the summer of 1943, I was working on a youth work site in Požega, not far from Užice. Every morning, on our way to work with pickaxe and pail, we would cross the main street, singing. Every time, without fail, the face of a young girl disfigured in a train fire would stare at us from the second floor of a house. The red, badly scarred flesh resembled an anatomical diagram illustrating the facial muscles. The eyes, miraculously saved from the flames, would peer out from behind this hideous mask. Serbia, occupied and ravaged by civil war, wore the same repugnant mask. Would the country ever regain its pure, serene face?

We were so impatient to make up for lost time, to live fraudulently if necessary, but to live. Damn the Master Design and everything else! Nothing was more important than life itself. That could have been our credo from the moment the Grand Master set up quarters on Dedinje Hill overlooking Belgrade, just as Nero overlooked the seven hills of Rome.

One October, I ran into N.N., a former classmate, probably the most intelligent man I had ever met. In class, this young boy grasped the most difficult mathematical lessons or grammar rules as if they were child's play. During study period, he would finish his homework so quickly that he didn't know what to do with the rest of his time. More often than not, he would read a novel or absent-mindedly look over the next day's lessons, which already felt vaguely familiar to him. To entertain himself, he would laugh at the poor souls struggling all around him. No one doubted that he had a brilliant future ahead of him.

Probably sick of our mediocrity, he quit high school around the end of the third year. But we never lost sight of each other. Whenever we met, we would exchange a few words.

When I saw him coming towards me on Prince Michael Street, I was struck by his appearance. Gone was the tie and elegant, classic overcoat; my former classmate was wearing a khaki leather greatcoat, split at the elbows. He looked as if he had just climbed out of the trenches of the First World War. He wore a military belt with a Nagan revolver, just like a Bolshevik commissar. Perhaps humans, as well as animals, are capable of mimicking their environment. I sniffed my way carefully over this new terrain.

"So, what do you think of all these upheavals?" I asked him.

"Whether we like them or not, they are inevitable," he answered.

"Are you a member of the Party?"

"No, but I am certainly not one of those who hang out at the American Cultural Centre."

The revolution was inevitable, so hurrah for the revolution. But he was not yet a member of the Party. Our thinking was shifting slowly, imperceptibly, like the shadow of a tree on a summer's day. Some consciences toppled brutally in an effort to flush away, once and for all, the past and its painful hesitations. Metamorphosis is not just the prerogative of the gods.

Luka M.'s case was an example of such a transformation, but hardly unique. A student at High School No. 3 for boys in Belgrade, for several months he was the punching bag of the young activists in his class. There weren't many of them, four or five at the most, but they had the upper hand. The boy's crime? He was the son of a hardware merchant who had amassed a fortune. Wealth had become shameful, criminal even.

One day, the pack of ruffians carried the joke a little far. They threw Luka out of the classroom window. Luckily, he had been on the mezzanine level and escaped with only a few bruises. He retained the lesson and thought it over. Why have these fellows made me their scapegoat? Because my father is rich and because I am not a member of the Young Pioneers? I can't change my past, but nothing prevents me from changing the present. On that day began the relentless metamorphosis of Luka M. A week later, he joined the Young Pioneers and, strangely enough, he was well received. His comrades erased his past. From then on, he never missed one of their meetings.

Six months later, his transformation was complete when he vigorously denounced our history professor, a timid old woman who had omitted to mention the glorious battle waged by the Grand Master during the war. Now he was ready to chuck out the window any person resisting the Party line, though no one had asked him to. Strangely, he started to think that he had always held these convictions. Later on, he pursued a distinguished career at the Department of Foreign Commerce. The new society was turning out new men.

To be part of the rank and file, not to rock the boat, to live simply, almost on the sly, to marry in order to curl up inside the narrow circle of a cozy family existence, this was a dream many of us had already entertained as we waited in the fine rain that October day. Oftentimes in my life, this temptation of a sweet death revisited me, but the siren's song would soon beckon, and I would lift anchor, hoist the sails, and embark on a long voyage to distant lands. To assume one's destiny, one must assume one's madness.

Two weeks after my return from Niš, an unexpected meeting took me back to a difficult time when I had been rotting away in the army in Ćuprija and Jagodina.

I was walking briskly by the former Russian Embassy. Occasionally, a face would stand out from the bobbing crowd only to fade away, leaving no trace. From out of nowhere, the face of Lieutenant Colonel Efrem, with his prominent cheekbones and his deep-set eyes materialized. I would have been less shocked to come upon a ghost. Instinctively, I turned my head sideways, but the colonel had already spotted me. He grabbed my arm.

"Wait, let me explain," he said.

"You don't owe me an explanation."

My anger subsided as quickly as it had flared up. After all, the lieutenant colonel was not a bad sort. And I had survived, had I not? The Armistice had put an end to the war just as I was about to be dispatched to the trenches. Anyhow, old grudges were tiresome to maintain.

In April 1945 the war was coming to an end. In Jagodina, the daily routine in the 47th Division had us all demoralised; only the occasional outings into the city brought a whiff of fresh air into our lives. Suddenly, news came that snapped us out of our lethargy: our cushy division of shirkers was about to be disbanded. Rumour had it that suspicious elements would be sent to the front. The politically correct, on the other hand, would serve in the Popular Defense Corps, a sort of Praetorian Guard serving the Grand Master.

My cousin Dimitri and I were on the list of suspects. At a time when the Master Design was taking over our lives and our minds, we felt honoured to fall into this category. Nevertheless, the question remained: why were we being treated as suspicious elements? What we were not yet aware of was that, in the country of the Master Design, the innocent were all presumed guilty, and whatever offence they had pinned on us, we had to dig into our past to disprove.

To be sure, we were both far from innocent: after all, we used to play cards in the home of a general's niece, and the general was in the royal army. We would pass the cozy afternoons pleasantly shuffling cards, sipping tea, and nibbling on shortbread. An unforgivable sin, exacerbated by another hapless incident. One rainy afternoon in March, my cousin and I were on our way to Jagodina Station, dragging heavy suitcases full of silverware, an indispensable attribute of every self-respecting bourgeois family. We were hugging the walls, like thieves with their spoils. In our efforts to avoid detection, we took the railway tracks. Our treasure belonged to a once-wealthy woman, a distant cousin of my Aunt Elisabeth, who had fallen on hard times. She was afraid of having her valuables confiscated and wanted to hide them at her sister's place in Belgrade. The Master Design proclaimed loud and clear that property was theft, especially when it belonged to the rich. It didn't help that this woman had married a German brewer whose family had lived in Serbia for over a hundred years. In those days aiding and abetting a bourgeois family was considered a crime.

I wasn't particularly frightened at the idea of going to the front. The collapse of the Third Reich was only weeks, if not days, away, but to be sent to fight under these circumstances angered me. Lieutenant Colonel Efrem owed us an explanation. After all, he was the one who had called us into the 47th Division. I found the colonel pacing back and forth with his assistant, Commander Jovan Barović, in front of the Park Hotel, which was now staff headquarters. They were deep in conversation. I greeted them. They pretended not to see me. I felt so angry that I decided to drop the whole matter. Better to go to the front than to humiliate myself by asking for an explanation. In any case, they probably would have said: in the army, you don't question orders.

The following day, which was Orthodox Holy Friday, we climbed into cattle cars littered with straw — the army was really coddling us. Our destination: Syrmia and the front.

Only later, once the war was over, did I discover a possible explanation for my hasty dispatch to the front. In Jagodina, I had been energetically courting Zora N., the daughter of a rich businessman. She had a pretty face, blond hair and a good figure. Not surprisingly, a captain also had his eye on her. Had he put my name on the list out of jealousy, and with the stroke of a pen rid himself of a bothersome rival? Given the atmosphere of suspicion in the army — and in the whole country — Lieutenant Colonel Efrem would not have dared oppose the decision to pack us off to the front. He might have been accused of protecting bourgeois elements, and my file would certainly not have been easy to defend. One thing struck me at the time: why did these men, so courageous when facing the enemy, grovel before the Party? Whatever the reason, my departure nipped a youthful romance in the bud. I had nurtured this infatuation with the intensity of my twenty years.

Before receiving the order to leave for the front, I had agreed to meet Zora at a *gloriette* owned by her family. It was situated on the outskirts of the city on a hillside covered with vineyards. This small structure, in its bucolic setting, overflowed with romantic charm. A week earlier, during a long walk, we had explored the little dirt roads that zigzagged among the vineyards and rustic cottages with their closed shutters. We walked with our arms around each other, stopping now and then to embrace passionately. Only the birds' chirping broke the silence. The setting was like something out of a Franz Lehár operetta. I could feel myself losing my mind at the sight of her body moving beneath the light cotton frock. Zora would laugh and push me away when I became too enterprising. When we arrived at the *gloriette*, we circled it but were unable to get in. She claimed to have forgotten the key and promised to bring it the following Saturday. This was said in all seriousness as she looked me straight in the eye.

I was in a state of feverish excitement with two days to go before our meeting. But on Thursday, the news of our posting put a brutal end to this delicious dream. Ours was a nascent love affair, already over. Before the convoy pulled out, Zora came to bid me *adieu*. On the little square in front of the station we kissed passionately, determined to trick death out of a few joyous moments. War was in its final death throes, but the bullets were just as deadly. The train arrived towards noon, and we parted, our passion unspent. As the train pulled out, I stood in the wide opening of the cattle car while the young girl, in her clinging dress, waved her farewell from the platform. The hills with their vineyards were slowly left behind, the *gloriette* hidden in dazzling spring greenery. The locomotive was panting hard. The dream of our amorous entanglement was quickly dispelled by thick sulphurous smoke.

The train accelerated. The wheels started to hammer: *to the front ... to the front ... to the front...*

War be damned!

---

Why do we act in ways we don't approve of? Why do we pursue a certain course instead of stopping while there is still

time? What mysterious force pushes us to do what we w
regret? Are we trying to punish ourselves for a sin that is secretly
tormenting us? Or does fatalism sap our will? The question still
preoccupies me when I think back to that visit I made to Vera
on a November afternoon in 1945.

She had been our neighbour during the Occupation. Often
in the evening, she would defy the curfew and come over to our
house to listen to the BBC. Aunt Elisabeth, Dimitri, Vera, and I
would gather behind closed shutters in the modest living room,
and sit in total silence waiting to hear the opening chords of
Beethoven's Fifth Symphony. These four knocks at Fate's door
would announce the BBC broadcast. The knocks could just as
well have been the Gestapo coming to arrest us. This possibility
gave our evenings a conspiratorial hue. Finally, the deep voice
of the announcer would break the silence: *This is the BBC calling.*
Immediately, we were all eyes and ears in our eagerness to hear
the latest news from the front. We were particularly interested
in the Eastern front, which snaked across the great Russian plain.
Armchair strategists all, we anxiously followed its complicated
progress, but none more passionately than Vera. Her husband,
who had joined the Party before the war, was already living in
Moscow working in some mysterious capacity.

Sometimes we could hear boots out in the street as the
German patrols did their rounds. In the dimly lit room, the green
light of the radio's magic eye quivered in direct response to
the intonations of the announcer's voice coming to us through the
ether. We lived moments of intense fraternity created by our fear
and hope.

So much had happened since the previous autumn. The Red
Army had liberated Belgrade at the end of October 1944. Vera's
husband showed up in Užice, impressive in his officer's uniform.

With his chauffeur-driven Jeep and his attendant, he awed the people of our street. Soon, his young wife and their two children joined him in Belgrade.

A year later, I debated the idea of visiting Vera. I realised that our evenings in Užice belonged to a distant past, and that we no longer had much to say to each other. Yet something urged me on. Was it curiosity or a desire to be provocative? I'll never know. The idea wouldn't go away. By that time, Vera and her family were living on a quiet street behind the National Theatre. In front of their prosperous-looking building, a sentry stopped me abruptly. I had to be given clearance. After verifying my papers, he allowed me to enter. The Party made sure that the bigwigs were well protected.

As I climbed the stairs to the third floor, I suddenly had the urge to turn back, but the guard at the entrance might have found such behaviour bizarre. I continued to climb. My hand hesitated one last time before ringing the doorbell. I jumped at the sound of it. Had I been the one to press the button?

Vera opened the door. For a fraction of a second she froze, and then, with a forced smile, invited me in. It was obvious that she hadn't expected a visit from me, but how could I back away without looking ridiculous?

The young woman walked ahead of me. I followed, already regretting my hasty gesture. We went through a conservatory filled with large-leafed plants and rattan furniture. The apartment exuded comfort. Only the eclectic furniture introduced a discordant note, most probably because it consisted of belongings seized from collaborators or from Jews who had been sent off to the concentration camps.

Our conversation languished pitifully in the living room. We recalled anecdotes from the days of the Occupation, but we quickly ran out of subjects. Vera and her husband lived in a world that was inaccessible to most people. With an outsider like myself, she could discuss neither her husband's nor her brother's activities. The husband was a senior public servant in the Department of Justice, and her brother a colonel with the secret police. These high-level party members had already created their own political bubble.

And yet, when the punitive German expedition rolled over Serbia in the autumn of 1941, my cousin Dimitri had risked his own safety to protect Vera's brother. Pursued by the police, this young man had found temporary shelter with Dimitri's sister in Užice, in a hideout that was anything but safe. The city was crawling with German soldiers and agents of the Gestapo. Getting out became a matter of life or death for him. My cousin and I accompanied him to my Aunt Elisabeth's estate, an hour's walk from the city. We climbed up a narrow path trying to avoid the large golden-brown thistles. Užice, with its red tile roofs, gradually merged with the greyness of the valley. A light fog hovered above the river, and the noise of shunting trains drifted up from the rail yards.

Every now and then, we would turn around to check if we were being followed. No one. But we hurried on regardless. After passing the last house, which belonged to Raško the tailor, we were hidden by a wall of hazel trees and thorns. Already we felt safer. Under his raincoat, Vera's brother carried a powerful pistol. He had the haggard look of a hunted animal, and was prepared to blow his brains out rather than fall into the hands of the Nazis. After spending the night on the farm, he left the following day before dawn. Dimitri accompanied him a fair distance along the way to Zlatibor. Beyond the forest was the rearguard of the Partisans.

I didn't bring this anecdote up with Vera. If I had, she might have felt obligated to me. In any case, the past was just a necropolis of heroes. The adherents of the Master Design were feverishly building the new Tower of Babel and didn't have time to look back. Above the Party's immense construction site shone the sun of a future so brilliant that whoever looked straight at it could be blinded. This utopian vision, which had inspired so many thinkers and painters in the past, was once again becoming an obsession.

Our dialogue remained halting until I got up to leave.

"If my understanding is correct, you are not yet a member of the Party?"

"I never will be! You know me well enough for that."

"It's true. Already during the Occupation, you didn't know at what altar to worship," she said.

"That's right," I replied. "But the men caught in the wheels of the civil war went on killing one another through a kind of inertia, without really knowing why."

"You really think that? You'll always be a Klim Samgin, incapable of making up your mind for or against the revolution," she said.

"I have never read *The Life of Klim Samgin*, and Gorki never appealed to me either, as a man or as a writer. As for being for or against the revolution, that feels like a false dilemma —"

"What do you have against Gorki?" she asked.

"His silence during the Russian famine: the kulaks were being exterminated, and cannibalism had been reported in the Ukraine, yet during this time the great author was relaxing in Capri or Sorrento."

"Our comrades did not take such extreme measures lightly, but they had to save the Soviet homeland," she said. "You have a lot to learn ... but never mind, you can still be a good engineer."

Indeed, I still had many things to learn. Was this last statement a barely veiled threat or condescension towards a young man who was only good for running some machine? She had the unshakeable conviction of someone in possession of the one and only truth. My blood ran cold at the thought of how the struggle for a noble cause was used to justify the worst acts against humanity. Nevertheless, when all was said and done, I preferred my doubt and hesitations to Vera's convictions.

As I ran down the stairs, I was furious with myself. What evil force had goaded me into setting foot in this apartment haunted by the ghosts of the dead, and their stolen belongings? Why had I felt the need to see this woman again when we had nothing in common anymore? Why had these men and women, who had fought in the revolution in the name of the humble, the humiliated and the rejected, formed a new and privileged caste in such short order? To be sure, they continued to love the proletariat, but from afar, just as Tristan had loved Isolde.

Ah, if Vera only knew what I knew. Before the war, when the Party went underground, she and her husband had broken down during a special police interrogation, and betrayed their comrades. They had been expelled from the Party. The solicitor dropped the charges against Vera who was pregnant with their first child, but her husband received two years in prison for his clandestine activities. Thanks to the intercession of an uncle with a high position in the Department of External Affairs, he was able to finish his sentence in Ćačak, Vera's native city. During the day, he worked in the prison's accounts office and at night, when the little town quieted down, the door of the jail would open discreetly. The prisoner would glance furtively to the right and to the left and then slip out. Sticking close to the walls of the badly lit streets, he would make his way to his wife's cozy apartment. His second child was conceived during his incarceration, and to hush up the affair, Vera moved to her mother-in-law's home in Užice. These events occured at a time when a cruel and corrupt bourgeoisie was, luckily, still in power in the country.

※

University started late, in November. Some courses interested me more than others. For instance, descriptive geometry bored me terribly. I failed to see its usefulness. However, the presence of pretty young female students, from Belgrade's old families, did much to cheer us all up. These girls hoped to regain their social status, now threatened by the revolution, by earning an architect's degree.

The course Elements of Machines had nothing very exciting to offer, either. Drawing nuts, screw pitches, valves, and pipes on an old rococo table soon became exceedingly tedious. According to our professors who were still "old school," future engineers needed to possess a wide spectrum of knowledge, much of which turned out to be useless.

Apart from these existential problems of the post-war period, teaching materials were in short supply. In order to buy a compass, Bristol paper, China ink and precision rulers, we would stampede the Papyrus Bookstore across from the Royal Palace. Quite often after a long wait, the clerks would announce that the supplies of this or that had run out.

Professor Rašković was a brilliant teacher of statistics, but there again, the class questioned how the subject could be useful to us. A tall man with a bony face, Rašković would walk into the auditorium with the expression of a death-row prisoner, march up to the blackboard, meticulously draw the vectors and diagrams of the various forces, and then leave without uttering a single word that didn't have a direct bearing on the course. Rumour had it that the new powers-that-be were trying to pick a quarrel with him. He was their declared victim, and several times he was removed from the faculty only to be reinstated for lack of a more competent professor to teach physics. What did they have against him? Was it that he had completed his studies before the war, on a scholarship, no less, which was awarded by the royal army. Sheer stupidity rather than simple meanness was propelling the country towards disaster.

The only course to find favour in my eyes was the one on differential and integral calculus. It alone satisfied my intellectual curiosity. The assistant, Gojko Vujaklija, would line up formulas and exercises with such rigour and clarity that I had the impression of grasping everything immediately, which was not, of course, always the case. Had his courses been recorded, they could have been published as a manual.

The man had an aura of mystery about him. Given his age, he should have been a full-fledged professor, yet his doctoral thesis was still unfinished. The faculty kept him on as a permanent assistant because of his undeniable pedagogical gifts. They turned a blind eye to the small mimeographing business that allowed him to make ends meet. He was reputed to be an inveterate bridge player. He lived opposite the college, and every evening, without fail, between eight and nine o'clock, his neighbours would see him pace up and down the sidewalk. If it rained, he carried his umbrella with touching dignity. He would walk slowly, and his sphinx-like gaze fixed mysteriously on the middle distance, a pipe clamped between the teeth. What was he thinking about? No one knew. Was he dreaming of a more brilliant career?

My courses turned out to be a cruel disillusionment. When I left the army in October, I thought — naïvely— that I had escaped, once and for all, the gloomy and mind-numbing sessions of ideological indoctrination. November brought with it a rough awakening. The Master Design hadn't changed one iota. In fact, it was present in a more insidious form. Several times a week, just as a professor was leaving the auditorium, a student would pop up like a jack-in-the-box, mount the podium, and launch into a speech that was half sermon, half harangue. Those who thought they were being clever would dash for the door, only to be stopped by big beefy fellows blocking the exits. We would be forced to go back in, arm ourselves with patience and listen to the insipid speeches and odes glorifying the Grand Master, and exhortations to join a study circle, the famous *kružook*. Why had they resurrected this wretched Russian word that evoked the revolutionary fervor of the czarist period? Was it concern for our academic progress or did our activist comrades simply want to keep an eye on us?

Docile as sheep, we, whose ancestors rose up bare-handed against the Ottoman oppressors, would listen to all this nonsense. What had turned us into such cowardly, pusillanimous beings? I was deeply revolted and afraid that I might get up and scream at the top of my lungs: "Enough! We've had enough!" But I remained seated, fuming with rage. For how much longer?

This harassment by fellow activist students wasn't the only sign of the change creeping into the university, the city, and the whole country. One day, as we were leaving the lecture hall, we discovered a new mural-like bulletin board in the corridor that displayed a mish-mash of practical information likely to attract the attention of students. It was a barely disguised call to vigilance against reactionary elements. These boards were popping up at other institutions, like an invasive vine spreading its tendrils. One of the more dedicated students even asked our friend Slobodan P., a student at the Fine Arts Academy, if he would draw them a poster exhorting comrades to denounce the enemies of the people. Nobody took these warning signs seriously. This proved to be a mistake.

My life rapidly became routine, hedged in by courses and deadlines. There were technical drawings to hand in by a set date. On my way to the university, I would pick up Milenko, who lived on Galsworthy Street, a stone's throw from the austere granite building. After classes, we would head for his place to continue our discussions or listen to classical music. *La danse macabre* by Camille Saint-Saëns was our favourite record. We listened to it so often that Milenko claimed he could hear the bones click while I not only heard their sinister cracking but could almost see the bones performing their macabre dance, no doubt influenced by my visit to the Paris catacombs in 1937. The underground ossuary was stacked high with bones. And so Milenko and Saint-Saëns took over my musical education. Sometimes Slobodan P. would join us to listen to these old pre-war records.

Some evenings, I would linger at Milenko's until midnight, helping him hard-wire one of his inventions. The device was an impressive metallic desk bristling with calibration instruments and radio tube sockets. Milenko was working on ways of quickly detecting problems in the radios that were brought to him for repair.

Such was my life at that time.

Aunt Lou, who had retired a few years earlier, was called back to work at the Ministry of Transport. They needed her extensive experience in the purchase and distribution of railway ties, to "rebuild the nation." As she never came home before two-thirty in the afternoon, I ate lunch at the university in a restaurant known as *The Three Skeletons*. It got its name from a famous poem about three skeletons that haunted the sleepless nights of a pasha. The stuffed cabbage and white beans, regulars on the menu, were our survival food. In those days the most meagre portions still seemed like a miracle.

Even today, when I think back to those young men and women struggling courageously to build themselves a future, I have a lump in my throat. We were so poor and yet rich with youth, that irreplaceable wealth.

༄

Election Day, scheduled for November 11, 1945, was preceded by a campaign that resembled a country fair — half theatre, half Venetian carnival, a noisy farce staged under a gloomy sky. The boundary between reality and delirium was being wiped out. Spectators were merging with the actors. Sane men and women thought they were going mad while the gullible believed they were living in the best of all worlds.

The country was sliding into unreality. Like the negative of a photograph, black became white and white became black, justice became injustice, courage cowardice, slavery freedom, hatred love and vice versa. The day after the elections, caught up in the dementia I felt the need to walk like a blind person, with arms outstretched, so great was the darkness in daylight.

Every morning, according to a pre-established order, the front pages of the newspapers introduced us to the main protagonists in this monumental farce. The phenomenon had been ongoing for quite some time, but after the announcement of the general election, it took on extraordinary dimensions. There they were in their grotesque get-ups. The Grand Master, a locksmith by profession, always occupied the front page, either disguised as a marshal or as an admiral. His ample chest studded with numerous decorations made him look like a

Christmas tree decked in tawdry jewelry. His fleshy mask stared out at the world with supreme contempt, or so it seemed to many of us. But to the disciples of the Master Design his expression was proof of masculine self-confidence. To each his own interpretation.

Looking as if he had just come off the mountain, a young activist "philosopher" with thick wavy hair and a Zarathustra-like mask was often featured on the front page, but below the Grand Master, as befitted his rank. Lower still was the teacher, the official interpreter of the Master Design, disguised as an ordinary guy and resembling the man on the Gillette razor-blade package. The ex-village tailor, in the uniform of the Director of the Secret Police, usually appeared on the second or third page.

In the city's business centre, the same faces were reproduced on huge banners, several storeys high, and hung from the balconies of buildings and let to float in the breeze. The unfortunate tenants living behind these banners did not complain: the honour of contributing to the glory of these great men was secretly mixed with the pleasure of not having to look at them.

As the elections approached, average citizens, factory workers, and government employees took to the streets and walked in lengthy processions. A pedestrian emerging from a side street could suddenly run into a colourful and rambunctious crowd, moving slowly like an old-fashioned religious procession. Instead of banners and holy pictures, this human river carried red flags, streamers, and signs proclaiming their undying fidelity to the Central Committee. Up front the marchers carried large posters of their beloved leaders, and of the founders and inventors of the Master Design — Marx, Engels and Hegel — all of them already beatified. But what was Hegel, Prussia's official philosopher, doing in their company? Vera was right, I still had a lot to learn.

Who was this puppet theatre intended for? Why bother staging mock elections in a country governed by a single party? Since the Party preached dictatorship by the proletariat, was it necessary to stage such a show?

Stalin's promise made to Churchill and Roosevelt at the palace of Livadia in February 1945 had to be honoured, so free elections had to be held in all the countries of Eastern Europe. The ambassadors of the great Western powers were under no illusions; nevertheless, they observed this farce without protesting. Actually, it was no farce. If the Western powers allowed themselves to be duped, surely it was because they wanted to be duped. But our new leaders were very serious about their masquerade. They needed to confer some false legitimacy on their actions. Upon further reflection, did not this attitude betray a hint of the bourgeois code of behaviour?

In the wings, the Grand Master was busy pulling strings with his pudgy fingers, a five-carat diamond ring flashing on his left hand. On stage the puppets in their new costumes were getting restless. The cheering of citizens sounded forced, but no one dared rebel. Fear had infected us with the habit of submission to authority.

The performance unfolded according to a tight script. Candidates were picked during electoral meetings. Some were former Resistance fighters, while others were old hacks who had followed the erratic Party line for ten or twenty years. They looked harmless, if somewhat surreal to a keen observer. The participants knew their roles by heart. Each one in turn would get up, recite his or her lines and sink back into anonymity, like the cuckoo of a Tyrolean clock. The audience would applaud or boo, as planned by the comrades. Afterwards the audience would disperse, feeling as if they had been performers in a crazy play. Sometimes a crank, in a fit of madness, would stand up and say what had been bothering him for a long time. The panicked organisers would rush at him, forcing him either to sit down or leave, and everything would settle down again.

To make the people swallow the rigged elections, the Party invented the Popular Front as an alternative, and plucked a few docile old gentlemen with starched collars out of mothballs to be candidates. By appealing to their vanity — the last consolation of old age — the Party bought them off with honours rather than with cash. In Belgrade, the Party dug up a biology professor, and made him the leader of the Popular Front. He had lived peaceably enough through the Occupation, but after Belgrade's liberation, he suddenly discovered a belated vocation as a revolutionary, a not infrequent phenomenon in those post-revolutionary times.

No one was duped. The dice were loaded and future deputies had no worries about losing. However, in an effort to emulate democratic countries, the leaders would go into the factories and onto the job sites to whip up enthusiasm and support for the candidates. At times, the Grand Master himself would make an appearance to harangue workers and peasants, seeking their votes — already decided in advance. The poor devils would applaud frenetically. The Grand Master and his acolytes had reinvented the electoral machine — and it was a masterpiece of ingenuity. The uncertainties of a democratic electoral system were safely shelved. On the day of the vote, I had a close look at just how the machine operated.

In October, the appearance of a weekly newspaper called *Democracy* gave us a glimmer of hope. It was the organ of the Democratic Party whose president, Milan Grol, had just returned from three years' exile in London. The necessity of creating a semblance of free elections had earned us this first and only voice of the Opposition. It appeared like a ray of light in a leaden sky. People would rush out to buy *Democracy* much as thirsty nomads hasten towards an oasis, but because they were afraid of being seen by the Party henchmen, they would ask for *Politika* and then whisper: "Stuffed." The vendor would hand them the daily stuffed with *Democracy*. Predictably, the newspaper was short-lived. Many copies were destroyed in bonfires around the city.

One day, near the Theatre of the Performing Arts, I saw a pile of newspapers burning on the sidewalk. The blackened pages were twirling almost cheerfully in the air before being scattered by the wind. A laughing group of young people was gathered around the fire, going through the motions of a ritualistic dance. A man of about twenty, with a bloodied face and a hand clamped over his mouth, brushed past me.

"What's happening?" I asked him.

"Don't ask! They're all bullies ... brutes! They broke my tooth. They're burning copies of *Democracy*."

The young man hurried away towards Slavija Square. An old man who had witnessed the scene, and shaking his head disapprovingly gave me a brief explanation. The young man was likely a student, and had been selling *Democracy* for the past week. The bullies had singled him out and threatened to beat him up, but he refused to be intimidated. That day, they had carried out their threat and confiscated his newspapers, which they proceeded to burn.

The next day, the sidewalk was marked with a black spot, an ephemeral reminder of the demise of *Democracy*. The winds and rains of November would soon erase the mark. But the old man would probably recall this scene until his own death erased the memory of these toughs and the courageous student who stood up to them. Nothing remains, everything passes.

The paper ceased publication a week later. The ambassadors of the Western powers protested meekly, just for show, but the government declined any responsibility. The pretext given was that the typographers' union had refused to publish a reactionary newspaper. Wasn't that proof enough of the freedom that reigned in the country? Drowning in lies, hypocrisy, and deceit, we couldn't summon up the energy to protest.

While the Opposition newspaper was burning in little piles around the city, the streets were being invaded by mysterious troops. Men and women, dressed in sloppy grey uniforms, marched to a martial beat and sang at the tops of their lungs:

*Comrade, Marshal, white violet,*
*We love you, we want you to know.*
*Comrade, Marshal, morning flower,*
*The entire country is behind you.*

A detachment of soldiers crossing Ilija Street reminded me of the final scene of the old film *We Are Not Alone*, showing English soldiers from the First World War going down the road on their way to battle, singing, while in a London prison, an innocent man, played by Paul Muni, was about to be hanged. These soldiers would also die for nothing. I was eighteen when I saw the film and these images had upset me.

The young recruits crossing the street in front of me were not about to die, however. But their cadenced step and the innocence with which they hailed the glory of a self-proclaimed marshal left me pensive. They would probably never even get to meet the Great Man, and as for him, he was haughtily ignoring them, perched on his mighty throne. History! A succession of crimes!

In the final days before the election, these soldiers would haunt the neighbourhood, marching in lockstep. Where were these men and women going, where were they coming from, belting out this moronic song into the fresh autumn air? Was it sheer coincidence that they popped up at every street corner or were they obeying orders to intimidate us and to make us forget our dream of freedom? I will never know, but I still can hear their boots and the ridiculous lyrics:

*Comrade, Marshal, white violet,*
*We love you, we want you to know.*

Finally, the big day arrived. For the first time in my life, I would be voting, but in rigged elections. I felt sickened and humiliated by the whole procedure. The entire country suffered from a split personality. Everyone knew that the chips were down. Nevertheless, preparations were undertaken as if we lived in a normal country. Fiction and reality coalesced, forcing us to live through this nightmare. Aunt Lou was probably going through the same misery as I was, but she never complained. Men and women brought up on freedom cannot understand the despair we felt.

On November 11, after breakfast, anxious to be done with this farce, I hurried over to the polling station located in a *café* at the corner of Ilija and King Milutin Streets. The newspapers had explained in great detail the voting procedure, but one of the returning officers insisted on refreshing my memory. He handed me a small red rubber ball. I was supposed to drop the ball into one of a succession of boxes to indicate my choice. Theoretically, this procedure was to give me the illusion of choosing a candidate, but since the candidates were all marionettes manipulated by the Party, the choice was between a white hat and a white hat.

But I almost forgot: there was a box reserved for the Opposition. After dropping my red ball into that one, I had to show the officer in charge my empty hand as proof of having discharged my duty as a citizen.

There was no denying the secret nature of the vote, but this secrecy served no purpose because the person elected would belong either to the Party or to the Popular Front. Depositing my ball in the box reserved for the Opposition was meaningless. Citizens could, at the very most, shift the percentage of voices in favour of candidates, but nobody was under the illusion that the Opposition box would contain more balls than the Party boxes.

The election of the deputy to the Chamber of Republics merely followed the same burlesque script. The box reserved for the Opposition was unofficially referred to as "one-eyed." The term *one-eyed*, in the vernacular, evoked a squinting, repulsive bum. The newspapers and the pamphlets vilified this ballot box as if it were evil. Only vile reactionaries would deposit their balls into such an abject container. Moreover, rumours claimed that the sound of the ball falling in that box would betray the unwise voter. He or she would expose themselves to unforeseen consequences. True or false, this rumour transformed the Opposition's box into an object of evil.

I decided not to be intimidated. The returning officers, members of the Party, looked at me as if they could read my heretical thoughts. I plunged my closed fist into the urns of the official candidates, but without releasing the ball. My heart beat wildly, like a captive bird's. After introducing my hand into the accursed box, I released the ball. It made a discreet sound. Panic-stricken,

I turned around and peered at the returning officers as if to beg their forgiveness. They smiled back at me with malicious smiles. They had heard that muffled sound. After showing them my empty hand, I went back to the table for a second ball, the one for the Chamber of Republics. The president of the polling station smiled in a friendly fashion, as if to say: "It doesn't matter, young man. Your vote won't change anything."

Afterwards, the whole procedure went very quickly. Feeling distraught, I released the second ball in the first box, the official-candidates' box, and inserted my hand into the other boxes as a matter of course. The officers gratified me with an ironic "Thank you, comrade" and a "Good day, comrade." At least that is what my pathological sensitivity had me believe. As I left the polling station, I had the impression of having passed before a strange tribunal that never reveals its sentence, but from which there is no escape.

Once back in the street, I was really annoyed at myself. Why the devil had I not voted for the Opposition in the second round as I had in the first? I had lost my nerve when I overheard the slight noise. As for my aunt, I didn't dare ask whom she had voted for, but I could guess how distressed she was feeling. We carried our secret like a hidden shame.

I spent the rest of the day in a state of nervous agitation, walking back and forth between Galsworthy and Ilija Streets. I was hoping for a miracle against all hope, an awakening of our people's conscience in a nation that had once prized its freedom so highly. But this was only a pipe dream. The Party had invented a diabolical electoral machine, suppressing anything unforeseen or random.

That evening, after the polls closed, I was a bit encouraged by the results posted outside the polling stations at Ilija and King Milutin Streets as well as at Harvig Street. Amazingly the

Opposition had not won but it had carried a third of the vote. True, this didn't change anything but a sliver of hope glimmered amidst the greyness. There were still courageous individuals out there. My aunt did not share my optimism and called me naïve. My one half agreed with her but I continued to hope against hope. Physically and mentally exhausted, I fell into bed and slept like a log.

The next morning I was in for a big surprise. *Politika* announced the results of the vote in Belgrade and throughout the country. The Party candidates had won by an astounding margin, sometimes by 99 percent. Incredulous, I read and re-read the numbers, as if by dint of looking at them, they would change because only the day before the bulletin boards had said otherwise. All kinds of strange ideas came crowding into my head. I accepted that the Party had falsified the results, but to that extent? No, they wouldn't have dared. Someone once said that the greater the lie, the more believable it is. The art of lying is in the daring.

I decided to go back to my polling station. The results posted the day before might still be there. Obsessed by this idea, I almost ran to King Milutin Street. Not a trace of the station or the bulletins. The *café* had resumed its usual appearance. And yet yesterday, the men in charge of the boxes had sat there like stern-faced judges. Their sly smiles had intimidated me. Who knows if they were not already enjoying the knowledge of my future punishment?

Without knowing exactly why, I went in. The strong whiff of tobacco smoke made me feel nauseous. Two or three customers, seated at tables with wine-stained cloths and cigarette burns, were drinking *sljivovica*. They looked at me indifferently. I backed away, overcome by a visceral revulsion. Outside, under a grey sky, another autumn day was beginning.

One possibility remained. I could go to the publishers of *Politika* and then ask, if by chance, a small error might have falsified the results of the election, at least for our district. But why bother? They would only laugh at me and might even denounce me as a subversive. I walked up the street quickly. Were these elections just a bad dream?

As I was about to open the door at 42 Ilija Street, I heard soldiers singing in the distance. I stopped to listen. The ghostly company was approaching from Slavija Square. Finally, they appeared, pounding the pavement with their determined step, belting out the usual refrain:

*Comrade, Marshal, white violet,*
*We love you, we want you to know.*

The company crossed Ilija Street and disappeared towards the School of Nursing. Their song lasted a few more minutes and then stopped. The elections had indeed taken place. Behind the visible one, there existed another secret and tormented Belgrade.

Without a doubt, the city reflected the deep changes that slowly but surely were taking place in all of us. Nobody was able to resist the changing times.

# IV

# The Abyss

> ...*human adventure will exist as long as a desire for the abyss still exists.*
> — GUIDO CERONETTI

THE SIGN ANNOUNCING the lecture was written in sprawling letters: *Does God Exist?* It hung in all the faculty halls of Belgrade University. In the mood of that era, it simply meant: God is dead! For the second time! Years earlier, a German philosopher had proclaimed His death *ex cathedra*. But God was tough. He still haunted the sick and the aged hovering on the brink of death. Sometimes, those who had denied his existence since their youth invoked him as their existential flame began to flicker. A wise precaution in case He really did exist. Of course, a few priests continued to sing hosannas. Was it merely habit or were they possessed by an ardent faith?

As the year 1945 drew to a close, God's condition was becoming ever more dire. Not that the number of atheists or agnostics was suddenly on the rise but, for the first time in centuries, a secular government thought it could do without God. In the past, coins used to proclaim: *God Save Yugoslavia*. In the schools, catechism was taught, soldiers swore fidelity to the New Testament, the Koran, or the Torah. But since the Revolution, the State had thanked God for his services. Fired, banished, chased from the schools, the barracks and the hospitals, He was now only tolerated in the cemeteries. In fact, having become a pariah and a laughingstock, as in the days of the Nazarene, He had no reason to complain. Had He not proclaimed: "My kingdom is not of this world?" His new situation had a certain advantage: the lukewarm, the hypocrites, the bigots, and the Pharisees were repudiating Him publicly. Yet curiously enough, His desperate situation attracted sympathisers among the indifferent and even the agnostic, as if He represented a last rampart against thought that had congealed.

I took the streetcar to National Theatre Square. Large snowflakes were falling on the city and a soft white blanket muffled the noise of traffic. I walked towards the Faculty of Philosophy, feeling a bit nervous as if I were about to take an exam. Milenko had categorically refused to accompany me. "If you want my opinion, the lecture is a total fraud and you'll only waste your time." He was probably right, but, as usual, curiosity drove me to attend this lecture that promised to galvanize minds and consciences.

In Students' Square, dark silhouettes converged on the old building. Inside the hall, the atmosphere was effervescent. My cousin Sofija beckoned to me. Recently demobilized, she was still wearing her military cape. Her presence didn't surprise me. She had always been *avant-garde*. A stone staircase, worn down by generations of students, led up to the large conference room. It was full to capacity and people still kept piling in. The attendance at the lecture probably exceeded the organisers' most optimistic expectations. Was it simple curiosity that had brought these droves of young people out on a December evening, or a desire to witness the public execution of God? Or did they assistant kept nodding his head in approval. Another student quoted Dostoyevsky, who had wanted to be with Christ even though he had been told God didn't exist. The student was advised to take up healthier reading, and several voices accused him of obscurantism. There were a few forced laughs, but it was impossible to tell why or who they were laughing at. Another student who stood head and shoulders above the crowd asked to be heard several times. Finally, he was given the floor, but instead of asking a question, he screamed at the top of his lungs: "May God bless you all." His words provoked a wave of hilarity and brought the evening to an end.

Gradually, the hall emptied. Something felt unfinished, for believers and non-believers alike. God's death by decree felt as illusory as the theologians' confirmation of His existence. A curious affinity was emerging between those who were non-believers because they had never seen Him walking the Milky Way and the ecstatic types who claimed to have seen the Virgin in their hallucinatory visions. Both groups needed to see a thing in order to believe, yet does not the word "belief" imply trust?

Everyone understood: from now on, God was officially outlawed. If He existed, he would have to hide in one of those ancient, ruined churches frequented by bats. During the war, I had once entered one of these profaned temples. Weeds were pushing up between the tiles. The blue sky with small white clouds could be seen through the collapsed roof of the nave. From the top of the still-intact cupola, Christ offered forgiveness for mankind's folly. Only the chirping of the birds interrupted the silence. God's mystery will continue to exist until the last Judgment, or the death of the last member of the human race.

As I was leaving the Faculty, a couple of students walked by me. They had their arms around each other. The boy whispered to the girl: "The atheists will end up resuscitating God." Outside, the snow was still falling on my beloved city. Did God exist?

⁂

New Year's Eve at the Moscow Hotel left me with a sour taste in my mouth. Much adored by the citizens of Belgrade before 1914, this establishment, with its elaborately carved chairs and red marble tables on heavy pedestals, was now seamy and rundown. Clusters of globes diffused a gloomy, jaundiced light. The decor of this turn-of-the-century hotel belonged to a world that was fast disappearing.

On this last day of 1945, musicians in worn tuxedos played listlessly, and the evening felt flat before it even started. The memory of those marvelous balls at Alexander I High School made me even more morose. War and the Occupation had stolen the best years of our youth. They had deprived us of the full potential of our pleasure at a time when our lives were just beginning.

I danced, pretending to enjoy myself and to court a young girl with a dark complexion, long black hair, and large oval eyes who reminded me of the queens on the frescoes, but my heart wasn't in it. All evening a voice kept whispering to me: *This is your last New Year's Eve in Belgrade. The years will go by and every year men and women will gather here to celebrate, smelling of perspiration and perfume, and awaiting who knows what elusive miracle, while you will be far from Belgrade, in another city, another country.*

At midnight, just as the lights went out, I deposited a chaste kiss on my partner's lips, feeling that I was committing a sacrilege against love. When the yellow globes came back on, some fool threw a handful of confetti in our eyes. Streamers floated above our heads while all around us couples engaged in long sensual kisses. I saw skeletons and skulls everywhere, and the English waltz failed to drown out *La danse macabre* playing softly in my head. Perhaps I was unwell.

The evening finished awkwardly. I bid goodbye to my partner in front of the Moscow Hotel in the early hours of the morning. She left on the arm of her brother, an artist, seemingly surprised to have fallen upon such an eccentric. The idea came to me to excuse myself, but why? I left heading for Slavija Square, happy to be walking in the cold air of the New Year. Large snowflakes melted on my flushed face. Near the Theatre for the Performing Arts, a drunken reveller wished me a happy new year. Happy New Year! You had to be pretty stupid to think the year ahead would be good. I slipped into bed quietly so as not to disturb my aunt. The big tile stove was growing cold but the room still retained a soft heat. If only dawn would never come.

The next day I had to buckle down and memorise the answers to 140 questions in inorganic chemistry. But, in reality, why bother? Because the faculty insisted, just as it insisted on a whole lot of other useless things. I was never good at it, unlike Milenko, who was passionate about chemistry. He had even set up a laboratory in the woodshed behind his home. An experiment that had blown up the shed almost cost him his eye. The next day, his mother dismantled what was left of the lab.

The exam was an oral. We took it together late one January afternoon in a poorly heated amphitheatre full of shivering students, each awaiting their turn. Professor Leko, in his overcoat, questioned us with the respect that old-timers showed to the humblest of their students.

Oh, my venerable professors, if you only knew the affection I felt for you, how I respected and pitied you for having to submit to the wishes of a few upstarts who, empowered by the

Party, insisted on turning this time-honoured institution upside down.

With our chemistry exam successfully behind us, Milenko and I once again became preoccupied with the thought of going into exile. In fact, since our first meeting on the day after my return from Niš, the idea had never left us, though at times it faded. Some days, the very thought of leaving the country filled me with terror. How would we cross a border we knew nothing about? I imagined it policed by guards with sharp-fanged dogs. The thought of being captured by these brutes was not especially appealing. And what if we managed to cross the border without mishap, what would we do in *terra incognita* without a passport, money, friends, or knowledge of the language? Unable to picture it, I kept repeating to myself that somehow we would manage, like all those who had gone before us.

Or should we stay? After all, my life was unfolding peacefully enough between university and Ilija Street. The road ahead was clear: studies, an engineer's diploma, marriage. It all boiled down to stopping my ears and closing my eyes in order to accept the world my generation had been handed by fate and history. Toe the line and bow to this absurd and omnipresent system? Remain silent? Everything was pointing to a choice between exile and a life reduced to nothing. Could I be content with such a life?

In this state of confusion, I thought of visiting our classmate, Aleksandar Veljković. And why Alex in particular? Because the idea of leaving the country must certainly have occurred to this passionate anglophile who worked at the British Embassy. One afternoon in January, I found myself in front of his villa at 80 Ilic Street.

Alex's mother opened the door. She looked at me with a frightened expression, as if she was expecting bad news. The bourgeoisie were living in a state of constant anxiety, fearful that their homes would be requisitioned for housing for the Party cadres. But her case was more serious. I found Alex in bed, not really sick, but wild-looking and demoralised. Ever since the New Year, he had been expecting to be arrested.

"Why?" I asked.

"On New Year's Eve, I was in the American Embassy jeep that hit and killed an officer of the Yugoslav army."

"But you weren't driving. What do they have against you?"

"Don't you understand? It makes no difference to them. They're out to get me! They swore they would quite a while ago. They'll arrest me, I know it! If you don't want to get into trouble, you're best not to stay here. They could become interested in you, too."

"Calm down and tell me quietly what happened."

His background, though unusual, was not surprising in the world we were living in. During our years in school, mathematics had been Alex's pet hate, whereas French or German grammar and spelling held no secrets for him. As if that were not bad enough, he started learning English at age fourteen with the passion of the self-taught, as much out of love for the language as for the country of Shakespeare. Unfortunately, that had caused him problems.

In February 1941, during the last winter of peace in Yugoslavia, he came back to the boarding school well after hours one Sunday evening. He was very upset. The police had stopped him coming out of the British Embassy and had confiscated his English magazines, illustrated and published in Greece, a country already at war with Italy. Alex had offered to translate the subtitles of the photos, type them and glue them over the original texts. That way the whole class could look through the magazines that showed the English submarines docked in a Greek port, and the landing of British troops in Piraeus.

Yugoslavia, still spared by the war, had to respect its neutrality, at least formally. However, the people of Belgrade liked the British. It was an open secret. And this attitude explained the brevity of our friend's arrest.

After the war, thanks to his knowledge of English, Alex got a job with the British Embassy. He spent his days happily, with a more-than-adequate salary plus goods he received in kind, a considerable bonus in those days. This state of affairs might have lasted a long time had the secret police not zeroed in on him. A man working in the embassy of a capitalist country could pass on precious information. Our friend was called into the office of a colonel of the Secret Services. He proposed that Alex collaborate with them, and even dangled before him certain material benefits, but Alex refused outright. He refused to spy on the United States which had been our ally in two world wars. The colonel suggested he take a little time to reflect, but Alex was firm.

"You're free to refuse, that's your right, but watch out, we'll be waiting for you around the next corner," said the colonel.

This expression, common at the time, was very threatening. Eerily enough, it applied in Alex's case almost to the letter. The Embassy jeep, driven by a tipsy American, had knocked down a Yugoslav officer while rounding a corner onto Mostar Square, even as I was celebrating my lackluster New Year at the Moscow Hotel. Was he innocent or guilty? It was of little importance. The tribunals didn't condemn people for real crimes. Instead, imaginary ones were substituted. It was all fiction. In any case, the Grand Master had said to one of his friends: "You can always invent guilt."

It was already night when I found myself back on the poorly lit street. My shoes made a strange muffled sound in the melting snow. The cold gripped my body and soul. Once again I had the bizarre impression of moving through a liquid that was gradually thickening and threatening to trap me, of being suspended in a kind of transparent sap. I was condemned to the same fate as flies that millions of years ago were imprisoned in amber. Escape! Escape! Escape this terrible death. Unfortunately, I could do nothing for Alex. A month later, we learned of his arrest. He was sentenced to five years in prison for conspiring with a foreign power.

When I was living in Paris at the Hotel du Château, a recent Yugoslav refugee told me the epilogue of this unfortunate New Year's Eve accident. Alex spent five years in the Zabela Penitentiary, near Požarevac. He did all kinds of manual work with the political prisoners and the criminals. During that time, amnesty was sometimes granted to common-law offenders on national holidays, but his sentence was not shortened by a year, a month, or a day. When he was released, he managed to finish his studies by giving private English lessons. Later, he lived modestly by tutoring future airline pilots. In another country he would have been a brilliant philologist. In ours, he was a convict and lived the life of a pariah — and his was not an isolated case. The lives of thousands of men and women were upended to the detriment of us all. Ours was a country of broken destinies.

During this time in the West, intellectual progressives were agitating, responding to Stockholm's call for peace, signing petitions, supporting countless noble causes, attending conferences held by the Soviets and dreaming of a big red sun rising in the East. We knew it was nothing but a dead star.

February was crammed with courses, diagrams and assignments to be handed in, and cabling the tube-testing device Milenko was constantly working on. We continued going to the opera and eagerly awaited Djordje Le Voyageur, the brilliant flutist from the Prague Conservatory who was always the last one in the orchestra pit. We knew that he had just swallowed a glass of red wine at the bistro opposite the artists' entrance. In the foyer during intermission, Milenko made eyes at a singer who was not performing that evening.

Life was fairly uneventful. The snow started to melt as we headed into March. Winter was coming to an end and I hadn't once put on my skis or gone dancing — except for that gloomy New Year's Eve at the Moscow Hotel. The time for amusement was definitely over.

On March 25, 1946, towards four in the afternoon, the doorbell rang. As I was shaving before going out to see *The Marriage of Figaro* I opened the door with my face all lathered up. The janitor was standing there. He was going door-to-door, urging tenants to show up at President Wilson Square in front of the railway station. The Grand Master of the Keys was returning from Warsaw, and Belgrade was getting ready to welcome him. My answer was immediate: "I'm shaving, and then I'm on my way." I had to make an effort not to laugh. The poor man bowed, and thanked me profusely, probably overwhelmed at meeting such a zealous citizen.

All over the city, thousands of concierges were canvassing people door-to-door in an effort to drum up enthusiasm. The huge square had to be filled to welcome back the great man. Poor Belgrade, so tightly monitored by concierges and street secretaries. Not only were they to be on the lookout for enemies of the people, but they were to whip up enthusiasm among the population, a sentiment that was sorely lacking. As for going to greet the Grand Master, the idea had never even occurred to me. My one run-in with the man in November 1941 had more than sufficed.

The day after his triumphant homecoming the truth exploded. At first there seemed nothing unusual about the photograph splashed across the front page of *Politika*, showing the crowds gathered in the square for the Grand Master's arrival. But a few skeptics examined the photo more closely and discovered that it was a photomontage. The reporter, panicked by the poor attendance, had come up with the unfortunate idea of photographing the crowd twice, hoping to multiply the number of people in the same way Jesus had the loaves and the fish on the shores of Lake Tiberias. The discovery of this deception tore through Belgrade like wildfire. The "hundred thousand people" who supposedly had turned out to welcome the head of state, as announced by *Politika*, suddenly collapsed like a pricked balloon, and the "glorious welcome" became an object of derision. The hapless reporter became the scapegoat in this affair and paid a high price for his stratagem: the authorities accused him of falsifying the photograph in order to tarnish the glory of the great man.

The new lords of the land took advantage of the leader's return from Poland to mount a propaganda campaign, the true purpose of which they kept secret. A journalist asked the Grand Master, as he was stepping off the train, if it was true that General Mihajlović, head of the Nationalist Resistance, was in the hands of the English. The president answered as haughtily as usual: "I don't know, but I think he will soon be in our hands." As we later discovered, the general was already imprisoned on Gypsy Island. In whose head had this grotesque lie germinated? Was it to convince those still in doubt that the new rulers were now firmly in control? Many years later, the second in command, by then turned renegade, admitted that the leaders at that time believed in their absolute power.

The news of the general's arrest was officially confirmed a few days later. A handful of activists from the university hurriedly improvised a demonstration celebrating his capture. The students coming out of class were herded towards the entrance hall to listen to the harangues of the youthful orators. We were treated to the sight of a few parading toadies who during the war had been careful to hide their true colours. Once the balance of power had swung safely to one side, they emerged from the wings to proclaim their allegiance to the new masters. The details of these speeches evaporated from my memory a long time ago, but this spontaneous demonstration taught me one thing: when a man is down, the cowards are the first to pounce on their quarry.

One April morning, as I was about to board a streetcar in Slavija Square, I ran into my former classmate, Angel. We had spent seven years together at Alexander I High School, sitting on the same benches and sleeping in the same dormitory. This sort of experience forges strong links.

Our last meeting had taken place back in June 1941 — the day Hitler launched Operation Barbarossa against the Soviet Union. Belgrade had been under German Occupation since April of that year. That Sunday we were taking our orals for the baccalaureate. Angel, lucky enough to have received a dispensation because of his high marks, had come to say goodbye. He was returning to Novi Sad, which had been annexed by Hungary after the Armistice in 1918. In those uncertain times, it seemed highly improbable that we would ever see each other again.

My friend was now barely recognizable. Formerly one of the smallest boys in the class, he was now taller than me. In school, he had always been impeccably dressed and groomed. In fact, everything he owned was top-of-the-line, as befitted a senator's son. I still remember his wooden clothes hangers, which were shaped like a pair of shoulders. His father must have bought them abroad. Dressed in old army gear that made him look like a newly demobilized soldier, Angel did not look like a boy born with a silver spoon in his mouth. And yet the face hadn't changed: clean-shaven, with a pink complexion, as if he descended from English gentry.

I was very happy to run into him at the streetcar stop. I remembered Angel as a very likeable person — serious, honest, modest and moderate. There was a lot of Voltaire's *Candide* in this young man's make-up.

We talked about all kinds of things, but particularly of our boarding school days. We also recalled, albeit a bit uncomfortably, our plan to resist the Nazi enemy around the time we were taking our exams. Milenko was going to build a transmitter-receiver and send Angel instructions in Morse code on a 31-metre wavelength. The message would be signed Caligula, Milenko's nickname which only his classmates knew. In hindsight, this "operation" seemed terribly childish, but in 1941 we were just emerging from adolescence, and were bursting with impatience to oust the enemy from our country.

We also talked about our adventures during the war and Angel told me about his time in the Resistance during the summer of 1944. I asked him what he was doing now. He was taking courses at a new school for journalists and future diplomatic staff. Without a doubt, he had an enviable career ahead of him. Before leaving each other at National Theatre Square, we exchanged addresses and he promised to come and see us soon on Galsworthy Street.

On my way to pick up opera tickets, the memories of our time together at boarding school came rushing back to me. Angel had always followed through with his ideas. If memory served me well, he had been headed for the Foreign Service College. Every Thursday he would receive a French comic book through the mail. And he played tennis with a Slazenger racket. Knowing French and playing tennis would not be sufficient to get him into External Affairs, but it certainly would not hinder him. Had it not been for the war, Angel might have been third secretary in one of His Majesty's embassies. But it was never too late. The Popular Republic of Yugoslavia needed ambassadors. Kingdom or republic, what difference did it make if one had the vocation to serve one's country?

Two or three weeks after we'd met, Angel showed up one morning at Milenko's, still wearing his ragged clothes, which were hardly flattering. Milenko and I were trying to connect a cable to the measuring device when he appeared at the window. After the initial pleasure of seeing each other, we started sizing each other up. In those days, meeting old friends was a delicate game of hide-and-seek, each one trying to guess the other's ideas without revealing one's own. By using short innocuous sentences, we could show our true colours without actually compromising ourselves. If we sensed a kind of resonance in the other, we could reveal our hand further. Otherwise, it was best to withdraw carefully. In such a way ideology unravelled old friendships.

That morning we talked about the revolution and the many upheavals that had occurred in the country since the war began in 1941. Angel adhered to the new order with all the enthusiasm of his twenty years. It was not unexpected given his educational and professional path. We listened politely, but without sharing his zeal. He could not have had many doubts about where we stood. Angel sensed our reticence and regretted it. But he felt that as engineers, we could contribute a lot to the building of a new future for the country. I could almost hear Vera's *"You could at least become a good engineer."*

Had Angel guessed our heretical thoughts and our vague project of leaving the country, would he have betrayed us, or tried to dissuade us? Not to denounce a defector was tantamount to being an accomplice to a traitor and a villain.

He approved of our interest in the sciences because he believed that science could help humanity attain a Golden Age. In his opinion, that was the true purpose of science. This utilitarian concept of science, which reflected the thinking of the times, carried a whiff of beatific optimism about it straight out of the nineteenth century: Progress through science! I was reminded of the Crystal Palace built in London in 1851, which had inspired Dostoyevsky's *Notes from the Underground*. The inauguration of the Eiffel Tower in 1889 had stirred up a similar frenzy for progress.

We argued with him: "Scientific discoveries can be as deadly as they are beneficial, but that doesn't explain mankind's interest in the sciences. How do you explain this innate curiosity, this desire to understand the world?"

"But how are we more advanced by simply trying to satisfy our curiosity?" asked Angel.

"We're not. It is just a gratifying reaction, but why does everything have to serve a purpose?"

"To improve our lives," he answered.

From then on, our conversation resembled a serpent trying to bite off its tail. Angel's view of science was decidedly anthropocentric. For him, science was just another human activity that should serve history. For us, science was an exciting intellectual adventure, not lacking in beauty; an end in itself. At some point, feeling carried away, I had even written in my journal that science and poetry would eventually meet and merge in infinity. The gap separating Angel's thinking from ours could never be bridged.

Angel left, and we never saw him again. We were left to wonder about his enigmatic metamorphosis from a boy born into a liberal and cultured bourgeoisie into a man devoted to an egalitarian utopia subverted from the very start. No doubt the Party had a few brilliant thinkers in its midst, but their ideas were rendered powerless because the last word would always come from uncouth creatures in whom deviousness and cunning took the place of intelligence.

No matter how much I thought about his mysterious transformation, I could find no explanation for it, though Milenko and I did come up with a few hypotheses. Children from wealthy families sometimes suffer from belonging to the privileged class. They feel uncomfortable in their skin, weighed down and isolated by their status. They are moved by feelings of fraternity for those less fortunate. Had Angel felt something similar? Like many innocent young people of that time, was he dreaming of a just world from which corruption would be banished? Did he need to slum it in order to feel like a man? Or was he already driven by ambition and the desire for power, the supreme opiate? So many questions, so many mysteries.

One rainy day when we were sixteen or seventeen years old, Angel, Milenko and I sat in the deserted study hall discussing the exploited workers and the poor left to fend for themselves.

At the time Angel defended an idea as daring as it was utopian: a man of integrity, concerned about the underprivileged and the poor, should be able to gain power legally via the ballot box, and as leader of the government impose radical measures to help the disadvantaged. This was the only way to bring social justice into the world.

Did Angel view the revolution as a shortcut to his utopia? If so, he would commit himself body and soul to the Master Design, with all the passion and intransigence of the idealist. Nothing would make him deviate from this course, not a muzzled press, not rigged elections, nor prisons filled with the falsely accused or people condemned to death in mock trials; not even institutionalized corruption which, by its very nature, is unassailable. He might see this but would not want to accept it because the only thing that counted was the glorious halo that, one day, would wipe out the villainous acts and sufferings. Yes, even if revolution were purgatory, it would eventually lead to an earthly paradise.

We were at the end of the spring session when Kosta, our regular professor, required us to buy a perfectly useless book, a rhymed work in German and printed in Gothic characters. Even though the author was our German professor's brother, we wondered what had got into Kosta. Not surprisingly, the class objected. Feeling a revolt brewing, he decided to nip it in the bud and called a meeting.

I can recall the scene clearly. With his salt-and-pepper hair in disarray and his eternal scarf around his neck, Kosta paced nervously at the front of the classroom, like the pendulum of a clock, before tossing out this question to us: "Who among you refuses to buy this book?"

Like cowards, not one of us answered. In the deathly silence that followed, Angel got up: "I do, Sir."

His gesture did not lack for drama. Kosta, furious, felt like squashing him like a bug, but he knew that he was in the wrong so he swallowed his rage. Angel's refusal had no negative consequences. We discovered a new personality trait in our comrade who was usually so submissive to authority. His gesture was an important lesson in civic courage.

Almost thirty years later, our classmate Beli told us an anecdote that left most of us perplexed. Immediately after the war, Beli was sentenced to two years in prison for having fought in the Resistance under General Mihajlović. During his stay at Zabela Penitentiary, another prisoner told him about being beaten during an instruction period by a young man called Angel. According to his story, the instructor had almost "killed his soul."

Whose soul? Beli's story remained vague on this point but it triggered a vast reflection on the soul of a torturer and that of his victim. Beli could not confirm whether the Angel in question had been our comrade.

Sometimes when I think back to Angel and those times, I am forced to recognise that History had swept us up in its violence. The climate inspired weak and confused men to rise up, and it hurled them, one against the other, like wisps of straw in a storm of dust, tears, and blood. Few escaped unscathed.

༄

There are times in our lives when fate sends us a signal, a warning about impending danger, and yet we go along blithely, ignoring it.

Such was the case during my last spring in Belgrade. At the beginning of April, a group of activist students decided to celebrate May Day their own way. One day, after our compulsory mathematics class, they blocked the doors of the lecture hall and asked us to form teams of volunteers to landscape the lawn in front of the university. The May Day celebration was approaching and the city was expected to look festive. But exams were also approaching, and the volunteers were few. The activists insisted and a number of hands went up, limply. We were told that those who didn't help would be viewed poorly. A few more hands were raised. I refused to be coerced into volunteering even though collective action had always appealed to me because of the way it sparked solidarity. However, this forced volunteerism didn't inspire me.

For a week or two, groups of students could be seen digging, raking, and seeding the lawn with brand new tools. I was dubbed a shirker but the matter went no further. Probably a few students secretly approved of my action. I was disgusted to see my classmates busy toiling over a lawn when they should have been studying for their exams. What fool had had the temerity to cook up this scheme after the schools had been closed for four long years during the Occupation, depriving us of our education? Was it to ingratiate himself with his leaders?

On the last Sunday of April, aided and abetted by beautiful weather and a few spring showers, tender green shoots made a timid appearance. I felt ashamed at not having contributed to this new growth.

May 1 fell on a Wednesday. A reviewing stand was erected on Alexander I Boulevard in front of the Hotel Madera, seat of the Central Committee. In the morning, the army marched by with its floats and its hardware while the crowd, mainly government department employees, factory workers, and school children with their teachers, applauded our worthy military. The parade moved down the boulevard past the School of Engineering. The soldiers goose-stepped proudly past the imposing grey granite building. They were hailed by the activists and the volunteers who had gathered for the occasion, and mindlessly chanted slogans in honour of the army, the unions, and the factory collectives who filed by in an endless stream. Flags snapped in the breeze, and everyone had a great time. In the brouhaha, nobody paid attention to the lawn. Towards one in the afternoon, as the last marchers — members of the sports clubs — filed by in joyous disorder, our lovely tender lawn suffered its death throes. Trampled by thousands of bystanders, it reverted back to its original state — hard-packed earth.

Rest in peace, you tiny blades of grass, you who enjoyed the spring sunshine for only a few days, but rest assured, your death will not be in vain. It gave me an excellent lesson in the enormity of human stupidity. And you, my dear comrades, who wasted so much youthful energy digging, raking and planting, all for naught, I can still hear your songs praising the Master Design, and your lugubrious caterwauling.

Two days later, as I was came out of school, I couldn't help but view the trampled lawn with a certain malicious pleasure. It symbolized all the busyness and enormous energy that was spent on ridiculous work. But my modest triumph was short-lived.

As I walked past the two pink marble sphinxes, I met the Grand Duke, a first-class engineering student. He came by this rather fancy nickname because of his height and his Russian mother. He greeted me: "Congratulations, old man! You were lucky enough to make the bulletin board!" His words, heavily laced with irony spoiled my good mood.

The short text posted cut short any desire for mirth. A typed, apocryphal statement quoted me as saying: "I categorically deny having worked the most hours on the remaking of the lawn." A fairly harmless joke, though of questionable taste, it was nevertheless a clear warning: "Comrade, we're watching you!" At the time, the whole affair merely irritated me, and in a few days, I totally forgot about it. How foolish I was to do so.

༄

As a teenager, I spent my summers in Užice. Sometimes, my cousins and I would row on the river by the Grand Park, a favourite place for our walks. The river flowed lazily towards a dam and continued on through gorges of wild beauty. Hundred-year-old trees were reflected in the dark green water. At the time, we considered our youth a God given and inalienable gift.

One day, one of us invented a game, as diabolical as it was dangerous. We stopped rowing, and allowed the boat to drift slowly towards the spillway. At the edge of the dam, a thick body of greenish water plunged down into an abyss of rocks and foam. As we approached the falls, our boat accelerated, drawn by the current. We knew that beyond a certain point, we would be pulled over. The roar of the water filled us with terror. At the last moment, panic-stricken, we started to row frantically and wrenched ourselves away from the pull of the abyss. This was the only time we ever played this horrifying game.

When I think of my first and only year at Belgrade University, the memory of this dangerous game still comes back to me, but then I was drifting towards a different abyss. I had refused to work as a volunteer on the university lawn, I was not part of a study circle, and I never joined the communist youth group. Slowly but surely, I was heading toward the cataract.

Professor Rašković had just finished his lecture on statistics. The blackboard was still covered with his drawings of vectors and parallelograms. The students were gathering up their books, preparing to leave the hall. Suddenly, a gang of tough-looking characters blocked all the exits. A comrade took the stage on a mission to improve our political education, or so I surmised.

This kind of farce occurred two or three times a month. We had grown used to it and would simply return to our seats. But this time we were told we would be attending the funeral of a student who had died during the Resistance. We would go in groups at such and such an hour and place, to follow the funeral procession.

Men who die for their ideas have always elicited my respect, even when I do not sympathise with their cause. But how could one not resist those who were treating us like cattle, we who were searching for a little place in the sun? In whose name did they want to turn us into puppets? My stomach knotted into a hard lump of revolt.

As if in a trance, I got up and walked down the steps. Was it really me? Heads turned in surprise as I descended. The speaker lost his train of thought. Like an automaton I continued walking towards the exit, disturbing everyone. My friends thought I had suddenly gone crazy. I reached the door after what seemed like an eternity. Two of the guards blocked my way.

"So, comrade. Are you deaf? Everyone in their seats!"

"Comrade, I feel nauseous."

"Oh, indeed!"

The two beefy guards, struck speechless by my insolence, hesitated. Should they hit me in front of almost a hundred students, or allow me to leave? Well-trained but unsure of what to do, they turned towards the man perorating on the stage. Disdainfully, he signalled them to let me go. The meaning was clear. We'll settle his case later.

Had I pretended to be really sick, they might have let me go scot-free, but instead, I looked the guards in the eye and taunted them. Was it me carrying on like that? Or was it someone else, a distant ancestor reincarnated in my flesh, who was appalled by his descendant's cowardice?

The door guards let me go but their expressions were anything but reassuring. Now, it was merely a question of time before the university expelled me. That day, I passed beyond the point of no return.

As I went down the monumental staircase of the School of Engineering, reality struck. I was horrified by the enormity of my gesture. I felt numb with fear. Before the war, even during King Peter's reign, the commissars would regularly beat up students who refused to give money to the Party, such as my friend Ivan Pajić. Now they were in full control and my capriciousness would not go unpunished. Once again, my quick temper had prompted me to make a dramatic move that was beyond my capabilities.

Outside, the weather in this, our first peacetime spring, was lovely. The streetcars were trundling along, and at the corner of Students' Park, old Vuk Karadžić, resplendent in bronze, remained impassive. How would the man who reformed the Serbian language have judged my behaviour — had he not been dead for over eighty years — a man who went from being a self-taught shepherd to a tower of strength, intelligence, and determination? Would he have understood my behaviour, he who corresponded with Goethe and the brothers Grimm, and who often had turned to the West for enlightenment and justice for the humiliated and the abused? Would he have upbraided me like a father, or would he have approved of my act, this man who had had the courage to stand up to an illiterate prince? Vuk Karadžić had preferred to remain poor but free rather than submit to the will of a despot. Now forever silent on his pedestal — a beggar for eternity — his eyes were turned heavenward still pleading for his enslaved people.

In a funny kind of way, I felt at peace with myself as if I could see beyond this world, now that I had plunged into the deep.

# V

# The Die Is Cast

*Everything has different facets,
everything is real, thus is the world.*
— MADAME DE SÉVIGNÉ

THE MORNING AFTER the incident at the university, the cooing of the pigeons woke me up early. The room was flooded with sunlight and the shadows of the leaves danced on the walls. It promised to be a radiant spring day. Aunt Lou was already out on the balcony feeding the birds. The world was peaceful and quiet. Unfortunately, behind this tranquil surface, lurked a frightening reality. I had only to consider the fate of my classmates to arrive at this conviction. Alex Veljković was serving a five-year sentence at the Zabela Prison, near Požarevac. Sili, exceptionally gifted in mathematics, was also stagnating in the same establishment, repairing prisoners' shoes. He was lucky to have received only two years for distributing Opposition tracts during the November electoral campaign. Beli too was lucky. Sentenced to one year for having fought with the Nationalist Resistance troops, he was granted amnesty after six months, but was barred from returning to university. He worked as a metal worker in a mechanics factory. There a metal sliver flew into his eye, and he would suffer the effects for the rest of his life. Žare Nikolić could also consider himself fortunate. After handing down his sentence, the judge, Milonja Stijović, came up to him and gave him a friendly pat on the shoulder: "It's because you're a decent sort of chap that I gave you only three years. You are young ... you'll see, they'll pass quickly."

Bora, alias The Wasp, determined to stow away on a freighter sailing under a foreign flag, had headed for the Adriatic. But his ship never sailed. His grieving mother, her mind disturbed by his disappearance, continued to believe that her Bora was alive and living in a faraway, exotic country. The only reason he wasn't writing to her, she said, was because he didn't want to compromise her safety. Belgrade was full of the walking dead.

Several other classmates spent a few months in filthy, overcrowded cells before being released as innocent. One day, after his arrest, a literature student was asked to fill out a questionnaire. The first question read: "Have you ever been arrested, and if not, why not?" Mystified, he answered: "I was lucky."

Another of my friends spent only three months in jail. On the day of his release, the guard, following regulations, handed him back his money, which had been confiscated at the time of his arrest. The bills were riddled with strange little holes. Delighted at having recovered his freedom, my friend had no intention of asking for an explanation, but the guard hastened to say: "The holes are caused by the mice in the storage room. We can't get rid of them."

That same day, when he went to buy cigarettes, the tobacconist commented: "Ah! You too!"

"What do you mean?" replied my friend.

"Are you just out of jail, by any chance?"

"How did you know?"

"Sir, when they released me, my money had also been gnawed. They can't get rid of the critters."

Former inmates formed a secret brotherhood whose members recognised one another by subtle signs. What a strange time: prison terms had ceased being marks of infamy; instead, they were a sign of honour.

As for my own future, it looked as dark and stunted as that of my comrades. One didn't have to be clairvoyant to know that I wouldn't last much longer. In the hall of the Faculty of Law was posted a long list of the names of students who were not authorized to take the final exams. No reason given. Who had compiled the list, and by what authority? Total mystery. If a student showed himself too curious he could get into even deeper trouble. Arbitrariness and absurdity became our daily lot, so we no longer paid attention. Rumour had it that expulsions from the Faculty of Science were being carried out publicly in accordance with a set ritual.

My classmate Miša was one of the first to experience it. He crammed for his chemistry course while his activist classmates, unbeknownst to him, were plotting to get him expelled from the university. Jelena Bilbia activated the lever, and Miša was catapulted from the faculty to the sound of snickering that resonated in his ears for a long time, like the sinister tinkling of tiny bells. He was barred from the university for a full year. He had to go through hell before being readmitted to the lecture halls and laboratories thanks to the intervention of Professor Pavle Savić, a true scientist lost among the worshippers of the Grand Master of the Keys.

And then there were the scientists afflicted with a strange mania. They thought a society could be built in the same way you build a railway bridge. Why did they expel a brilliant student who had never even been interested in politics? Because the son of a general in the Royal Army had no place at the university regardless of how brilliant he was. How many lives and how many futures were crushed, wrecked and ruined to accommodate a world forced to conform to the warped ideas of the Party and its cohorts?

My own case was different. My activist comrades probably considered me harebrained, prone to acts of bravado and deliberate provocation. They couldn't understand that my behaviour was more an expression of despair than an attempt to ridicule them. In any case, they felt obliged to react in order not to lose face. They viewed me as someone volunteering for expulsion, which was humorous given my visceral abhorrence of any kind of volunteerism. All I could do was to wait and see. Sometimes my curiosity made me forget my anxiety. What would they accuse me of?

My participation in the Resistance, modest but undeniable, protected me from being accused of collaborating with the enemy. At least that's what I thought, though the comrades had fertile imaginations when it came to inventing crimes. A friend of my father's, Professor Radoje Knežević, had been the moving force behind the March 27, 1941 uprising that put Yugoslavia on the side of the Allies during the Second World War. He spent the war in Lisbon and London, which did not prevent the puppet judges from condemning him *in absentia* to eight years in prison ... for having collaborated with the enemy.

The reign of the Master Design had given birth to a new breed of jurists endowed with rich imaginations. The prosecutors, judges, their substitutes and their assistants had become novelists capable of turning every man's life into fiction. Taken to extremes, their actions confirmed an uncanny link between literature and life.

"Nothing counts but the present," an architecture student had once warned me. At age twenty-four, he had thrown himself into the Party with all the enthusiasm of a neophyte. It was his way of telling me not to rely on the past for protection from the vicissitudes of the future. The comrades could find a reason to boot me out of university. And what could I do? Go and see them, beg their pardon, and promise to remain forever silent? Never. Better to die.

All this waiting around for a denouement gnawed away at me slowly but surely. For the first time in my life, I started to drink. Adulterated red wine with a sour tannin taste made me sick. Hard liquor knocked me out and cut my legs out from under me. My choice therefore became beer. It was not very strong, and it made me feel euphoric. On those hot May days that already had a hint of summer about them, the cold amber-coloured drink topped with froth slaked my thirst deliciously and gave me courage.

I had plenty of opportunities to quench my thirst. Since the first bombardment in April 1941, the taverns and refreshment kiosks had multiplied like mushrooms. People needed to toss back a drink to stiffen their spines. These places repelled me: they smelled of tobacco smoke and floors mopped with a petroleum-based cleaner. Leaning on a zinc counter, I would down a glass of beer and immediately head out into the streets and walk frantically, as if I could wear out my anxiety by getting tired.

After a glass of beer, my fears would fade and life would take on a kinder hue. I would fantasize. "Everything's going to be alright." My friends might consider my untimely exit from the lecture hall a bad joke and the matter would soon be forgotten. If ever the authorities insisted on showing me the door, I could always leave the country. If I survived Užice under siege in October 1944, and escaped the German and Bulgarian machine guns, I could certainly cross a border. The border I had in mind was in northern Slovenia, a mountainous region with deep gorges and ravines. Milenko and I were sure to find a way through them. The Party could not keep the entire country under a bell jar.

And somehow we would manage abroad. How? Like all those who had gone before us! Once the Yugoslav border was behind us, crossing the others would be mere child's play. Whatever the obstacles, we would eventually end up in France, home to all peoples without a country. Everything would become easier. The Serbs had counted on the French ever since the first insurrection when Karadjordje had written to Napoleon asking him for help against the Ottoman Empire. And the Serbs who sought refuge in France during the First World War had come back with extraordinary tales of people's generosity. My own father had told me so many stories about his stay in Rochefort-sur-Mer. To hear them talk, you would think that France had ceased to be a country and had turned into a beautiful woman, putting everything aside in order to come to the rescue of the Serbs.

But after a while, when the alcohol wore off, I would start to feel depressed again. How could the comrades ever pardon me for ridiculing them? They would make me pay dearly. The burning of witches at the stake had returned. As for France, better not to have any illusions. The war was over, the French soldiers who fought in the East were slowly dying out and Serbia had disappeared from the map. France had concerns other than looking after the Serbs.

I imagined how the activist students would organise a public trial at the university. They would plant guards at the doors of the lecture halls. A zealous Party member would rise and ask if I was worthy of walking the corridors of this venerable institution. The big boys would stand up and cry: "No! No! ... Out!" They would accuse me of imaginary crimes and expel me by force, even though I had champed at the bit during the four years of the Occupation, impatient to return to my studies.

The army might decide to re-enlist me and, because of my poor record, throw me into the disciplinary unit stationed at the mildewed barracks at Petrovaradin Fortress. The place was picturesque enough with the Danube flowing beneath the towering ramparts, but the soldiers of the disciplinary unit did not often see the river or the sky. Each one was being transmuted into a link of a monstrous human chain.

In the centre of the fortress was an open shaft. A door at ground level opened into a narrow whitewashed gallery that went down some fifty steps and ended under an impressive cupola. In the centre was a well with stone walls. From the well, underground galleries fanned out to the various bastions of the citadel, like a giant warren. In case of attack, these tunnels provided the garrison with access to water without exposing the soldiers to the bombs of the enemy. To reach the water level, a staircase spiralled down inside the well. The soldiers of the disciplinary battalion had to climb down there with pails and haul up water for the vegetable gardens and the flowerbeds in front of the commander's office. Hour after hour, the human chain went round and round. The poor devils who passed through this disciplinary unit emerged as wrecks.

To chase away these dark visions, I needed another beer so I would sink into the infernal circle of the drunk who drinks to drown his troubles.

In the evenings, I had to make a superhuman effort to hide my nervousness from Aunt Lou. The slightest movement of my head felt as if a steel egg were banging against the insides of my skull. More and more, flight seemed to be the only means of extricating myself from this nightmare. But where to go?

On Monday, May 6, a seemingly innocuous incident reinforced my status as a pariah. In the past, on the Orthodox feast day of St. George, many people in Serbia, particularly the young, would get up early and go for a picnic in the countryside. They were commemorating the *haidouks*, guerrilla fighters who fought the Ottoman oppressor. When the warm season arrived, the *haidouks* would emerge from their mountain hideouts and take up arms. On November 8, St. Dimitri Day, they would return to their hideouts to spend the winter. Now, celebrating St. George's Day aroused suspicions of a certain elitist nationalism. So on that day, the activists at the university, with their mania for seeing enemies everywhere, organised their own collective excursion for students wanting to revive this patriotic tradition.

Milenko and I had no intention of being caught up in this herding exercise. On my way to his place early that day, I met a group on their way to Deer Park. I had nowhere to hide. They were coming straight towards me. The leader, a student called Jacques, walked alongside the procession.

"So, comrade individualist, feel like joining us for a little country outing?" he asked.

He could be so irritating. At the time of the Occupation, Jacques had been as silent as the tomb whenever we discussed politics. Since the Liberation, he had discovered a vocation as a progressive and a revolutionary, a vocation as ardent as it was belated. I felt tempted to tell him off but I lacked the courage. To justify my absence, I babbled some excuse, pleading the need to study for exams, but I don't think I convinced him. The others laughed at me. They were such creeps — despicable critters crawling out of the shadows. When the sun goes down for good on this planet, they will be the last ones to die. Their instinct for preservation is so well honed.

Milenko bucked me up by saying I attached too much importance to these morons. To snap me out of my mood, he suggested that I go with him to House Painters Street opposite the School of Engineering. He needed help carrying a large radio. The day before, he had been unable to repair it at the client's apartment, and he wanted to bring it home and examine it in peace.

A plump older lady and her daughter awaited us in a spacious but empty apartment. Chatty as a magpie, the woman told us her story with machine gun-fire rapidity. Her husband, a colonel in the royal army and a former prisoner of war, had preferred to remain an exile in Germany rather than return to the land of the Grand Master. Having fallen on hard times, Madam Colonel had sold her furniture to raise a little money to open a perfume shop, one of the few private businesses still tolerated by the authorities. "As you can see, we are living close to the bone," she said. She might have been exaggerating slightly; her physique did not suggest a state of hunger. In any case, she wanted the radio in working condition so that she could sell it.

We listened politely to the woman's laments. This kind of grumbling was not uncommon in Belgrade. Thousands of people, suddenly deprived of an income, had recently come down in the world. But everyone had problems, so nobody listened to their stories anymore. It was a pity to see such a beautiful apartment empty. Even that they were in danger of losing should the apartment be requisitioned for a Party favourite.

As we were leaving the building, I recalled another unfurnished apartment I had visited when Djordje, a childhood friend, had dragged me out to listen to classical music in the home of two weird brothers. Only a week earlier, another friend had mentioned a woman, the widow of a general, who was selling off her furniture. Belgrade was in the throes of a mysterious epidemic of unfurnished apartments.

Three days later during this memorable week, as I was coming out of class, I saw a poster in the entrance hall announcing

Professor Dragiša Ivanović's inaugural lecture. This sort of event did not usually attract many people besides a clique of professors and a few students who wanted to be seen. But the title of the lecture was surprising, to say the least: *The Theory of Bohr's Electrons and Dialectical Materialism*. I read and reread it, but I couldn't understand what Niels Bohr's physics theory had in common with Marxist philosophy.

I felt like stealing the poster to show to Milenko, but it was too risky. I hurried over to his place to tell him about this unusual lecture. Five minutes later, I burst into his room. Milenko was sitting in a cloud of smoke, lost in thought in front of a radio transmitter that a customer had brought in that morning. He was searching for the problem. He used to enjoy this kind of detective work, but now that it had become his job, he was bored by the routine. My arrival was a good excuse for him to take a break. I came right to the point.

"Time to get out of here, old pal! Dialectical materialism has reached the atom!"

"What's this nonsense you're talking?" he asked.

"It's not nonsense! Professor Ivanović's introductory lecture is called: *The Theory of Bohr's Electrons and Dialectical Materialism*."

"But he's going to be the laughingstock of the entire faculty," says Milenko.

"Well, they might laugh at him behind his back, but he doesn't seem to care. The man is the eyes and ears of the Party at the university and no one dares poke fun at him openly. He is drawing up confidential reports on all the professors. In other words, he is the university's chief spy. Apparently, he wrote a report on Professor Popovič, who holds the English chair, in which he called him 'a real bourgeoisie,' and declared: 'he hates us but does not dare say it openly.' Apparently, Ivanović can read people's minds. And the Theory of Relativity is his pet peeve."

"What does he have against it?"

"Who knows! He abhors the word relativity, maybe because it threatens his own convictions. In the magazine *Tesla*, he treated Einstein and the relativist physicians like a bunch of idealistic eggheads. I won't even mention his run-ins with the great Russian physicist, Kapica, who refused to take him on as doctoral student. To make himself sound important, Ivanović invoked his past as a combatant, but Kapica cut him off: 'I can't accept as doctoral students all those who fought in the war.' Apparently, in Chicago, Enrico Fermi also gave him a very cool reception. As a last resort, he had to fall back on Belgrade University."

"So you think it's time to get out?"

"Yes, but how?"

"Right now, I don't have the slightest idea. We'll have to ask around... I could take a trip to Slovenia and check things out. There must be people there who can smuggle us across."

"Probably, but do you want to go to Slovenia?" I asked.

"And why not?"

Though the idea of leaving the country had been germinating for some time, since meeting up again in Belgrade to be exact, the announcement of this outrageous upcoming lecture was the actual catalyst.

Later, when Belgrade started to slip into the mists of memory, that afternoon would remain a turning point, the day when our destiny changed irreversibly. We could have said: *alea jacta est*. The die is cast — in honour of Berko, our Latin professor.

Preparations for our trip of no return progressed slowly. If passersby on Galsworthy Street had paid attention to No. 31, the old one-storey house with the peeling paint, they might have noticed that the shutters remained closed for hours at a time. In a room with carefully drawn curtains, we were bent over maps of Slovenia, discussing our escape plans at length.

Where to cross? Italy or Austria? Each country had its advantages and disadvantages. If we crossed the Italo-Yugoslav border, we would find ourselves in a country bordering France. This would shorten the distance to Paris, but it also meant crossing a contested border zone heavily patrolled by border guards and the army. Conversely, if we went through Austria, which was divided into three occupied zones, our route was quite a bit longer, but the Austro-Yugoslav border had the advantage of being more porous. Whichever route we chose, we were under no illusions. The venture was risky. The important thing was to aim for Paris. We were very attracted to the City of Light, and I in particular, with my memories of the World Exhibition in the summer of 1937.

We knew nothing about life on the other side. Italy, Austria and all of Europe were *terra incognita* for Yugoslavs, who had access only to confused and contradictory reports served up in our press. Right after the war, a spate of articles accused the Allies of favouring Yugoslav exiles in Italy and Germany in order to recruit them in an army of mercenaries to fight the Soviet Union. In reality, these men, most of whom had fought in the Resistance, guarded warehouses and military installations in the former Axis countries now occupied by the Allies. Using the simplistic jargon of Agitprop, these articles were intended to incite the population against England and the United States. They had the opposite effect: they encouraged a number of young people to try their luck at escaping abroad.

When the masters of propaganda finally realised their error, they reversed course. From one day to the next, the press started to describe the poverty of these exiles in the West, and launched teary appeals asking them to return to the country of their ancestors.

One day, while Milenko was busy tuning a radio, we came across a programme on Radio Zagreb about the capture of young fugitives who were trying to cross the border clandestinely into Italy. We could hear the barking of dogs and the border guards shouting *Halt*. Real or rigged, this reportage only strengthened our determination to leave a country bent on preventing the free movement of its citizens. But we were under no illusions: crossing the border would be no picnic.

The second half of May was spent discussing various options, all as daring as they were unrealistic. I even proposed hijacking the Belgrade-Podgorica plane and forcing it to land in Bari, in southern Italy. Milenko considered this notion too outrageous and risky. We dropped the idea, but it was in the air, for some time later, a passionate young Montenegrin woman pulled off a highly dramatic exploit. Wishing to marry an Italian doctor who had been a captain during the war — love can transgress the barriers erected by men — she hijacked a Yugoslav plane and ordered it to fly to Bari. Ready to risk her life, she pointed her automatic pistol at the pilot. Her fate was decided in a matter of seconds. If the captain had detected the slightest hesitation in her voice and movements, he would have refused to comply, and the gamble would have finished with the arrest of a hijacker. But, as a woman deeply in love, she had already accepted her death, as well as that of the passengers and crew. We were not ready to go that far. Milenko was right to reject my suggestion.

We were such poor sailors that we could not even contemplate crossing the Adriatic in a makeshift boat. Finally we concluded that the only way out was through Slovenia.

Before leaving, we needed to break the news to Milenko's mother, my aunt, a few trustworthy friends, and my father who was living in Prizren.

I decided to be direct with Aunt Lou even if it meant trying to cushion the blow afterwards. I chose an evening towards the end of May. It was almost as hot as summer. We could hear the customers of the Bistro *Chez Brale* chatting under the chestnut tree. Upstairs, we were having sausages and beer. Belgrade was luxuriating in one of those lovely spring nights that I was so fond of, and this set me dreaming about my future life.

I saw my whole life go by in a flash. I would live peacefully with a woman I loved and who loved me, surrounded by two or three children and a few faithful friends, aspiring neither to riches nor honours but pursuing my career passionately studying a subject that interested only a few people. That evening, I realised this was all a silly dream. Reality would more likely be a bitter struggle for survival.

"You know, Auntie, Milenko and I will be leaving soon."

"Leaving to go where?"

"Abroad. To a foreign country."

Her fork froze in the air. She was speechless as she searched for a response.

"What foreign country?"

"Well, France to begin with, and then we'll see ... maybe we'll end up in America ... who knows?"

"And how do you intend to get into a foreign country?"

"By crossing the border ... clandestinely, of course."

"And you think you can cross a border like you cross a street?"

"Of course not! There are risks, but people have also died crossing a street. After all, life is a series of risks."

"Except that some risks are riskier than others. And what will your father say? Have you thought of him?"

"Yes, I have. In fact, I have thought of both of you, but you can't imagine what is going on at the university. If you knew, I'm sure you'd understand."

Aunt Lou knew that I had gone my own way ever since the war started, but she hadn't expected me to push things this far. We talked a little. I tried to make her see our reasons, while I fabricated scholarships that awaited us in Paris. She was visibly shaken. After all, I was her only family, the only son of her sister who died at age forty. Her sorrow made me sad, and a bit ashamed of my selfishness, but the decision to leave the country was irrevocable.

I wondered why I couldn't just be like everybody else? I ought to be more flexible and accepting of the indoctrination and harassment going on at the university, as it was not directed at me personally but at all of us. I needed to look at the future with a degree of optimism, and believe that one day the stupidity and absurdity of our leaders would self-destruct.

I didn't like calling attention to myself, or standing apart from everyone else. On the contrary, all my life I had dreamt of a simple existence far from the turmoil and clamour of the world. Unfortunately there were always obstacles, always a hitch, some real or imaginary circumstance that prevented me from leading such a life. First the war and then the Occupation had interrupted my studies. Now, when a more or less decent life could have been mine, the tentacles of the Master Design were insinuating themselves into everything. In my nightmares, I could see its hideous tentacles slithering up the stairs at 42 Ilija Street and wriggling under the door. Sometimes, I felt I would spend the rest of my life waiting for my real life to begin — and in the meantime, it would be over before it even started.

Two or three days later, Milenko talked to his mother. When I arrived at his place one morning, she who was usually so cheerful and playful opened the door with a taciturn expression. Did she blame me for having planted the idea of exile in her son's mind? Maybe, but she never breathed a word, not even on my last day in Belgrade when Milenko had already left for Zagreb. She was not the only one to entertain doubts. Several of our fellow students suspected that I was the instigator of this adventure. Others accused Milenko of having dragged me into the Resistance. People are like that. They need to oversimplify in order to understand.

At the beginning of June, for reasons of his own, Milenko told a classmate and fellow student, Janot the Rabbit, of our plan. Two days later, I ran into Janot on the street. When he saw me, he burst out laughing. His strange laugh always reminded me of an imp popping out of a box of surprises.

"So, you little sneaks, you're skipping out and leaving your old friends behind. And yet you fought for this lost paradise!" he said.

"Janot, it's not a joke! The war carried us off ... like poor devils. And as for the paradise you're talking about, you know what I think —"

"It's alright. I'm just teasing. I won't hold it against you. My best wishes for a good trip. But we can't all run away. Who'd be left in the country?"

We parted, amicably. Once again I forgot to ask him where he got his nickname, Janot the Rabbit. If ever we meet again, I'll ask him. I went my way, feeling reassured. Janot was not the kind of guy to spill the beans.

The situation was quite different with Slobodan P., whom we called the Painter. A student at the Fine Arts College, he used to stop in at Milenko's from time to time, like all of us, to listen to classical music or simply to talk. Milenko's good humour and optimism attracted friends. Like many young people at the time, the Painter saw the new regime as a calamity, and he was not shy about saying it in our little circle. He too dreamt of leaving, but he found our project too risky. His attitude started to irritate us. Of course it was dangerous to escape, but if he hoped to find a failsafe route, he might as well stay home. Many more young people would have fled the country if they could have metamorphosed into Daedalus and flown off to clement skies.

So we decided not to tell the Painter our final plans even though we felt a little guilty. That way, if we were stopped and interrogated, he would in no way become involved. What right did we have involving someone who was so undecided?

Fortuitous circumstances can determine fate. Our lives were beginning to resemble a roulette wheel. My friend Mirko's case showed the difficulty of predicting the future. On a day in June, he was waiting in a Slovenian inn for a man to smuggle him and his friend across the border into Austria. The man was supposed to arrive at two in the afternoon. At a quarter to three, there was still no sign of him, so Mirko, feeling very edgy, decided not to wait any longer. He swore to himself that if the man was not there by three, he would go down into the valley, take the first train back to Belgrade and abandon the idea of exile. At three o'clock, the cuckoo clock struck the hour and the man in question walked in. Instead of returning home, Mirko and his friend found themselves that afternoon in Austria. Paris was no longer a pipe dream, and a possible life in Belgrade remained unlived.

There was another candidate for the trip, Mate, a Croatian from Dalmatia. During the Occupation, he had worked at the head office of the railway company. This key post enabled him to pass on information about German troop movements to the resistance fighters. Once the war was over, the new authorities fired him from the Department of Transport. The poor chap had supported the wrong resistance movement. He could consider himself lucky not to have been condemned for conspiring with the enemy. Now he earned a meagre living as an accountant and a jack-of-all-trades for Djordje the Traveller, owner of the radio shop for which Milenko did the repairs. Mate dreamed of setting sail, nothing extraordinary for a man born on the shores of the Adriatic. Every time the talk in the shop came around to get-away schemes, his eyes would light up like electric bulbs. Unfortunately, he was almost fifty and we were afraid he might not be strong enough to withstand the stress of crossing the border.

After I left Belgrade, I sometimes would think of him as a tragic figure trapped by fate. Tall, thin, with a face like Pushkin's, always wearing the same old railway worker's overcoat, he had the look of an officer in reduced circumstances. But how many others were struggling in similar situations?

If we felt guilty about dropping Mate and the Painter, we really regretted not bringing along two other classmates, Sili and Beli. Sili, in my opinion, might have had a brilliant career as a mathematician in the West. Strangely enough, his passion for mathematics was matched by an equal passion for history and politics. Hidden behind his calm and serene appearance was a born conspirator. He reminded me of Evariste Galois who, the night before he died in a duel, jotted down notes on set theory. Sili was eventually locked away in the Zabela

Correctional Institute. I can still imagine him, lost in thought, seated on a three-foot stool, hammering away at a new sole on a prisoner's boot. And once again, I am beside myself with rage. As for Beli, he eventually became an agricultural engineer and an eminent soya specialist. But in those days, we didn't know of his whereabouts.

How many others were locked away in the Grand Master's prisons? *Adieu*, friends and men of courage! We will keep alive our anger toward your jailers, and carry you forever in our hearts.

∽

One hot summer evening in early June, I accompanied Milenko to the station. He was off to Slovenia on a reconnaissance mission. We got off the streetcar in front of the station at President Wilson Square, scene of the infamously doctored photo of the Grand Master's triumphant return to the city. People were seated on the terraces of the restaurants and the rotisseries, drinking and eating grilled meat rolled in finely sliced onion. The whole neighbourhood was filled with the delicious aroma of food. *Caleches* and a few ramshackle taxis were dropping off travellers and picking new ones up. Commuters were waiting to storm the streetcars.

Life appeared to be going on as usual, peaceful and routine, just like before the war when, on summer evenings, Aunt Lou and I would come here for a bite. Occasionally, I felt a twinge of nostalgia for those teenage years that had vanished so quickly before we had time to taste our fair share of happiness. The war had stolen our youth, and when it was finally over, a mournful greyness had settled over everything like fog. The thought that it might hang there forever made us feel even worse.

Life also carried on secretly. We tried to snatch a few moments of happiness here and there, more often than not in the tender arms of a young girl. If only we could have sent out a clarion call to the powerful of this world: "Give one hundred years of freedom and peace to this country and you will see what our people are capable of!" But the great powers would probably have answered: "It's all your fault!"

Just as the train started to move, Milenko leaned out the window and waved. He looked confident, as if saying: *Don't worry, everything will be fine.* Or was it sheer bravado, the reaction of someone who has taken on a challenge bigger than himself?

Feeling pensive, I left the station. It was a wonderful June evening, just the kind of evening to abandon oneself to euphoria. The flowering linden trees filled Nemanja Street with their perfume. I walked past the squat Ministry of Transport building, turned up Prince Illiterate Avenue and arrived back home on Ilija Street.

The long walks and strolls along the streets of Belgrade had exercised a mysterious fascination on me since childhood. The desire to know every nook and cranny of my city had created an almost physical bond between us. Belgrade was not just an agglomeration of houses, streets, and boulevards but a living entity with its own destiny, often tragic, and a soul that I loved passionately. Now that my days in the city were numbered, I wanted to take with me a storehouse of memories from these promenades.

If Milenko were to fall into the hands of dishonest smugglers and end up in prison, or, even worse, fall into the hands of the border police and possibly an executioner, would he betray me under torture? I didn't think so, but our friendship, well known as it was, would be reason enough to warrant my arrest. Best not to dwell on it!

I sauntered up Ilija Street. In front of the tavern at the corner of King Milutin Street, the people of the neighbourhood were drinking beer or the ever-popular wine spritzers. The city appeared peaceful, serene. Nobody seemed even remotely aware that only last November 11, this fashionable restaurant had doubled as a polling station. In a few weeks, all this would be so far behind us.

Three days later, I received a telegram from Milenko in Ljubljana: "Short on money. Stop. Please send five thousand dinars post-haste. Stop. Leaving for Malibar." That afternoon, before going to the post office, I went to his mother's to reassure her and let her know he would soon be back. When I got there, Boris Kočutnik, a Slovenian student of stomatology, was at the door. He was a member of the inner circle that met regularly at 31 Galsworthy Street in a semi-clandestine atmosphere to listen to music, criticise the absurdity of the world around us, and keep the small flame of freedom burning. He knew nothing of our plans to escape.

"So where have you been keeping yourself? Milenko is never here and his mother is quite evasive," he said.

"Boris, I'll tell you what is going on. Milenko is on a trip."

"On a trip! Where?"

"Somewhere in Slovenia. At the moment he is in Ljubljana, but he leaves for Maribar in two days."

"Monsieur left for Slovenia and he didn't even bother telling me! Don't you realise my parents live in Celje?"

"I know, Boris, but I haven't told you everything. Milenko is in Slovenia trying to find someone to smuggle us across the border. We want to escape to Austria and then later on head for France."

"So that's it! I felt you were up to something! But you're not very smart. If there's someone who can help you, it's me! I have a cousin Milka who lives three kilometres from the border. And you're looking for a guide in Slovenia?"

"Boris, we trusted you, but we were afraid to mix you up in this affair."

"Well now I am mixed up in it. We'll talk when Milenko comes back."

"Great."

Milenko's trip resulted in nothing concrete. A so-called safe lead dried up and the vague promises of an engineer whom Milenko met at a hydroelectric plant north of Maribor smelled fishy. In this kind of transaction, everyone suspects the other one of being an *agent provocateur*.

As Boris was ready to help us, the rest no longer mattered. Our plan began to take shape. All three of us would travel to Celje to the home of Boris's parents where Milenko and I would hide for two or three days, long enough for Boris to visit his cousin in St. Ilj and to organise the details of our escape. But first Boris needed to finish his exams at the Faculty of Stomatology, which meant that we would leave towards the end of June. We had two weeks to settle our affairs and to pick up our baccalaureate diplomas from the School of Engineering. And I would have time to visit my father in Prizren and bid him good-bye.

This visit, almost certain to be followed by a permanent separation, was already making me very anxious. I was torn between the feeling of betraying my father and remaining faithful to the ideal of freedom that had fed my youth. During the Occupation, my father had also transgressed the rules by going on mysterious trips to the remote St. John's Monastery hidden in the gorges of Ovčar and Kablar. There he entered into contact with members of the Resistance. He also forged baptismal certificates for his former Sephardic students, Alex and Marko

Ćelebonović, so they could seek refuge in Dalmatia, then occupied by the Italians, to escape the Nazi concentration camps. Like many others, he spent fourteen long months in a Gestapo prison for refusing to sign their Appeal for Peace, Work and Order. If I were to remind him of his courageous actions, he could not help but approve our escape plans. All the better if this far-fetched reasoning helped reassure me. I knew, deep down that this upcoming adventure was stretching my resources to the limit. By always placing the bar too high, I condemned myself to perpetual failure.

After our meeting with Boris, plans were set in motion that could not be reversed. We were burning our bridges behind us.

How did I manage to lose my way in the huge, deserted building of the School of Engineering? Professor Rašković's course finished at six, and normally I would have gone home, or detoured by Milenko's, but it was past midnight and I was still in the building, which was dark and silent at this hour.

How did it happen? My head was abuzz and my mind felt as if it was emerging from a thick fog. What if all this was just a dream?

And yet the miserable little light at the end of the long corridor was real enough, though it made the ambient darkness appear even more sinister. Other hallways led to the back of the building. They connected the wide staircase to the different wings, turned at right angles, crisscrossed and formed a labyrinth studded with doors to the right and to the left. These doors opened into lecture halls, laboratories and offices. Each one had a brass plaque on the door giving the names, the impressive titles and the positions held by the occupants: Chairs of Fluid Mechanics,

Aircraft, Fixed Machinery, Resistant Materials. Faced with the extraordinary sum of knowledge concentrated in this one building, I became painfully aware of my own ignorance, to the point where I felt as if I was choking. I had only one idea: to get out as quickly as possible and inhale deeply.

At the top of the staircase, the huge window diffused the moon's pale light, or was it a halo hovering above the city? Leaning on the banister of the first floor, I looked down the stairs, hoping to see someone, anyone, but the building was disconcertingly empty. This strange situation, at first annoying, started to frighten me. Was I about to spend the night as a prisoner of these dark corridors? The concierge must have fallen asleep in his loge in the entranceway.

Feeling extremely tense, I slowly descended the stairs in the semi-darkness, as if I were moving through the muddy water of a pond. Somewhere, on the ground floor was the amphitheatre — and the bulletin board where I had been ridiculed before my peers. The note must still be there. The idea came to me to look for it and tear it off. But why bother? I had been branded and nothing would change that. In any case, I wouldn't be able to locate the infamous scrap of paper in the dark.

As I entered the hall, I felt a ray of hope. A night light was glimmering in the concierge's loge. But no one was there. I tried the knob of the large exit door. Locked. I retraced my steps and passed in front of the two pink marble sphinxes. Whose tomb were they guarding?

As I climbed up to the first floor, I was struck by the silence. Two months earlier, a gang of rowdies had made a racket in this very spot as they shouted for joy at General Mihajlović's arrest. Now, not a trace of them. Everything passes, all is forgotten, the cowards and the courageous alike.

My attention was drawn to a thin ray of light under a door down the right-hand corridor. It was like a breath of warm air. No doubt it would lead me to some doctoral student struggling with a problem of tensorial calculus or a differential equation. I hesitated for a moment, and then knocked twice. Silence. I tried again. Nothing moved. Just as I put my hand on the knob, the door opened, as if some spirit had leaned on it from the inside. The bright light hurt my eyes while reassuring me at the same time. The room, probably the office of a professor, was empty. A study lamp lit up a drawing table. Papers, sketches, and rolled-up plans were scattered about. Foreign-language books, sturdily bound, covered a whole wall, and a handsome model of a suspended bridge sat imposingly on top of a filing cabinet.

I approached the window, which was wide open. The air was hot and humid. A storm was brewing. There was not a living soul on the sidewalk. The city was fast asleep. Suddenly, a tram appeared coming from Terazije Square. As it trundled by the faculty, I could make out the face of the conductor. He made me think of a ghost haunting a city deserted by its citizens. In front of the Vuk Karadžić monument, the empty streetcar turned onto New Cemetery Avenue, headed for the depot. The squeaking of the wheels tore through the calm of the night, and the trolley spit out clusters of sparks. Then the street sank back into silence. Should I call for help? But who would hear me?

Feeling totally helpless, I turned towards the door. The light in the room projected my shadow onto the floor. Where to go? Explore this maze of corridors in the hope of finding a teaching assistant, still busy correcting exam papers in his office? He might be able to help me by opening the main door and letting me out, with the reassurance: "Don't worry. It can happen to anyone." But the idea appeared preposterous.

At that very moment, a strange noise became audible in the empty building. At first it was muffled, but it grew louder. Strange as it might seem, the noise resembled the cantering of a four-legged creature let loose in the deserted corridors of the faculty. I could make out the ringing strike of hoofs on the tiles.

Guessing that I was in a nightmare, I made a desperate effort to shake myself into consciousness, but in vain. The bizarre sound resonated, growing sharper and clearer, though at times it ceased entirely. The animal must be stopping where the corridors intersect, undecided about which one to take, or else it was sniffing the air, exasperated by an unseen human presence.

All of a sudden, an infernal racket interrupted my thoughts. Terrified, I looked out into the hall and saw a black mass hurtling towards me, sparks flying from its hooves. It literally shook the floor. I barely had time to back up into the door frame to avoid being speared by an enormous black bull. The beast went flying past me like a cannonball, probably furious at being shut up in this labyrinth of corridors. As it brushed up against the door, the lamp in the office smashed noisily on the floor and the room was plunged into darkness. Like a person in a straitjacket, I struggled to free myself. The image of a bull was imprinted on my retina, and the staccato of its hoofs was perfectly audible.

Was this a students' prank? At the Faculty of Veterinary Medicine at Cordoba University, in the country where bulls are raised for the cruel game of bull fighting, I could imagine such a joke, but here in the School of Engineering in Belgrade, in this world of machines where they dealt only with horsepower, it seemed too preposterous.

The racket subsided, and once again everything lapsed into silence. The bull was probably catching its breath in some corner. My first reflex was to feel my way along the wall to find the light switch. But there was nothing there. My heart was pounding. What should I do? Little by little, I calmed down and my instinct for survival took over. After all, it didn't matter how the animal had got into the faculty building. What I had to do was hold out until dawn. Darkness wouldn't last forever, and the first glimmers of light would chase away the chimeras of night.

The concierge was sure to show up. He would unlock the door, and students and professors would rush in. The firemen and the guardians of the zoo would find a way of capturing the beast and removing it from the building. The rector would take the necessary measures to prevent a reoccurrence. The event would probably make the headlines and would be talked about for a long time, but no one would ever know who had introduced the bull into the faculty. I might even merit a modest amount of fame for my part in discovering the animal.

I had to find a safe place to hide until dawn. The crafty beast, with its heightened sense of smell, could still flush me out and gore me. Staying in this room was no solution, even if I managed to lock the door. With its powerful horns, the bull could smash through the door and splinter it like a box of matches. Better to go down to the concierge's loge. There, at least, I could play at being a matador around the pink marble sphinxes.

So, ready to flatten myself against a door at the slightest hint of danger, I inched forward, on tiptoe, towards the big staircase. An unbearable silence filled the corridors. Was the bull real, or was it just a trick of my addled brain? My head ached terribly. I arrived under the big window and leaned against the railing to catch my breath, struggling to grasp what was happening to me during this extraordinary night.

As I made my way towards the concierge's loge, my worst fears were realised. Something was moving in the corridor that led to the stairs. In my haste to see what it was, I turned around, my back to the railing. Too late! The black mass emerged from the darkness with a terrible drumming of hoofs and came straight at me. A serpent of fear slithered down my spine.

The crafty beast, hidden in an obscure corner, had been waiting for me to return to the window. Stunned, I just had time to duck to the left to avoid full frontal impact, but my manoeuvre didn't save me. The beast crashed through the railing and I fell backwards into space, my head turned up towards the window as if imploring heaven's mercy. The beast and I, in a shower of marble chips, plunged into the abyss, side by side at arm's length. Suddenly, a streak of lightning lit up the window and on the powerful neck of the bull I saw the huge head of a man with long black sideburns. I had always thought the Minotaur had the head of a bull and the body of a man! Greek mythology never dealt with this reality. What was even more curious: I had seen his head in the Faculty corridors.

A reverse Minotaur was haunting the darkness of this huge granite building. How had it got in without anyone noticing? We were always asking this question about the strange goings-on that surrounded us all the time. Would I carry this secret to my grave? Tomorrow, when people found the monster's cadaver beside mine, no one would be able to resolve this enigma, unless ... unless ... And that was my last thought.

An inhuman shriek from the depths of my being woke me with a start. Where did that cry come from? Who had shouted? Was it me or was it the double fraudulently installed in my body? I had heard this glottal cry one summer a long time ago when I had almost stepped on a venomous serpent.

"What's wrong?"

My aunt lit the bedside lamp. Frowning, her hair in disarray, she looked over at me. Outside, the rain was battering the leaves. Lightning flashed incessantly, illuminating the room as if it were day. Huge waves of thunder rolled overhead. The first storm of the year had unleashed itself over Belgrade.

"It's nothing, Auntie, nothing. Go back to sleep. I'm sorry. I had a nightmare. Tomorrow, I'll tell you all about it."

My aunt switched off the lamp and turned her back to the wall. The storm wandered back and forth over the city, then departed for the mouth of the Save River to maraud on the Pannonian Plain. The rain continued noisily for a little longer. When everything became silent again, I heard a truck with a pierced muffler backfire as it drove up Ilija Street. I could hear cows lowing on their way to the slaughterhouse. Their cries always made my Aunt Lou shudder. "Animals can sense death," she would say.

I couldn't fall asleep. My thoughts slipped back to my childhood years when my mother was still alive, and we lived on Queen Nathalie Street opposite the primary school. My parents used to hold my hands when we walked in the street. They would run and lift me up between them. Like a bird, I would fly and sing for joy. Once, they woke me in the middle of the night to show me the fire ravaging the Theatre of the Performing Arts at the end of the street. The air had a scorched smell as the immense flames flickered and glowed against a black sky. An image of the apocalypse, so close at hand and yet so far.

I fell back to sleep at dawn, just as the birds were starting up their morning chatter.

# VI

# Pilgrimage to Prizren

*There comes a time when those
who are closest must leave one another.*

— BUDDHA

IT WAS WITH a heavy heart that I decided to visit my father in Prizren, a small town in southern Serbia where he was the Orthodox bishop. I dreaded our meeting. He would be shocked by the news of our departure, but I couldn't leave without offering him an explanation.

The trip to Prizren was my maiden flight. Early that morning, when Belgrade was barely awake, I boarded a nearly empty streetcar at Slavija Square that deposited me in front of the Putnik Travel Agency. There I climbed into a covered truck with the other passengers. Twenty minutes later, we were dropped off at Zemun Airport. A DC 3, a relic from the war, awaited us on the runway. This plane provided service between Belgrade and Skopje. Its pilot and the mechanic still wore British army uniforms. The passengers sat on benches affixed to the sides of the cabin. All we lacked were the parachutes and the weapons to persuade us we were on a war mission rather than simply travelling to another city. The plane bounced along the runway and, with a mighty heave and roar, finally tore itself off the ground. It rose like an arrow into the lovely blue sky. For the first time in my life my body had lost contact with the earth.

An abyss opened up before my eyes. My heart was beating so hard I was afraid it might jump out of my breast. Was it fright ... or pride in being a member of the human race? Through the porthole, I saw the Danube and the Save, two powerful rivers shimmering in the brilliance of a beautiful summer day. Belgrade and its suburbs were soon left behind, and a quilt of fields clothed the earth in a harlequin pattern. We flew over Sumadija, the cradle of Serbia liberated during the 1800s, following the long Turkish occupation. Towards the west, the blue mountains of Bosnia and Montenegro were falling away. After a short forty-minute flight, we landed in Skopje. Big-bellied planes, marked with a red star, were lined up alongside the runway.

A ramshackle bus about to leave for Prizren stood in front of the terminal. I took a seat among the taciturn passengers. The Albanians from Macedonia and Kosovo wore white skullcaps. They all had craggy faces that harmonized with the landscape of gorges and bare rocks we passed through. After two long hours travelling over potholed roads, we entered Prizren shortly before noon. With its old houses covered in Roman tiles, its tiny craftsmen's shops, its medieval churches and its mosques, the city still bore traces of Ottoman rule.

The Orthodox cathedral and bishopric, both surrounded by a wall, were situated on a quiet little street at the foot of a hill. Trees growing on the church square extended their shade into the enclosure. Everything seemed so peaceful, a perfect setting for quiet and contemplation. I pulled a cord by the carriage entrance. Somewhere inside, a bell rang and a man came to open the door.

Moments later, I walked into my father's office. He was seated in a chair, reading by the window. His white beard stood out against his dark cassock. Such a familiar and reassuring sight. My father seemed to live in a world of peace and serenity undisturbed by the rough and tumble of life. Even during the Occupation, he had maintained this detachment despite the state of perpetual and latent anxiety in which we lived.

My father, astonished to see me in Prizren, peered at me over his glasses and smiled. We embraced and before I could even get a word in edgewise, he asked me: "Have you come to tell me you're getting married?"

His words felt like a whip. For some time now, he had been hoping that I would start a family, and here I was about to announce to him that soon I would be a nomad — without home or hearth. I felt deep compassion for him, just as I had three years earlier, in July 1943, when a teacher at Požega Station told me he had been arrested by the Gestapo. Despite fearing for my father's life, I felt his imprisonment was a kind of honour. Even today, I feel guilt mixed with sorrow at having abandoned him on the threshold of old age.

I needed all the courage I could muster to tell him the truth. "No, I came to tell you that I'm leaving the country."

"You're leaving? Did you get a scholarship to study in France?"

"No, Milenko and I are leaving the country illegally."

My father stared at me, appalled and incredulous.

This was the beginning of an intense discussion that continued in the austere dining room of the bishopric while the gatekeeper served us a frugal meal in silence.

My father thought that Milenko and I had decided to leave on an impulse. To dissuade him of this, I described the suffocating atmosphere at the university, how it was riddled with accusation and suspicion. Did he know, from his haven of peace, that henceforth the Party had decided to "evaluate" all the citizens in this country? A toxic little piece of paper, often signed in an awkward hand, shadowed every man and every woman. It attested to their allegiance or hostility to the Master Design. Sometimes, this classification even followed people beyond the grave. How to explain otherwise the sudden disappearance of certain street names and library books except as a result of this deplorable posthumous classification? Some had been long in their graves, but this made absolutely no difference.

The irony of fate: while some names were disappearing, mine was displayed in full view on the infamous bulletin board at school as a warning that I was being watched closely, every gesture noted now. The countdown had started. The end result would be my expulsion from the university. The stage was already set, plotted to the smallest detail.

Because he was leading such a secluded life in Prizren, my father had difficulty understanding why I couldn't be like everyone else and learn to live under the new regime. He spoke of the long battles waged by the Christian churches, the necessary compromises they made in order to safeguard the essential doctrine. He criticised me for my intransigence, my partisan attitude. By dint of berating the fanatics, I would start to resemble them.

What could I say? He was right in so many respects. I disliked my brusque nature and my fiery temper. Torn between the desire to melt into the crowd and the urge to rebel, I was often caught in an exhausting inner struggle. At times society seemed intent on totally controlling the individual and creating an immense barracks where love and laughter were regulated by law; whereas at other times, I was conscious of my morbid predisposition to paint the devil blacker than he was.

While I was ready to admit to a tendency to exaggerate, I absolutely refused to live in a country governed by absurdity.

Why had nobody spoken out against the necessity to remake the lawn in front of the School of Engineering the day before the May Day parade destroyed it? Why had we accepted that allegiance to the Party should replace all other values? How had we reached that point? What magician had bewitched us to be as docile as the poor decrepit beasts of some small provincial circus?

I told my father about the strange dream I kept having: Lost in a large and dilapidated house, I would find myself climbing an unsteady staircase. The mouldy air was making me nauseous. Eventually, I would arrive in front of a door and feel compelled to push it open. On the other side was a bucolic landscape. In the middle of a bright green field, a cow grazes peacefully. A solitary tree stood silhouetted against a blue sky scattered with small white clouds. I need only to cross the threshold to enter this idyllic landscape and escape the haunted house, but somehow, this beautiful scene inspired me only with dread.

My father listened patiently, and then proceeded to upbraid me for my pride. This was not the first time. A few years previously, he had come across one of my letters to Milenko in which I had written: "You know that for us, every word has its own meaning; synonyms are the mainstay of confused minds." He had become indignant: "Who do you think you are? Kant or Spinoza? You're setting yourself up for a painful fall, my son." Christian humility had no doubt marked him for life. He was partly right. I found it difficult to deal with my pride, which, strangely enough, co-existed with extreme humility.

Towards five o'clock, our discussion was interrupted by the ringing of a bell calling the faithful to vespers. My father suggested that I accompany him to the old church, which had been built in the Middle Ages by a king from the Nemanjić dynasty. Was he hoping to distance me, for a moment, from the outside world?

The inside of the stone church was dark and cool. Small oil lamps flickered in front of paintings on the iconostasis. From the fresco-covered walls, saints and pious donors looked down sadly on what remained of the flock: at most six or seven old people. A priest was officiating. Three seminarians were singing psalms in Gregorian chant. The Slavonic liturgy and the ritual, which I didn't understand, belonged to an unreal world, far removed from the one bustling around me in Belgrade and throughout the country. My quarrel with the activists at the university and even my planned escape suddenly appeared futile here. In this five-hundred-year-old church, the frescoes depicting the birth of St. Nicholas and the Blessed Virgin's Dormition reminded me of what really counted: life, suffering, and death. I started to feel very anxious, as if being torn between a mystical world and the real one. Suddenly, I had no place to turn.

As we left the church, the few parishioners gathered around my father. This allowed me to slip away and go for a walk. I started to climb the street in front of the bishopric. I supposed it would eventually lead to the foot of the old fortress whose walls towered above the city. Ever since childhood, ruins, old stones, and the remains of medieval *châteaux* had always fascinated me. It was as if I secretly hoped to uncover the traces of a fascinating past and imagine the men who had once lived there. The fortress dominating Prizren had been built in the fourteenth century during the reign of Emperor Dušan when medieval Serbia was at the height of its power.

After passing the Orthodox seminary and the last of the houses, I followed a narrow path that wound its way up through wild grasses and burrs. Half an hour later, I found myself in front of the fort. Stones, whitened by the sun and the rain, lay in piles under the crumbling ramparts. The impressive portal bore witness to the past splendour of the citadel. I went inside respectfully, as if fearing to disturb the dead. Thorn bushes had taken over the interior. The dying rays of the sun lit up the walls, and insects buzzed in the bushes. I tiptoed towards the ramparts. Only a few vaults remained of the former stables under what once had been the parapet. In the cavities, clusters of bats were sleeping in anticipation of dusk.

Wandering among the ruins and the desolation, I let my imagination loose. I could almost hear the neighing of the horses in their stalls. Yesterday, Dušan the Powerful, Emperor of the Greeks and the Serbs — a title bestowed on him by a chronicler of the times — had crossed this very courtyard, followed by courtesans wearing garments of rich brocade. His men, middle-aged, were probably discussing their newest conquests. How could they have imagined that thirty or forty years later, thousands of horsemen from across the Bosphorus would cover the great plain of Kosovo visible from the dungeon, and that their empire would dissolve like a huge block of ice that calves off a glacier.

A hissing of serpents in the ruins interrupted my dreaming. In the west, the sun was still on fire, but down below, the town was already plunged into shadow. I hurried to retrace my steps. On my way down the narrow path, I thought of all those men in the fort, so obsessed by power and glory. On the plain, other men were building churches, painting frescoes, and aspiring to eternity while giving praise to God and the Apostles. All of them feared death and sought desperately to leave behind a trace of their existence here on earth.

Back at the bishopric, my father reproached me for having disappeared. He had wanted to introduce me to the people attending Vespers. He was so proud of his son. And here I was about to abandon him to a solitary old age.

He suggested that we spend two days together at the

monastery of Dečani and continue our talk in the shadows of the old sanctuary. The suggestion delighted me. Perhaps there, through some miracle, we might arrive at a peaceful resolution.

~

The next day we left in an even more dilapidated bus than the one that had brought me to Prizren. The passengers still wore the same craggy faces. The vehicle jogged and coughed its way across this ancient land soaked in history. On June 12, 1389, on this softly undulating plain covered with wheat fields, the Serbs had fought the Turks in the famous battle of Kosovo. One month later, when the news of the Serbian victory had reached Paris, the bells of Notre-Dame Cathedral rang out triumphantly to herald the victory of the Christian armies.

But the news turned out to be false: the Serbs had actually lost the battle of Kosovo. Their defeat opened the doors of Europe to the rugged Turkish warriors. They besieged Vienna twice, and in 1683, the city was saved only by the intervention of the Polish army under King Jan Sobieski. In Serbia, the victory of the Turks cut short a flourishing medieval civilisation. But the tragedy of this defeat forged the character of the Serbian people. For almost five centuries, the Serbs lived under the domination of the Ottoman Empire, yet they never lost hope that one day they would regain their freedom. The Turks, on the other hand, remembered the battle of Kosovo as a great victory over the infidels. All nations cultivate their own version of history — and tomorrow, the tragic cycle of war and peace will start up again.

The bus bumped and snaked between the hillocks, kicking up a large cloud of dust. Not far from there, five hundred and fifty-six years earlier, almost to the day, cavalry and foot soldiers had rushed to battle with an immense clamour. Swords and shields had clashed in a ferocious hand-to-hand combat. The battle, which lasted barely a day, decided the fate of the country for centuries to come. Once the carnage was over, the vultures, attracted by the smell of death, made their appearance, wheeling grimly above the battlefield. The wounded lay for days in the terrible summer heat. According to legend, a young girl went among the soldiers with a jug of water in order to quench the thirst of the wounded and the dying. Our national poetry commemorated the red peonies that were said to have sprouted from earth drenched with the blood of the Serbian heroes. Sagas embellish death; up close, death is always hideous.

I remember the poor young man who, in December 1944, had died in front of the soldiers of our unit, his throat pierced by shrapnel. What did he care whether death was heroic or not? His bulging eyes seemed to cry out: "Do something. I'm dying. Keep me alive!" But he couldn't talk. His throat was nothing but a horrible wound emitting a death rattle. We heard it, but could do nothing to keep him alive.

My father and I were headed toward the mountains of Montenegro. They rose up, trembling in the June heat. The bus stopped at the lowest foothills in a great cloud of dust. A dirt road climbed toward the forest and at the first turn, the monastery of Dečani appeared, nestled at the bottom of a small wooded valley. A group of buildings formed a sort of enclosure surrounding a pink marble church. In the outlying vegetable garden, two monks were busy digging. We used the carriage entrance and soon found ourselves in a setting that hadn't changed since medieval times. In the courtyard, monks went about their daily chores; one was cutting wood, another was crossing the courtyard with a bag on his back. The scene might have been lifted straight from the illuminated pages of *Les Très Riches*

*Heures du duc de Berry* painted in the fifteenth century. It was comforting to see man's activities bridging centuries and cultures.

Archimandrite Theodosia, a former officer of the Czar, hurried up to greet us. My father immediately told him my reason for coming to Kosovo. We walked towards the church built in the fourteenth century by King Etienne Uroš, father of Emperor Dušan.

Inside the church, the past was tangible on the walls and arches that were almost entirely covered with frescoes. All of medieval society was portrayed here — crowned heads, dignitaries, but also artisans, builders, fishermen, blacksmiths, soldiers, monks, and peasants. They came alive in the faces of the biblical figures and saints and the wealthy donors. According to Father Theodosia, the walls of the church were covered with the faces of some ten thousand people painted by anonymous artists, only one of whom had dared to sign his name: Serge the Fisherman.

I also had the privilege of being shown a small room behind the iconostasis, where the treasures of the monastery were stored. Among the manuscripts and sacred objects displayed, I was particularly struck by a chalice. Apparently, it had served at the solemn communion of Prince Lazar and his army the day before the bloody battle of Kosovo. In retrospect, this last communion was more of an extreme unction. Almost all the men were to die the following day. Taken prisoner, Prince Lazar was decapitated and followed his men to their deaths. The richly carved chalice left me pondering. More than five centuries before, Prince Lazar, whose mummified body would become a revered symbol, had sipped wine from this sacred vase. Instinctively, I touched this mystical link to our past.

A little before noon we left the church to eat lunch with seven or eight monks in the refectory. Their presence prevented us from continuing the discussion we had started the day before, but after the meal, I found myself once again alone with my father and the archimandrite.

My father worried about how we intended to cross the border. I explained Boris's plan to him. He was skeptical, as was the father archimandrite, who told me how, during the Bolshevik Revolution, units of the notorious Tcheka, or secret police, organised false escape routes which often ended up in the cellars of the Ljoubljanka, the infamous prison in Moscow. There the escapees died with a bullet in the head. Milenko and I had complete confidence in Boris, however, plus I was counting on the luck that had carried us through the war, but I dodged the topic of the unpredictability of Lady Luck.

My father wondered how we intended to survive in Austria, and later on in France. How would we continue our studies? I had no answer for him.

"It's true, father, that on the other side of the Mura River, we are entering *terra incognita*, but we are relying on chance to help us out. Others have done it before and survived. Why not us? In fact, after the defeat of 1915, you yourself walked through the snow in the Albanian mountains, half-starved and exhausted. You didn't know that you would end up three months later in Rochefort-sur-Mer, in a quiet little town with friendly people. Life is unpredictable and, anyhow, you used to say to me: 'What is important is to serve the Supreme Master. The rest will follow.'"

"And who is your Supreme Master, my son?"

"I admit that I'm not too sure. Sometimes, I think it is Freedom ... sometimes Truth, or the Spirit, but maybe they are three aspects of the same entity."

As soon as I had spoken these words, I realised how pompous they sounded. Would my father think of me as a pretentious fool? He didn't say anything, but only looked at me as if to ascertain whether I was sincere.

Encouraged by his silence, I continued: "Father, freedom is not just some vague abstraction. We are aware of it only when we lose it. You yourself told me how often you thought about these things when you were a prisoner in Vojlovica, watching the German soldiers march back and forth under your window. It was snowing outside and your cell was barely heated."

My father remained silent, although he was listening intently.

"It's true that I've never been to prison but the entire country has become a vast prison. And the worst part is, we're not allowed to talk about what we see. The Master Design has forced us to live in a divided universe. All day long, we're brainwashed by the newspapers and the radio, which promote an unreal world of cardboard and theatre props. Every day, we suffer because we're not allowed to talk about what is going on around us. Some people turn it into a joke: 'If we want to know how happy we are, we only have to listen to the radio.'"

My father remained silent.

"This divided universe ends up by splitting us in two. We are living in a continuous carnival where everyone wears the same mask. We all have to meet the same norms. We are all being standardised. It is only when we find ourselves alone, standing in front of a mirror, that we can glimpse our true identity — humiliated, ridiculed, crushed human beings angered by our lack of power. Worse still, the Master Design has seized control of our language and distorted the meaning of words. People can no longer communicate among themselves. The new order has condemned them to a life of juxtaposed solitudes."

I finished my indictment, surprised at my clear-headedness and awaited my father's remarks. Instead of commenting, he changed the subject.

"You know, my son, I wonder if you're not making a mistake to study engineering. You plead quite well, and I think you have the makings of a lawyer or a philosopher or, who knows, even a writer."

"But, father, I can be an engineer and a writer. Dostoyevsky did it and he wasn't the only one."

"You're right, my son. In any case, we often ignore our true vocation. Look at Father Theodosia who started out as an army officer. Never could he have imagined that one day he would become the Archimandrite of Dečani Monastery."

Father Theodosia smiled.

"It's true, Monsignor, in my youth I dreamt of battles and the glory of bearing arms, but war, with its dead bodies and its survivors who are wounded in flesh and spirit, changed my path and directed me towards God."

"Father Theodosia, do you regret having shot men who were your brothers, and even possibly killing some?" asked my father.

"You know, Monsignor, I commanded a battery of long-range cannons. I would shout: 'Fire!' The soldiers carried out the order and the missiles went far, very far. Who is to say where they fell? So I'm not too haunted by the invisible dead, but I am guilty and a sinner. There is no doubt about that!"

My father already knew Father Archimandrite's answer, but he wanted me to hear it for myself. Occasionally, his mischievous side would cut through his episcopal reserve.

※

Our discussion, interrupted by the prior's recollection of his war experience, left me feeling hopeful. My father seemed to be softening up to the idea of my leaving, though we had yet to really talk about it.

After vespers, we played out the final act of our discussion as we strolled among the old tombstones of the little cemetery behind the church. I tried to read the time-weathered, centuries-old names of the archimandrites and bishops buried there. We didn't talk, but I felt that the denouement was rapidly approaching. I decided to break the silence and put an end to the ambiguity.

"Father, if I remain here, I will end up in jail."

The old man looked startled. "Why jail?" His voice betrayed his anxiety.

"Because I can't adjust to the new order. I can't remain quiet. Something always impels me to make a scene. After the university throws me out — and they certainly will — I could end up back in the army, and be sent to a disciplinary unit that closely resembles a penal colony."

My father stopped in his tracks and looked at me. After a moment's silence, he said: "My son, if you must choose between prison and exile, then go and God be with you."

I was expecting a long and bitter argument. This sudden acceptance caught me off guard. Had he thought about it during vespers or did he know the dilemma I was facing, and had resigned himself to my decision? In any case, what did it matter? He had accepted the idea of my leaving.

My relief was mixed with guilt. I had purposefully dramatized my situation, and in a sense almost blackmailed my father into giving me his blessing. My expulsion from the university did not necessarily mean that I would be inducted into the army, but it would cause me no end of trouble. And if I had any doubts about that, I had no illusions whatsoever about my future in the country.

Surely between prison and exile, there must be a third path, the possibility of a metamorphosis, perhaps even a radical one? Why not? It happens all the time in nature. A chrysalis opens up and a beautiful butterfly emerges. Flitting from one flower to the other, does the butterfly remember its past as a caterpillar? Why can't a person do the same? Change from one day to the next, and become a new person? All one needs to do is slough off old thinking, and immediately the world around becomes friendly and benevolent. Luka M., the third-year student who had been thrown out the window, had managed to grow a new skin. Why couldn't I?

⌒

The rest of the visit remains vague in my memory, like a distant dream. My father and I slept in a room with whitewashed walls and rustic furniture. The smell of the forest drifted in through the open window. Several times during the night, the cry of a bird shattered the silence. I remained awake for a little while. I could almost feel the slow breathing of the earth and the trees as the monastery slumbered.

In my dream, I was wandering around the deserted courtyard of the cloister. Behind the chapel, the ancient tombstones were bathed in moonlight. Perhaps there, among the Orthodox monks, rested the remains of Brother Vito, the Franciscan who had built this church. Or had he gone back to die in his native Dalmatia, fleeing some silly quarrel over dogma between the Eastern and Western churches? In my dream, I pushed open the heavy door of the church and found myself among the silent people of the frescoes who had been watching over us for centuries. Perhaps among these ten thousand faces was an ancestor begging me to remain in the country. Too late. A secret voice was urging me to embark on the long, uncertain voyage.

Birdsong awakened us early. The monks were already out in the courtyard, attending to their daily chores. Towards ten o'clock, Father Theodosia accompanied us on foot to the bus stop. The same bus arrived in its usual cloud of dust.

A little before twelve, we arrived back at Prizren. After lunch, I prepared to leave. My father walked me to the bus stop. We said our farewells, and pretended that we would be seeing each other soon. I climbed aboard to cut short any show of emotion. I waved to my father one final time from my seat by the window. The last image I have of him is etched on my memory. As he stands in front of a miserable little shop, his white beard stark against his black robe, he could be a symbol of the loneliness of old age in a painting. As the bus started to move, I was tempted to ask the driver to stop so that I could run back and tell my father that I would stay after all. But I didn't. The bus accelerated and I lost sight of my father. A minute later we were out on the open road and the cloud of dust blotted out the city with its mosques and its churches. That same evening in Skopje I boarded the night train for Belgrade.

# VII

# The Round of Farewells

*Is not leave-taking what
resembles death most closely?*
— J. BARBEY D'AUREVILLY

ON MY RETURN from Prizren, I was plunged into the furnace of a Belgrade summer. The streetcars with their wooden benches smelled of grease, and the asphalt, softened by the heat wave, turned into a rubbery carpet.

Partly relieved to have obtained my father's consent but increasingly anxious about our approaching departure, I moved restlessly from one end of the city to the other, busying myself with real or frivolous chores, trying to exorcise my fears in activity. Sometimes, I just wanted to revisit the places that I had really cared for. I needed to kill time.

This last summer in Belgrade reminded me of pre-war summers when I would spend a week or two in the city after the end of the school year and before the summer holidays in Užice. I would take advantage of these first days of freedom to go swimming with friends at the public baths of the Seven Poplars. We would spend hours tanning ourselves on the wet wooden boards. Their smell evoked long days of delicious idleness, swimming in the shadow of the old fortress, and summer pranks. September meant going back to school and the bustle of the city, seeing friends and going to the afternoon dances at the school. But all this had slid irrevocably into the past.

The war, with its trains full of starving men and women desperately searching the countryside for food, the curfews and the lists of detainees felled by firing squads, their names displayed on the walls of our cities like leprous lesions: all this had destroyed the innocence and freshness of our youth. Today's youth, wearing a rictus of happiness, was dying on the immense work site of the new Tower of Babel. The party was definitely over.

Strolling about the city, I stopped here and there in the *cafés*, with their wine-stained tablecloths. To quench my thirst and staunch my anxiety, I would have a beer at the counter, but the more I drank, the greater was the thirst and the anxiety I was trying to drown. A little drunk, I would get up and hurry out to escape my fear, but it stuck to my skin like tar.

I would come home to Ilija Street late at night, watching my shadow alternately shorten and lengthen on the sidewalks. As I'd approach a lamppost, my shadow would slide behind my back but when it preceded me, I would stare at it anxiously. Was it the shadow of a Party henchman trailing me? But, no, the streets around Slavija Square were deserted. As I'd approach my aunt's apartment, I would look at the light shining from her window onto the leaves of the chestnut tree. What if a militiaman were waiting for me upstairs? I would climb the stairs and open the door, my nerves on edge. Nothing would have changed. Aunt Lou would be calmly reading a newspaper.

On my way to the university to pick up my baccalaureate diploma, I ran into T.N., a military judge I had known in Jagodina during the war. A rather colourless but dangerous character, he brought back memories of those Sundays when the officers in our unit would meet to play football. T. N. would call out: "Hangman, throw me the ball." The executioner, perfectly comfortable in this august company, would run after the ball. The spectators would laugh, enjoying the convivial atmosphere. That gave me the shivers. Whoever said that executioners were held in contempt? In Belgrade, in the hard heat of June, this puny little judge was still wearing his captain's uniform and carried a big automatic pistol in a black leather holster. Was it to give himself confidence? We exchanged banalities. If he had known what I was planning.

Fifteen minutes later, I was walking down the cool corridors of the School of Engineering. My baccalaureate diploma had been sleeping in a filing cabinet of the secretariat since last autumn. I wanted to retrieve it with the hope that one day, I would continue my education in France — or elsewhere. However, before withdrawing it, I had to strike my name off the faculty list. This meant postponing my education indefinitely, a decision that was very painful.

At the secretariat, a grey-haired lady received me sympathetically. She tried to dissuade me: "Young man, you shouldn't abandon your studies." What could I say? Feeling like a thief, I shoved my diploma into my briefcase and left the office. In the hall, the sign announcing the first lecture of *The Theory of Bohr's Electrons and Dialectical Materialism* had disappeared, but the memory lingered like an insult.

Milenko and I weren't the first to withdraw our documents before vanishing into thin air. Faces started to disappear mysteriously from the once overcrowded lecture halls. Some would reappear months later in Paris or elsewhere. One day in Paris in 1947, I came across the Grand Duke in the waiting room at 6 Tournon Street. Like other students in exile, he was waiting to receive a scholarship from the Inter-university Assistance

Programme run by the remarkable Madame Meuvré. We reminisced and laughed about those days when stupidity and absurdity were the order of the day.

Eventually, the secret police caught on to the students' stratagem. Shortly after our departure, the secretariats of all the faculties were asked to advise the relevant authorities whenever students asked for their documents. By that time, we had already left the country.

⁂

As the day for our departure approached, I seesawed wildly between optimism and blackest despair. My imagination was prone to conjure nightmarish misadventures. The least terrifying of them was of border guards stopping us as we were about to leave Yugoslav soil. They would bring us back to Belgrade under escort. In the train, the passengers passing our compartment turn their heads to avoid seeing our chains. Back in the capital, we would be kept waiting for months on end at the headquarters of the secret police located in a large white marble building. Others like us, who had also been waiting for months, had invented a way of obtaining news from the outside. In the washrooms, once the door was closed, they would climb up onto the sink and peer out at the roofs of the city. At night, the news headlines would be displayed on a luminous panel installed at the top of the *Albania*, the only high-rise building in town. The fleeting words would give us an inkling of what was happening elsewhere in the world.

In a more macabre version of the nightmare, we would be wounded during our attempt to cross the border and felled on the spot with a bullet to the head. All traces of us would vanish. Buried where we fell, like so many other young people before us, we would enter the world of the living dead, our lives frozen into the eternal youth of our last photograph. In case the secret police decided to return our bodies to Milenko's mother and my father, our corpses would probably resemble the remains of Aleksandar Cincar Markovic, shot in the autumn of 1944. His body was handed over to his widow with his head wrapped in bandages. Members of the secret police — such sensitive creatures — wanted to spare his widow the sight of his face, which had been blown away by a bullet.

My imagination, unhinged by fear, was constantly inventing new images, each one more horrific than the previous one. Barely had I chased away one image than a new one would swim to the surface. It was slowly driving me crazy. If Boris's exam at the Faculty of Medicine had not detained us, I would have jumped on a train, headed for the border and been done with it — whatever the outcome.

Prompted by an innate curiosity and a desire to provoke, I thought of paying a call on the Writer. He was the author of several books and had been the toast of Leftist intellectuals in Belgrade before the war. I wanted to know what he thought of the New Order, this man who, all his life, had secretly hoped for such an outcome. He was, of course, in no way involved in the execution of a hundred or more intellectuals in November 1944, nor in the rigged elections of autumn 1945, but he had helped to create an aura of moral integrity around the Master Design that had seduced many well-intentioned men.

The Allied bombing of Belgrade in the spring and summer of 1944 had forced the Writer, his wife, and a young architect in poor health to seek refuge at my Aunt Elisabeth's estate near Užice. All of us had spent the remaining months of the war in her large house.

The view from the estate was of a small valley filled with

corn and alfalfa fields. Gnarled plum trees covered with lichens grew up one side of the mountain. Above them a forest of beech trees clothed the mountain in a thick green coat. The peace of this rural landscape was deceptive, for behind the house a hundred or so Bulgarian soldiers were dug into their log blockhouses like moles. Sometimes, in the middle of the night, they would shoot blindly to exorcise their fear. The echo would ricochet through the valley. When the shots stopped, we could hear the muffled roar of trucks travelling with their headlights off, the sound of the German army withdrawing from Greece and retreating north through Yugoslavia.

We lived in an unreal world. The war was still grinding on all around us, but in the vast country kitchen, within the protective circle of light shed by the gas lamp, the conflict seemed eerily distant. The Writer would often take the floor and speak of literature, politics, Surrealism and people whose names meant nothing to me. The man manipulated language brilliantly, but what he said was rather bookish, detached from real life. Perhaps that is why I was rarely moved by what he said.

Only one name from this time has survived the wreckage of my memory — Louis Aragon — probably because of an anecdote related by the Writer's wife. One day, in Paris, the great poet was ten minutes late for his lecture because of a conversation with the Writer. Aragon had apparently told those urging him to hurry up: "Can't you see that I'm speaking to Mr. M.?"

The Writer probably thought me a cheeky ignoramus. One day, when I felt like teasing him, I had asked him whether he had written the even or the odd pages of the novel he was working on with a friend. He made a face, but didn't hold it against me. He probably took me for a young savage who needed to lose a rough edge or two. His erudition impressed me, but his commitment to the Master Design did not. It was incomprehensible to me that such a cultured man with refined bourgeois tastes and a Voltairian mind could belong to a movement that proclaimed: "The Party never errs."

One day, as I was walking near his home, I thought about how his life had turned out. Between the two World Wars, he had taken up his pen for the cause of the Master Design. Now that the Idea had triumphed, the new potentates kept him at arm's length. He knew them all personally. They could have appointed him director of the National Theatre or made him an ambassador, or even have created some prestigious post commensurate with his talent. But no, they deliberately ignored him. The Writer remained a simple high-school teacher until the day of his retirement. Why did they ostracise him? Some blamed him for remaining quietly in Belgrade during the Occupation while his comrades were fighting and dying in the Resistance. But others had done the same thing and it hadn't prevented them from achieving influential positions. The real reason lay elsewhere, in the vague rivalries among the leftist intellectual groups. Profoundly hurt but too proud to complain, the Writer suffered in silence. This regrettable outcome tempered my desire to provoke him.

I hesitated a moment before ringing the bell of his first-floor apartment. The Writer came in person to open the door. He was wearing a red dressing-gown, shabby but still worthy of a wealthy bourgeois. His emaciated face made me think of Voltaire. His cozy apartment, furnished with refinement, reminded me of the apartments of Paris intellectuals I had met during in 1937.

The Writer seemed very pleased to see me. I think I had interrupted his solitude and his isolation. After exchanging a few niceties, he went straight to the point: "How is university?"

"Not too good," I answered. "In fact, I'm no longer a student. I'm leaving the country illegally in a few days."

My words had the effect of a cold shower: "Don't do it. Why would you want to leave the country?"

"Look at what is going on. Think of the people who were shot here in Belgrade in November 1944 under pretext that they had collaborated with the enemy. Think of last autumn's rigged elections. Think of the new red bourgeoisie that is moving into the fashionable neighbourhood of Dedinje, evicting the owners from their own homes. Not to mention what is going on at the university," I said.

The Writer listened to me, looking decidedly uncomfortable, but he was more surprised by my decision to leave the country than by what I had just said. I wasn't telling him anything he didn't know, but my blasphemous remarks hurt him.

"No doubt there are excesses and errors but all revolutions begin this way," he said.

"Begin and end?"

"You haven't changed — always the sharp tongue. You'll see, this revolution isn't like the others. Not only is it against injustice, but it is creating a modern society. It might have crushed a few innocent people, but you have to judge it with an eye to the future, not the present."

"Heydrich said more or less the same thing when he claimed that future generations of Germans would one day be grateful to the *Führer* for his toughness. But the innocent people who were crushed, as you so tastefully put it, were men of real flesh and blood. It wasn't just a matter of erasing them from a list. They collapsed around the stake or received a bullet in the head, always in the name of an unpredictable future. Who will resurrect them the day the Master Design finally succeeds in creating a society of geometric justice?" I asked.

"Always the individualist. But this century is for the people, for the collective. The greatest men of our century all understood that: Joliot-Curie, Romain Rolland, Aragon, H. G. Wells. They all espoused what you refer to as the Master Design. As for the executions, don't exaggerate. There were many more during the Bolshevik Revolution."

"You might find me pretentious but I don't believe in great men. They make mistakes like anyone else. As for those who were shot, you're saying that we should be happy there were fewer here than in the Soviet Union? It's true, here we don't shoot everyone who doesn't have calloused hands, but —"

"I didn't say that, but be realistic. There were collaborators —"

"Probably, but in November 1944, of the men who were shot, some were collaborators and others were totally innocent," I answered.

"Well, you can't make an omelette without breaking a few eggs."

"Yes, but it's always the other person's eggs."

"Come now ... you're still young ... you have time to see things differently. Right now I'm writing a novel about youth ... you mustn't leave ... you'll see, everything will work out!"

And so ended our discussion. It didn't make sense to continue, for we were looking at the world through different eyes. Apparently, the Writer had remained faithful to his convictions, but was he still as steadfast as when we used to sit around the table in that big country kitchen? It's true he urged me to stay, but so limply that it made me wonder whether in fact he secretly approved of my decision. Perhaps, like so many other intellectuals of the Left, he too felt the worm of doubt gnawing at him.

Despite our disagreement, we parted on the best of terms, proof that his thinking had started to shift. As I closed the door, it occurred to me: what if the Writer reported me to the police? I banished the thought. Despite his connection with the new order, I didn't feel him capable of such a gesture. Poor man, he was still stuck with a bourgeois code of ethics.

༄

By the end of June, I had finished my round of farewells. I had spoken to a few friends and all of them, unlike the Writer, had applauded our decision. Most of them regretted not being able to join us. This reassured me and banished my doubts.

My leave-taking of Professor Ivan Djaja, who taught biology at the Science Faculty, was very different. I didn't know him and I had no intention of letting him in on our plans. I had bought two French-language books at an antique dealer, *Colloidal Suspensions* and *Secrets of the Life of Djordje Lakovski*, which I thought he might enjoy. Because my own interests were pretty far-ranging, I had bought the first one without even knowing what a colloidal suspension was. The second book was about a visionary, or a charlatan, who claimed to have detected electromagnetic rays in plants. I was averse to throwing away a book, no matter how insignificant. So I decided to offer them to Professor Djaja, one of the few men in Belgrade who could appreciate them.

How little we know ourselves. Today I understand why I gave him these books: I wanted to meet him. When I was in high school, I had read one of his books that had absolutely fascinated me. *Going Down the River* was a child's voyage of initiation down the Danube in a little boat in the company of an older man. When the sun went down, they stopped on a sand bar to gather dry wood and grill fish. They talked around the fire, their faces lit by the flames, about the stars, the sciences, and the world's mysteries. His book had totally enchanted me.

Diffidence made me hesitate to ring his doorbell. What right did I have, a student at odds with the university, to disturb a scientist and a former student of the Teachers' College of Paris, who was moreover a recognised authority in Belgrade and Paris for his work on the artificial hibernation of mammals? My idea of approaching him was a bit presumptuous but, as usual, my curiosity won out.

With the two books under my arm, I went to the professor's home at 8 Ban Jelačić Street located in a quiet neighbourhood. Most of the houses belonged to academics. I rang at the gate of a tiny garden. Immediately a very tall man, with a goatee resembling Napoleon III's and wearing a straw hat like Robinson Crusoe's, planted his spade and came over. I felt like running away, but it was too late. He was already standing in front of me.

"How do you do, Sir. I apologise for disturbing you, but I thought these books might interest you."

The professor looked at me with the curiosity of an entomologist. "Come in, young man. Come in."

I followed him, feeling slightly reassured. His simplicity made me feel at home. We sat down in the agreeable half-light of the living room, with its semi-closed shutters. He took a few moments to leaf through the books.

"So you want to give me these books. And why me, exactly?"

"You studied biology in Paris and I thought these books might interest you."

"How do you know that?"

"You wrote it in an article about André Maurois."

"You remember my article about André Maurois who is, in fact, Émile Herzog? Do you know why I wrote that article during the Occupation?" he asked.

"No, I don't. Did you want to send a message of solidarity to the Jews who were being hunted down by the Gestapo?"

"Your guess is correct. I have often wondered if people understood what I was trying to do — that I was thumbing my nose at the occupying forces, because the Herzogs were Jewish and belonged to a prominent Alsatian family. In the early 1900s, Maurois and I were at the same boarding school in the *Quartier Latin*. He was a brilliant young man who was studying for his university entrance exam. After we finished school, I lost sight of him until one day, I discovered that he wrote under the pseudonym of André Maurois. But tell me, who are you and what do you do in life?"

His simple and direct manner put me at ease, so I explained briefly my situation and that I was intending to leave the country. He listened to me attentively.

"Why do you want to leave? Why don't you wait until you have your degree?"

I told him of the inaugural lecture of Professor Dragiša Ivanović and the nonsense about the theory of Bohr's electrons and dialectical materialism. He smiled, but did not seem surprised. Science and ideology were fighting a covert battle in all faculties.

The professor's query obliged me to consider the most important reason for Milenko's and my departure. "I think ... I'm not sure ... maybe it is to keep my freedom of thought ... to be true to myself. If I continue to live here, I will become just another man. This might sound vague or irrational, but ..."

"Perhaps, but it is important. Unamuno wrote ... have you read him?"

"No."

"One day you probably will. In *The Tragic Sense of Life*, he says that the real world includes the irrational one and that without the irrational world, there is no creativity. The freedom you speak of might at first seem vague and abstract, but take it away, and the world goes to pieces."

The professor called his daughter, a girl of about twelve, to bring us some red wine. We drank a glass and talked for another half-hour in the coolness of his living room. He explained, though, and I am no longer sure in what context, that the inertia of the spirit is infinitely greater than that of material objects. To support his theory, he spoke of how the first cars resembled carriages "because the inventors, despite their great ingenuity, couldn't discard the image of a horse-drawn carriage."

At three-thirty, I got up to go. He wished me good luck for the border crossing and suggested that I go to see one of his friends in Paris, Professor Schaeffer, a well-known physiologist.

Walking down Ban Jelačić Street in the intense heat, I felt happy about having met such a remarkable man.

# VIII

# Yesteryear's Landscapes

*The only real landscape is the one we have lost.*
— MARCEL PROUST

WHY BE ASHAMED of feeling nostalgic for the happy memories of one's youth? Why fear becoming sentimental about the days when one was full of sap, still discovering the world and dreaming of going out and conquering it? Why douse the coals that continue to glow under the ashes of our lives? What prevents us from fanning our dreams back to their former brightness? By evoking joyful memories, perhaps we can rescue them from oblivion.

I left for Užice, my father's birthplace and cradle of my paternal family, under pretext of selling the bed linen in our apartment. The real reason for my trip was a desire to see, one last time, this town hidden in the mountains of Serbia where I had spent my first summers. Images from beloved places become all the more precious when one is about to go into exile.

My two uncles and my father owned a couple of buildings in Užice as well as a property in the countryside. They were the sole remnants of a fortune accumulated in the previous century by my great-grandfather and grandfather, both wealthy merchants of agricultural goods. By 1937, the three brothers had already divided up their inheritance. My father received an old house on land extending from Princess Ljubica Street to the wharf on the Djetinja River. That same year, my father tore down the house and built a two-storey apartment building. As his sole heir, I didn't feel rich but at least I knew I would never be in need. However, the war, revolution, and bombardment of 1944 wiped out this security. A bomb exploded in the middle of the street and sliced off a good part of the facade. With many of the rooms open to the street, the building resembled a huge doll's house.

My memories of this trip to Užice are both nebulous and sharp. On June 23, I boarded a wheezy old train at Belgrade Station. Small picturesque villages with familiar names rattled by: Jarkovo, Umka, Obrenovac ... each place meant something to me. After passing the city of Ćačak, the train entered the gorges of Morava. Old monasteries clung to the white cliffs or hung off steep slopes, the ultimate refuges of Serbian culture during the Turkish Occupation, where for centuries, the monks, far from the bustle of the world, had copied hagiographies and the chronicles of kings. The railway followed the restless river, which often pooled into quiet bays. The bridges, destroyed during the final fighting of October 1944 and hastily rebuilt with rough-hewn beams, seemed to belong in films of the far West. The train slowed as it travelled over these frail constructions, and the passengers closed their eyes, not daring to look down into the gorges.

In the afternoon, the train pulled into the Užice station where I had worked as a telegrapher during the Occupation. The former locomotive depot had been bombed, and only the charred walls remained. I emerged from the station and took the shortcut past the quays. Clear water lapped around the big white rocks. Although the day was waning, the sun lingered over the summits of the mountains. Were it not for a few ruined buildings, I might have been back in the town of my childhood.

Visiting Užice brought on a fresh wave of guilt. I saw myself as the prodigal son, come to sell off the remains of a dilapidated fortune to satisfy selfish passions. My poor ancestors had earned all this by dint of hard work. In the final decades of the nineteenth century, before the advent of local trains, they used to ride for days on horseback, rounding up large herds of cattle and driving them over long distances into special wagons waiting in a railway station. The cattle were then sold in Belgrade, Budapest, or Salonika. After an exhausting trip of several weeks, they returned home with gold pieces, and jewellry for their wives in Užice.

They would have turned over in their graves if they had seen how their fortune had dwindled. But they bore a share of the responsibility. Instead of inculcating in their sons a taste for business and commerce, they sent them off to Russia and Austria to be educated. The family fortune had run out by the time my cousins and I came along.

Soon I was walking along Princess Ljubica Street, with its worn cobblestones. Little had changed since the 1944 bombardment. The front rooms of our apartment building were still open to the street, now completely bare of any furniture. Seated in front of my cousins' house, old man Jeunot, with his yellowish beard, was blowing out long puffs of tobacco smoke. His wife Catherine used to sit beside him, busy spinning her wool, but two years before she had joined my grandparents in the little rural cemetery. In the country, master and servant sometimes find themselves buried side by side. This old couple, who could neither read nor write, had entered the service of my family in 1878, while Serbia was still at war with the Turks. Jeunot was doing his military service and Catherine, totally without resources, had sought refuge with my Grandmother Jelena. When he was demobilized, Jeunot, a carpenter by trade, joined her and they remained with my grandparents until they died. They were there for the birth of my uncles and indeed almost looked upon them as the children they never had.

I climbed to the first-floor apartment where I had lived during the Occupation with Aunt Elisabeth and Cousin Dimitri. Uninhabited for two years, the empty rooms were disquieting. In the hall, the head of Judas painted onto an old cupboard stared out at me as always. Poor Judas. Why did we condemn him for his betrayal of Christ if he was only fulfilling the prophecy?

My grandmother Jelena's blue eyes watched me from her portrait on the wall, with their curious mixture of softness and quiet strength. Those who had known her spoke of a strong woman who, when she became a widow, had had to battle creditors to preserve what was left of a shaky fortune.

I knew little about this only daughter of an Orthodox priest, born in a village on the other side of Zlatibor. A childhood trip into the country of my paternal grandmother had left me with indelible memories. I will always recall the long walks on foot or horseback, the high plateau where grass undulated in the wind, those clear, cold springs, the dense pine forests and the deep gorges. I imagined my grandmother on horseback, riding sidesaddle with her father to meet the man she would eventually marry. In those days, people got married and love came later, my great-aunt Catherine used to say.

As I wandered around the empty rooms, I came to the door to the living room. I opened it and looked out onto emptiness and ruin. The floor sloped badly, or the joists had been broken. In the street, the bomb crater had been temporarily filled with rubble, and people now walked around it without even glancing up at the collapsed facade.

One afternoon in December 1943, in this room, my father had reluctantly received the visit of Captain Robert Münster, the German commander for the region. The officer had made a surprising announcement: he considered himself first a Christian and then a German officer. At the same time, he admitted having written to his superiors not to shoot prisoners in case the Resistance decided to shoot him in retaliation. I clearly remember the profile of this distinguished-looking Viennese, a chemical engineer in civilian life, as he stood by the window. Outside, the snow was falling. Chance had dropped Captain Münster into this small, obscure Serbian town. Three months later he was demoted and sent to clear rubble in Hamburg where he died under a rain of Allied bombs.

In September that same year, Aunt Elisabeth had received in this same room Italian officers who had been taken prisoner after Italy's surrender that month. Expressing himself in impeccable Serbo-Croatian, Captain Latuino Sagermano had drunk a toast to peace and to the friendship of all peoples.

When I finally closed the door of the living room, it was with the strange impression that I was turning the page on an entire era.

The bedroom was still intact. I opened a lacquered wooden cupboard that smelled of dried basil. The shelves were filled with the household linens we had used when we lived here. Among the sheets was an old-fashioned linen towel decorated with red flowers and green stalks. Nobody had used it for ages. My father kept it in memory of my mother who had embroidered it as a young woman. My father's straw hat was also still there. In the summer, he used to wear it when he taught at a Belgrade high school for boys. I can still see him standing in the courtyard of the old house in Užice, cleaning his boater with an old toothbrush and white powder.

I also discovered a heavy braid of black hair wrapped in a cloth. In the late Twenties, like many women of the time, my mother had cut her hair in response to a wave of emancipation sweeping across Europe. Instinctively, I smelled the heavy braid, as if it might have retained the scent of the body that gave me life. Nothing remained of this woman who had once played, laughed, loved, and lived but her black hair, and it filled me with morbid thoughts. To chase them away, I closed the cupboard, and left to have dinner with a distant cousin, Cveta, who lived around the corner with her husband and two sons.

The next day, before I set out to visit other landmarks of my past, I offered the remaining mattresses to Dr. Oscar Gruden, a dentist that I had encountered during the Occupation. He was interested in buying them, and for good reason. His family was increasing at the rate of a baby a year. He found the price reasonable and we concluded the transaction over a glass of *sljivovica*. I almost told him of my plans, but didn't. It could cause him problems in case of our arrest. During the twenties, he had had to escape Fascist Italy atop a freight car.

That same morning, hugging the walls and avoiding the main street, I was able to bring Dr. Gruden the mattresses on my head without attracting too much attention. The sale of personal effects could arouse the curiosity of an informer. Walking on the burning pavement accompanied by my shadow, I hesitated between crazy laughter and tears. This time I was the prodigal son pillaging the last scraps of my parents' fortune.

Towards noon, at Vlajko's Bakery, I treated myself to a cream pastry, a regional speciality. Having discovered my bathing trunks in a drawer, I decided to go for a final dip in the clear water of the Djetinja River. I left the house around two in the afternoon and walked into a solid wall of heat. The streets were empty. The whole town was having a siesta.

To cross the river, I had to make a detour via the bridge by the cattle market. Sadly, the old Turkish bridge, dating back to the sixth century, no longer existed. On December 17, 1944, the German artillery blew it up as they withdrew from Serbia. The following day our own forces had entered the newly liberated city. At that time I had visited the ruins of the Turkish bridge and felt a great sadness. In the moonlight, you could see the river winding between the huge stone blocks that had anchored the structure. These were covered with the first snow. Built by a pious pasha, the old humpback bridge with its three graceful arches now lay at the bottom of the river. And yet the little track that crossed it had only gone to a few distant villages in Zlatibor. I sobbed dry-eyed out of sadness and rage as if the destruction of the bridge had killed the soul of the town. That night a monstrous realisation came to me; I could more easily have forgiven the invaders for the death of prisoners than for the destruction of my beloved bridge.

I continued beyond the cattle market shaded by large plane trees and followed the canal, which was bordered by tanning shops. As usual, skins and the innards floated on water that had turned milky from the tanning products. Ducks glided about gracefully on the calm surface.

I walked along the canal until I arrived at the public baths where we used to spend most of our afternoons. The building was in a terrible state. Over the winter, people had torn out the boards to heat their homes. Only the bare skeleton with its large beams remained ... would these last only until the coming winter?

A little further on, the half-open gate of the power plant invited me inside. I pushed it open with a distinct sense of breaking and entering. This was not entirely inaccurate. Access to the power station had always been forbidden, but during the summer we used to come regardless. We would buy off the old Finnish guardian with a few dinars. The poor man, stuck in the Balkans through some hiccup of history, could be persuaded to look the other way. In the machine room, the alternators hummed and the floor shook. Under the floor the powerful turbines could be heard rotating. Nothing had changed. I climbed up the steep metallic staircase to the terrace overlooking the entry point of the forced-water pipes. Not a soul anywhere, only ghosts.

The first ghost that came to mind was Joseph Tapeiner, an Austrian soldier who had escaped from the Eastern Front one winter. In the summer of 1944, he would lie outside tanning himself, and exposing the stumps of his amputated toes. The war had snatched this timid young man from a peaceful pharmacy in Innsbruck and thrust him into the bitter winter on the Russian steppes. How he must have suffered before learning how to walk again like some strange mechanical toy. His disability allowed him to work as the telegraph operator for his company. Later, we became such good friends that he would play us the BBC news from London that he was able to intercept on his transmitter-receiver. Had he been caught, he would have been shot as a traitor. Two days before the German retreat from the city, he had asked us to hide him. He wanted to desert the army. Although we felt sick at heart, we had to refuse. A fanatical Partisan could have shot him, and we would have had him on our conscience all our lives. I often wondered if he survived and returned to his pharmacy in Innsbruck.

The gorges of Djetinja were haunted by another ghost. Mucius Scaevola was born with one arm and was known by his classmates as Dusko the Orphan. One day during that summer of 1944 he went for a walk on the low wall by the canal that carried water to the pressure pipes. He seemed impervious to the noise of the war going on all around us. In any case, there wasn't an army on earth interested in a one-armed man. Mars, the god of war, only accepted healthy bodies for his sacrificial offerings.

Mucius had decided to go swimming. He inched his way along the wall. The water below flowed between rock faces and in some places splashed over the wall covered here and there with tender green moss. Mucius's bare foot slipped. His body toppled into air. He tried desperately to hang onto the wall with his left hand, but had no grip on the water-gorged moss. An inhuman scream echoed through the mountain. A few stones ricocheted off the steep rock face where his body struck, and then there was silence. His broken form lay lifeless on the large pebbles of the beach. High up, around the ruins of the fort, the vultures started to circle. A lovely young woman, Miss Mirkovic, who was out for a swim, closed his eyes. A pathetic consolation for a crippled child who had been rejected at birth by the woman who bore him. I sent a heartfelt blessing to the spirit of Mucius Scaevola.

Leaving the ghosts behind on the deserted terrace, I slipped into my trunks and started swimming against the current. At the small dam, I came across a solitary bather who had been a friend of mine from our military theatre days. Tall and well muscled, he reminded me of Prometheus leaning against the rock. We talked about everything and nothing. He ranted and raved against the new red bourgeoisie. A member of the Party who dared criticise his leaders? It felt too much like provocation. I stayed on my guard, and didn't say much. Sometimes modern Prometheuses are prisoners bound in invisible ideological chains.

In the gorges, the sun dips early. We parted around four and never saw each other again. To go home, I took the road that went by Miller Drago's mill. Its wooden, rust-tinged walls had a certain charm. As usual, wagons loaded with wheat and flour were parked in the yard. A fine mist rose from the turbines. I couldn't pass by the old mill without harking back to my childhood. At the time, Drago the Miller was fattening a sow so obese that she could no longer stand up. At night, the rats would come to gnaw the fat on her back, leaving repulsive holes in her skin.

༄

That evening, I visited Dr. Milan Zanković, a distant uncle of my cousins Nikola and Dimitri. I had struck up a friendship with him during the Occupation. He possessed a vast knowledge of European culture and possessed a Faustian intellect. Everything interested him — medicine, natural science, philosophy, literature, and politics. During the dark war years, we spent many hours discussing the situation at the front and other subjects, but psychoanalysis was our preferred topic. How many times had I left him barely five minutes before curfew, and hurried home as night was falling and the streets were emptying of people?

The man had a sad history. His father was descended from an Italian family with Slavic ties from Dubrovnik. His mother was the niece of Paul Arène, the Provençal writer. He had studied medicine in Vienna and spoke fluent German, Italian, English, and French. Two wars and an erratic civil servant's career landed him in this small Serbian town. In his twilight years Dr. Zanković led a lonely life in retirement.

He must have suffered from solitude because he seemed so happy to see me, and to recall our former discussions. When I told him my plan to leave the country, he approved of it wholeheartedly. All he regretted was that he could not join us, due to his age.

The old doctor had a curious way of stimulating the intelligence of the person he was speaking with. Oftentimes, he would squint his eyes as if to penetrate the meaning of what I was saying. This gave me the impression that my ideas were more enlightened and more daring than they really were.

He could paint a vast portrait of the world and its people as he had done so often during the war. Such talk might have seemed pretentious coming from an old man living forgotten on the outskirts of Užice, but this wise old doctor could see what lay beyond the mountaintops that hemmed in the little town. In his opinion, we were living, after the death of Nietzsche's God, in the age of science where man had substituted himself for the Creator and His original act of creation. The upheavals all around us resembled Genesis. From now on, man would rely on science to become master of his own universe, and it would be a source of pride. What undertaking could be more exhilarating, more exalting? The only drawback was that the world already existed, and a new one could not be created unless we levelled the one we already lived in. This would spell the disappearance of everything that man had built, and his own demise. The new potentates were split between the desire to start from scratch and the necessity of building on what already existed. Furthermore, how was the New Man to be created when he already possessed a deep, unchangeable nature? The old doctor saw no solution to this dichotomy underlying the Master Design.

By the same token, he considered the revolution to be a counterfeit of the Christian ideal, only coined by a group of atheists. He also thought that the wisdom, or ruse, of Christianity had been to promise man eternal life in an unverifiable hereafter. The error of the Master Design was to propose eternal life here and now. While triumph over death was never openly stated, the promise was implicit. He pointed out that in our society only heroic death was admissible. Death by sickness or old age was no longer allowed; it carried the stigma of shame and failure. The old doctor felt that by scorning the human condition, including suffering and mortality, the Master Design carried within it the seeds of its own destruction. In other words, the new masters had forgotten the revenge of Cronus, the Greek god who devoured his own progeny. He could just as easily devour the children of the revolution.

The doctor was trying to understand why men of culture and scientists were willing to submit to the authority of uneducated Party leaders. Were they fascinated by these men who claimed to possess the absolute truth? Meanwhile, the intellectuals had grown weary of their doubts, but he believed it was precisely this capacity for self-questioning that was their most precious asset.

The fresh night air was already entering the room when I got up to leave. Dr. Zanković looked tired and did not encourage me to stay. In rising, he made a movement as if he wanted to tell me something important. That we might never see each other again? He simply advised me to be careful going into town. His house was on a hill at the top of a poorly lit lane. The first fields began just beyond his house.

I left the old doctor with his books and his thoughts, which he would take with him. The image I carried away with me was of a small round man, framed in the light of the doorway.

Absorbed in my thoughts, I walked down the narrow rutted road winding between the wooden fences. A dog barked as I went by. Another dog answered. Then they fell silent. Stars glittered in the deep indigo sky, and below, the lights of Užice glittered back. The town and surrounding hills were gradually sinking into another short summer night. Everything reminded me of my summer holidays before the war when we would go up Malo Zabučije Road after swimming and eat pastries. It was difficult to believe that in the interim German panzers had rolled down these streets, prisoners had been felled by firing squads behind the cemetery, and that for four years we had gone to sleep at night to the sound of the German military police patrolling the deserted street.

An anecdote from the doctor's life came back to me. As a young student in Vienna at the end of the 1800s, he had bribed someone to bring him a dead frog which he needed for an exam in physiology. The examiner was suspicious, and guessing that Zanković found it repugnant to kill a little amphibian, he ordered his student to bring in a live frog and cut its head off in his presence. With great difficulty Dr. Zanković had done so, and the memory haunted him all his life.

༄

After the bustle of Belgrade, my stay in Užice felt like a short holiday. I was strangely calm on my last night in town. The mattresses were gone. I had seen Dr. Zanković. I had no further obligations. As for our trip across the border, I would trust fate and allow myself to be carried into unknown lands ... or over treacherous cataracts.

My guilt also started to fade. An inner voice told me: "You are not leaving your country to betray it, but to remain faithful to it." I imagined my future with a certain detachment, as if my conscience had deserted me and taken refuge in my double that was hovering invisibly overhead and observing me quietly.

I spent my last night on blankets piled on top of a box spring. The following morning, I woke up early, filled with a sense of freedom. I could have caught the first train to Belgrade but something told me to push on to Aunt Elisabeth's farm. After all, wasn't this the true purpose of my trip?

Since the last agrarian reform, her property, which used to belong to my grandparents, had shrunk like a favourite sweater. All that now remained of the fourteen-acre farm was the big wooden house and a small piece of land. As yet, no fence or markers indicated the new property line.

Around ten the next morning, I headed for Malo Zabučije Road and the hill that overlooks the city. My aunt's estate, invisible from town, lay on the other side of the hill. I walked slowly. I wanted to make the most of each moment, and dream myself back into the past.

After crossing the Djetinja River near the Sports Centre, I took the old road which used to go to Zlatibor. Neglected by the Roads Department since the construction of a new route, the old road was scarred with potholes and ruts from the farm carts, and it only went as far as a few villages. It began near a tavern frequented by peasants who came into town on market days.

It was at this precise spot, on April 12, 1941, that I witnessed the arrival of the first German motorcyclists, barely an hour after the surrender of the town's last defenders. They were wearing grey raincoats and looked well fed.

The road twisted up the mountainside. I had barely started to climb when I turned off at the shortcut that threaded its way through a veritable jungle of huge burrs. I remembered the last summer before the war when a group of us, on our way back from the beach, had gone through with sticks and beaten down the stinging plants that scratched our bare legs. The burrs looked as if they had been blasted by hail stones.

In front of Raško the tailor's house, I cut back onto the old road for a bit before taking another shortcut through an orchard of plum trees. In the past, when the fruit was ripe, I would help myself to two or three juicy plums on my way through.

The shortcut rejoined the road near the old antiaircraft machine gun nest where, in 1941, I had played at being a hero, taking shots at the German Stukas, those sinister metallic birds. This was back during the oh-so-brief existence of the Red Republic of Užice. The German planes used to divebomb ammunition stocks on the plain behind the cemetery of Dovarje. Whenever the weather cooperated, they would circle high up in the sky beyond the reach of our weapons. Then suddenly, like sparrow hawks, they would zero in on their targets. They looked like huge birds of prey, and their landing gear like giant claws. They would switch on their powerful sirens to demoralise us further. The sound was paralysing. Flying low in the valley, they veered so close to the mountainside that we could make out the silhouettes of the two crew members in the cockpit, which resembled a glass coffin.

Someone had filled in the dugout where the old Hotchkiss machine gun was hidden. All that remained was a slight hollow, a reminder of the men who tried to take on the Third Reich at the height of its power.

After covering a hundred metres on the old road, I turned left onto the path to my aunt's property. Behind a hedge stretched a golden wheat field almost ready for harvesting. To the right was an impenetrable forest of pine, hazel and other species. I knew every step of the way by heart. I had taken it so many times to go into town to buy cream puffs or to bring back the Belgrade newspapers that arrived by the morning train. Once, along this path after a rain shower, I had come across a pretty salamander with bright black and yellow spots. I felt sudden affection for this little creature, and observed it for quite a while, wondering why the ancients believed it to be a creature from hell. A little further on, near three pine trees, another path branched off towards the Great Park and led to a restaurant by the water.

There was not a living soul to be seen anywhere. I continued slowly, drinking in the landscape that I was soon to leave behind. The buzz of insects heralded another hot summer day like those when I would sit near the well under the willow tree reading or simply doing nothing.

At last I came out into the valley. In the past, when we spoke of "The Valley," it was always this one. The common noun had became a proper one. Our family's estate had begun here. There was no marker to indicate it but I felt as if I had crossed an invisible border into familiar territory. Was it because of the breeze, always fresh at this spot even on the hottest days?

The Valley opened up like a huge gash between the bald summit and a mountain covered with beech trees. A zigzagging path through a grove of mimosas led to the house. I preferred going up the valley, staying close to a wall of thick vegetation that ended by the big wooden house and its outbuildings. The barns and a few trees huddled near the top of the steep hill.

After the long school year in Belgrade, coming back to the big wooden house was an absolute joy. The two dogs, Bepo, a Doberman, and Bianco, a mutt, would dash out to welcome us, wagging their tails furiously.

A pear tree at this spot revived a nostalgic memory. At the end of our last summer before the war, my cousins and I had shot a scene of an amateur film under this tree. I was filmed coming down the hill, stopping under the tree and turning towards the house to wave farewell. It was all so naïve. While Nikola was shooting the scene, his brother Dimitri, perched in the tree, emptied leaves from a wicker basket.

Less than a year later, in the very same spot, harsh reality replaced this romantic image. War had broken out brutally on April 6, 1941. A week later, towards two in the morning, German panzers attacked Užice. The battery of our antiaircraft mortars on the hill near the cemetery took aim at the monstrous steel beetles as they crawled forward. Each time one of them was destroyed, another appeared like a hideous nightmare. We had little chance of stemming the invasion. We were a nation of shepherds; they were a nation of blacksmiths.

On that day, a Yugoslav officer, pale and frantic, had leaned against the same pear tree, his pea jacket unbuttoned, his pants half down, and his shirt slimy with blood. Part of his bowels protruded from a small wound in his stomach. Two young women, Klara and Stoja, were circling him, half crazed. A teacher in civilian life, Captain Jovanović died three days later of septicaemia.

I took my time climbing the steep hill and soon found myself on the terrace in front of the house. From there the vast landscape unfolded from east to west, sweeping the spectator up into its embrace. Two or three thorn bushes and a solitary almond tree occupied the hillside below the terrace. A wild vine, sole survivor of a vineyard that had disappeared a long time ago, clung to a pile of rocks. Lower down in the valley was a dirt road overgrown with weeds which was used only during harvest time by heavily laden carts. Late into the night, we used to hear the grinding of their wheels blending with the strident cries of the cicadas. On the other side, a wheat field bordered by plum trees with gnarled branches extended up towards the great forest of beech trees.

The view towards the northeast looked out over an even bigger valley surrounded by small wooded mountains and grey cliffs. In the middle was Dovarje Hill with its two knolls covered with gravestones. A tiny chapel between the knolls resembled a pendant around a woman's neck.

Also visible from the terrace was the modest provincial cemetery where my paternal ancestors were buried. They lay peacefully beneath a simple stone overgrown with lichen amidst bronze-coloured grasses: my grandmother Jelena, her husband Nikola who had always been in poor health and Petar, my great-grandfather who, senile and a little tipsy, had fallen asleep in a large, empty cider cask one fateful Christmas Eve, and never woke up again. Only the names and dates of birth and death remained of these people who had once loved, laughed, hoped and cried in their flesh and blood. This landscape, unchanging and yet constantly renewed by the years, the seasons and the hours of the day, brought together the living and the dead of my family.

Behind Dovarje Hill was the racetrack that came alive once a year on September 21, the Feast of the Birth of the Virgin Mary. Beyond it, the mountains, hills, and forests of my native land stretched in great rolling waves into the distance.

In September, the weather would deteriorate, the nights freshen, and rain would patter down monotonously on the leaves of the old walnut tree. Leaning on the windowsill, I used to spend long hours contemplating the misty landscape, and regretting the end of the summer holidays.

The war was still to come.

During the Occupation, things were quite different. I took refuge in Užice, and for the first time in my life, I saw the landscape evolve with the seasons. One autumn day, I remember looking out the window at a phantasmagorical scene: a sea of fog had filled the valley. Only the two hillocks and the small chapel emerged from the cottony shroud. The cemetery had turned into an island of death, drifting towards unknown shores.

One morning, winter arrived to stay. The landscape awakened under a soft quilt of snow, the whiteness brightening up the faded colours of autumn. The rust-coloured facade of the big wooden house softened into a warm pastel while the jet-black branches of the prune trees startled the eye. Thorny bushes pierced the snow in prickly brown arabesques while in the great valley below, the knolls of the cemetery swelled like the white breasts of a woman. For a time, the sleeping plants, the wild animals hibernating in their dens, and the larvae buried in the earth kept company with the dead. The landscape was plunged into a deep white silence. Only the smoke curling up from the railway workers' chimneys betrayed a human presence.

At the beginning of March, the sun waxed bolder. The snow started to drip off the roof, and in the morning, the eaves wore a necklace of ephemeral, translucent stalactites. Rivulets of water were starting to push their way through melting snow. Spring was arriving with fierce determination, and on the southern hillsides, large patches of earth had started to appear.

The day finally dawned when the last scraps of snow disappeared from the bottom of the dark ravine. Hoofs no longer sank into the water-gorged earth. Helped by the fine warm breeze, the hazel trees behind the house brought forth their blossoms. In April, with the southern slopes turning green, the landscape took on the colours of a child's drawing. The sap was rising in the tree trunks and one day, the plum trees got dressed up in their floral finery. Spring was definitely here to stay. The buzzing of bees and wasps in the fields were harbingers of the first heat wave. In the evening, the musicians of the insect world tuned up their instruments for the great summer concerts. And the mysterious cycle of life and death began all over again.

On this particular day the double doors of the country kitchen were locked, and all the windows shuttered. The two rain barrels at the corners of the house were in a sorry state. The dried-out slats were splayed like the petals of an immense black flower. Everything had an air of abandonment, including the gazebo below the terrace.

The gazebo, or *ćardak* in Turkish, had a past very much its own. This frail little structure, faithful companion of my youth, aptly illustrated Alphonse de Lamartine's famous lines: *Inanimate objects, do you have a soul that clings to our soul and teaches it to love?* Sometimes, when I spotted it from the valley after a summer's rain, the old *ćardak* looked almost cheerful, spruced up despite its venerable age. During the Occupation, on certain autumn evenings, I caught sight of it in the gloaming, with pewter clouds bowling over the roof, and thought it seemed haunted by the fear of death. As were we all.

In 1868, my great-grandfather had bought this estate, with the *ćardak*, from a Turk who left Serbia when it gained its independence. That year, the Ottoman garrison blew up the old fortress of Užice, built in the Middle Ages by Nikoa Altomanović. The soldiers and the faithful subjects of the Sublime Porte reluctantly took the road to Visegrad, one of the last bastions of their crumbling empire. As they passed the Serbian cannons recently built by Krupp and Schneider, they ran their fingers over them and wept to remember the first uprising of the *raïa* when the Serbs had fought with howitzers made from the trunks of cherry trees.

On the ground floor of the *ćardak* was a small room with an earthen floor. The hired hand had used the lattice lean-to to store empty beehives and the centrifuge for extracting honey. Upstairs there was a single room that opened on to a wide terrace. A sloping shingle roof covered the gazebo. The main room had a wooden floor and whitewashed plaster walls. The two windows, with openwork shutters, faced east and south.

I can still hear the squeaking of the hinges when, in the early morning, we would fling open the windows and brilliant sunshine would flood the room. Half asleep, we rejoiced at the beautiful weather and the prospect of swimming at the foot of the old fortress.

The exterior walls of the *čardak* had always intrigued me. The bricks were covered with wooden shingles in a fish-scale pattern. Never before nor since have I ever seen such a method of construction. The *čardak*, dating from the Turkish era, reflected the oriental philosophy, a mixture of hedonism and fatalism, which was not lacking in charm. I can still picture an old Turk on the terrace meditating in the moonlight on the brevity of human life, smoking his water pipe as he gazes across the vineyard.

The children — my cousins and I — liked to sleep in the *čardak* and occasionally it was used for our guests from Belgrade. After the main house was built in the summer of 1930, the grown-ups allowed us to use it as a playhouse, and the *čardak* became our Odeon Theatre where we put on plays for which we were the performers, set designers, and prompters. The name *Odeon* was still visible on the door. I pushed it open, curious to see if anything remained of our stage props. In the semi-dark of the shuttered room I could see nothing more than a pile of corn cobs in the middle. Everything else was gone.

A hundred years from now, who will remember the *čardak* and its little theatre? Most likely it will no longer exist. A summer storm could easily blow it away. The one remaining *čardak* of the country will be no more.

I paused for a few moments, and leaned on the ramp. Down in the little valley, a farmer was cultivating alfalfa on one side of a dirt road lined with blackberry bushes. On the other side of the road were a field of strawberry and raspberry plants and an orchard of shrivelled-up plum trees. I always felt sorry for these charred-looking trees eroded by lichen, as if the dark sap they sweated was the result of some suffering. Further up, a vast forest of beech trees blanketed the entire mountain and made it look like an immense bear asleep for eternity.

As a child, I used to think that the forest was endless, inhabited by nymphs, fawns and satyrs. As a teenager, I attempted to explore it several times but fear would always stop me in my tracks. I was always seized with a foreboding as I walked among the great silent trees with their greyish bark. Long creepers hung from the branches, like immense boas capable of squeezing and suffocating me at any given moment. Panic-stricken, I would start running down the slope, my feet sinking into the carpet of dead leaves. As soon as I was out of the woods, I would feel better and could breathe more easily. As a young man, I dreamt of crossing the forest in search of a secret village ensconced amidst tall, undulating grasses, but I never carried out my plan. My fear was that reality could never measure up to my imaginary hamlet.

An old wicker chair, a rustic table, and some benches still lingered on the terrace. Dandelions proliferated between the flagstones. In the summer, we would often dine out there under the immense star-studded sky. The acetylene lamp, hanging from a branch of the old walnut tree, would hiss and shed a bright light while the owlet moths, with their gold-powdered wings, would swoop out of the night to circle the flame. I remember listening to the laughter and voices of my uncles, cousins, and my Aunt Elisabeth merging with the clinking of dishes as I sat in the small circle of light, lost in the immensity of the warm night. Thousands of insects and nocturnal creatures would be stirring in the dark forest, the bushes, the pond, the fields, and along the old road. Sometimes, a firefly, temporarily lost, would swing by our table only to disappear again into the night. In the valley, the skimpy earth-bound constellations of railway workers' homes blinked tiredly. Sometimes, a light trembled in the cemetery chapel where a family held a vigil for a loved one. Off in the distance, the train from Sarajevo, always punctual, traced a long glittering curve through the wide plain of the valley before vanishing into the gorges of Djetinja. We would stay up late, and when the cool night breeze began to blow, we would gather in the kitchen to play cards or read novels.

Some evenings, we would walk up Malo Zabučije Hill behind the house. As soon as we moved away from the light on the terrace, we entered the disquieting world of juniper bushes which night transformed into great beasts. Below us, the valley sparkled with the lights of the town. We could see each house and street lamp. On the main street, young people would promenade between the Hotel Zlatibor and the grain market.

Sometimes, I would stretch out on the grass and stare up at the stars. I felt myself propelled into the vastness of infinity, intoxicated with the thought of being sucked into the dark abyss. I would think how the diamond dust from the Milky Way would still be there on the day I died, immutable and indifferent to my demise. In our rush to escape death, do we risk letting life pass us by?

On this, my last visit to the *ćardak*, I stayed a long time, soaking up the landscape and remembering times past. Finally, I shook myself and headed over to fetch the house key from Radovan the farmer. He lived nearby in a stone building that now belonged to him.

When I opened the door of the old house, I smelled the familiar odour of dried flowers and sun-warmed resinous wood. The rooms were virtually empty. Mattresses stuffed with corn husks covered the simple iron cots.

My imagination started to fill the empty rooms. In the final days of November 1941, many refugees had crowded into the house, among them Dr. Zanković. Women, children, and old men slept on the floor. The cast iron stove burned bravely, but the cold air seeped in through the cracks in the wooden walls. We shivered and were afraid. The ephemeral Red Republic, which lasted a mere forty days, was on its last legs. The Grand Master of the Keys and his acolytes had already left the city to hide in Montenegro. The city of Požega was now in the hands of a German punitive expedition, and the panzers were about to enter Užice at any moment. None of us knew what lay ahead. We were thinking of Kragujevac where, on October 20 and 21, the occupying army had shot many men between the ages of fifteen and sixty.

During those days, I would often climb the hill behind the house and scan the town. The streets were deserted. A large five-pronged star, frail symbol of a dying republic, shone from the cupola of the courthouse. We knew that as long as the star was there, the German troops had not yet arrived.

On November 20, 1941 at 4 a.m., the first tanks entered Užice. A hail of bullets pelted the five-pronged star and extinguished it. The day dawned anxiously for us.

Three years later, during the spring and summer of 1944, the Writer and his wife had moved into a small corner room. The heavy table with legs made of birch trunks which he had used during that time was still there. The Writer's ghost too, had stayed behind, still writing his book and occasionally looking up at the wild plum tree through the window.

As a child, burning up with scarlet fever, I once spent several weeks in this room. In my delirium, I kept dreaming of a spring of cold, pure water, the same one that we had drunk from one summer day in 1929 when my father, an uncle, my cousins and

I crossed Zlatibor to visit the village where my grandmother Jelena was born. We must have looked strange, riding through the deserted fields of the high plateaus wearing fashionable hats brought back from Paris by my parents.

On the little table of the front hall stood an old gas lamp from our house in the city. The lamp also had a soul, a past, and a memory. Its five-sided shade was decorated with hand-drawn bucolic scenes depicting hunters under a tree, their dogs stretched out beside them. These images belonged to a strange, faraway Germanic land. The lampshade obviously came from Vienna or Budapest. In the 1800s, the rising bourgeoisie of the small kingdom of Serbia ordered much of their furniture from the Austro-Hungarian Empire. My grandmother Jelena and her husband must have dined by the light of this lamp before the first hydroelectric plant was built in the gorge of Djetinja in 1902.

As the first fogs and rainy days of September moved in, we would gather in the country kitchen around this old lamp. We would read books by Blasco Ibanez, John Galsworthy, or Jack London, and play checkers. My Aunt Elisabeth, after much concentration, would finally win a game. The patter of rain used to fill me with melancholy but the prospect of returning to Belgrade invariably cheered me up.

Some summer nights, when I was sleeping in the main house, storms would break out and wake me with a start. Lightning would slice the sky above the valley and light up my room like an aquarium. Thunder claps would resound in quick succession, and echo back off the mountain. Then the rains would move in, hammering the roof like the furious sea. I listened happily, sheltered and protected by the walls of the house. After a time, the storm would pass. The flashes of lightning would become less frequent, and the thunder would die out. The pounding on the roof would stop until only a monotonous rain whispered in the leaves of the walnut tree. The storm would wander around the mountains for a while, and then everything would fall silent once again. Sometimes, a fat moon would show its face among the ragged clouds. The sky, appeased, gave promise of good weather the next day. In the morning, we would find the table on the terrace littered with branches from the walnut tree.

I opened a window and looked out into the valley. The hot air from the fields flowed into the room and a bee buzzed against the screen, reminding me of those long, lost, lazy mornings. I could have gone on forever conjuring up nostalgic images. But they belonged to a vanished world. This summer of 1946 still promised the same brilliant light, the same life force as always, with the heat trembling over the wheat field. But the great house was deserted. My cousins were in Belgrade, friends no longer came to spend a few days, and these rooms were desperately silent. Only the bees kept colliding absentmindedly against the screen. The summer holidays were over once and for all.

I knew how dangerous it was to look back at these memories of past happiness. Their sweetness draws us almost imperceptibly towards the void, the grave. But a secret alchemy of the soul has the power to transform these same memories, pluck us out of empty nostalgia, and project us towards new horizons.

Having feasted on these images, I had to leave if I wanted to catch the train for Belgrade and arrive in the capital before midnight. I bid farewell to the farmer, new owner of this part of the domain, and walked back to town down Malo Zabučije Hill past the stone quarries. I came out onto the old road near the frog swamp and continued walking past the cornfield belonging to Didan.

I couldn't stop thinking about the old *ćardak*. I realised that ours was the only one I had ever seen, yet the word had been familiar to me since childhood from a traditional tale entitled *The Ćardak, Neither on Earth nor in Heaven* which had made an impression on me. In the story, the *ćardak*, inhabited by a dragon, floated above ground. It couldn't land, and it couldn't rise above a certain height. As is usual in this kind of fantastical story, the dragon had kidnapped the king's daughter and kept her a prisoner in his unusual home. Luckily, the beautiful captive's three brothers undertook to find her and deliver her from the talons of the fabled creature. After many attempts, and despite the treachery of one brother, they succeeded in rescuing her. Sometimes, I pictured the storybook *ćardak* with its columns of whitewashed brick, suspended between earth and sky, its foundations wrenched from the ground with bits of earth still clinging to them. Obviously this vision was inspired by our *ćardak* slumbering behind the big house.

Such traditional tales intrigued me for a long time. Who was hidden behind all these kings, dragons, knights and achingly beautiful girls? Did any of these fanciful tales have a meaning, or were they just the product of a fanciful imagination? And what was the real meaning of the *ćardak* hovering above ground but incapable of lifting off?

Lost in my thoughts, I walked by Kuka Fountain. A powerful jet of water had been spilling into the drinking trough since time immemorial. Ten minutes later, I was back in town. I stopped to wolf down one last cream puff at Vlajko's Bakery, fetched my briefcase from the bombed-out apartment and left for the station.

The ticket agent remembered me from the time I had worked there as a telegraph operator and we spoke a bit about the Occupation. A thought came to me. How could I claim the right to leave my country and wrench myself away, while this man sitting behind his wicket would remain here until retirement —

or death? What made me think that by leaving the country, I could choose a new destiny? Was it not just an illusion?

A little before three, the train from Sarajevo pulled into the station. I hurried to grab a third-class seat beside the window, and ten minutes later, we were on our way. The train skirted the peaceful waters of the Djetinja River which flowed past the station. On the other side of the river lay first the orphanage, then the municipal slaughterhouse, and finally the Great Park with its pine trees. For one fleeting moment, I caught a glimpse of the *café* in the park, its terrace overlooking the water, and the boats for hire moored on the riverbank. The train picked up speed. The dam and the hydroelectric power station disappeared. The track rounded Dovarje Hill before coming out onto the small plain home to the racetrack. Just as the train was about to negotiate the long curve around the island in the river, I caught a final glimpse of our big wooden house and the little *ćardak* high up in the mountain.

When the image faded, my imagination substituted another one of an immense *ćardak* hovering above the mountains. Despite the distance, I could see every detail clearly. A crowd of men, women, and children were crowded onto its terrace. At any moment the ramp could give way, tipping everyone over the side. They were all shouting, laughing, and crying. Some insisted on throwing an anchor to catch a tree and pull the *ćardak* back to solid ground. Others wanted it to sail up into the sky. Was it their lack of agreement that condemned the *ćardak* to hover between heaven and earth?

Some, dressed in rags, had come back from the dead. Those who had been asphyxiated by smoke in the grotto of Deer Valley during the first upheaval of the *raïa*, stood around with lifeless faces. There too were the bride and groom, priest and witnesses who, one terrible autumn day in 1941, were discovered floating down the Save River with their hands tied. This strange blood-wedding party had come to rest in a bay, on its long voyage to eternity. The fishermen lifted them out with their boat hooks in order to bury them. I recognised two twelve-year-old boys from the village of Pribilovci, who had implored their executioner: "Uncle, we beg you, let us live." Also marooned on this *čardak* were the dead from the deep limestone gorges: men, women, and children who had agonised for days in the dark bowels of the earth, their lips chapped from thirst. In its extended flight, the *čardak* was gathering up my entire people, and this would continue until Judgment Day.

I could see myself among this cohort of the living and the dead, leaning against the rail and looking down on forests and fields, mountains and valleys, villages and cities as they slid by. I didn't know which was better: to anchor the *čardak* in place on this tormented planet, or to let it fly free.

IX

## Adieu Belgrade

*Adieu! I feel that I will never
See you again in this life.*
— ALFRED DE MUSSET

ON JUNE 26, 1946, I woke up a little before eight. It was a beautiful day and as usual the pigeons were cooing on the terrace. Aunt Lou must have gone to fetch bread and milk. An ordinary day in the city — in fact it was anything but.

Ever since our decision to leave, I had been sleeping badly. Exhausted, I would fall asleep as if I were plunging into a deep well, spiralling down the black walls as I fell unconscious. After my body had gathered a bit of strength, the nightmare would begin. I was walking along a long hall with olive-grey walls. A prison guard was taking me to be interrogated. If I woke up during the dream, I would think: *that could be my reality tomorrow.*

Too late to back down! That same evening, Milenko and Boris were taking the train for Zagreb. I would meet them the morning of the 29th and we would continue on into Slovenia. It seemed wiser to leave the capital separately. Wise precaution or paranoia inspired by reading too many spy novels? In any case, Boris's parents were offering us a place to hide.

In a way, my last three days in Belgrade resembled those of a man on death row whose last plea for clemency has been rejected. I looked forward to a good life under new skies where I would find new landscapes, friends and loves, but my eyes would no longer look upon my loved ones or the familiar streets of my native city. I was dying within the world of my youth. Far from my country, would I feel more dead than alive? Of course, memories of happy moments would endure, but their evocation would be painful. Belgrade would freeze into an immense postcard, increasingly blurred with the passage of time.

The metallic ring of the alarm clock put an end to my dreams. Already eight o'clock. Milenko's arrival was imminent. We had hatched a far-fetched plan for the day of his departure. He would go in search of Buca R., a youthful love of his. According to the rumours circulating among our former classmates, she had the address of one of her friends, Jelena Santic, now living in New York. Since we were getting ready to live in an unknown world every name and address was precious. This was the ostensible reason for our plan, but possibly Milenko wanted one last visit with the girl whom he had loved during the summer of 1942 in the bucolic landscape of a small provincial town. In occupied Serbia, the shadow of death hovered over our lives, and we snatched at every moment of happiness. In this way, we were marked more deeply by those moments.

We boarded the tramway on Prince Illiterate Street. The cars, almost empty, were hurrying along. We passed Guverevac, the Hospital for the Insane, and the *École Polytechnique* with its wooden pavilions, a gift from the American Red Cross to Serbia after the country was devastated by the First World War. The streetcar lumbered up Dedinje Hill past Mostar Square and the Hay Market. We got off at the stop between Alexander 1 School and the residence.

Our last visit here dated back to the first months of the Occupation in June 1941. It had left us with a sinister feeling. We got off the tramway the day after our final oral for the baccalaureate. The boarding school looked abandoned. The German tanks had been there only the day before but had left to take part in Operation Barbarossa, the invasion of Russia, which would become the greatest land battle in the history of mankind. The tracks from the panzers were still visible as large arabesques on the sports field and in the flowerbeds. We entered the building by the main door facing Star Square. Instead of the animated sound of the students' voices, there was only a terrible silence. In the library next to the entrance, the leather-bound classics of literature were scattered about on the floor.

On that visit, we had explored the building from top to bottom. A feeble light in the furnace room shone on the furnaces now out of commission. A wagon full of coal was waiting to be unloaded. We had the impression of visiting the machine room of a ghost ship abandoned by its crew. The great ship of our education, deserted by its captain, the teachers and us, its sailors, had been set adrift.

In the dormitories, the sheets and blankets had disappeared. Only the metal cots and mattresses remained. In the study halls, the bookcases and lockers yawned emptily. The principal's portrait, by the well-known painter Uzelac, still hung in his office. We took it off the wall to return it to him. On our way home, people looked at us somewhat oddly. The portrait of Professor Kosta could be mistaken for that of Lenin.

Since the end of the war, the new leaders of the country had transformed our boarding school into a school for Party executives. Mountain people, with their rough-hewn faces, gathered here from all over the country to study dialectical materialism and then spread the good word to the people. A sentry sauntered back and forth in front of the main entrance. This time, it wasn't possible to go in and look around at our poor old school, which had been desecrated once again.

We walked away from the traffic circle of l'Étoile with a twinge of sadness. Five minutes later, we were in front of de Buca Villa on Tolstoy Street. Buried in greenery, it looked asleep at this early hour. We rang the doorbell, but nothing happened. The silence was broken only by the chirping of birds in the trees. Perhaps the doorbell no longer worked. We walked around to the back but were no more successful. I hesitated a moment before turning the doorknob gently. The door opened. We had the disagreeable impression of breaking and entering. Not a soul anywhere. I knocked timidly at a door. Something moved inside.

A depressed voice muttered: "What is it?"

"We're looking for Miss R."

"Don't know her. Try the second floor."

It seemed so strange. The address was correct but this voice claimed he had never heard of the owner's daughter.

Like thieves we climbed the stairs on tiptoe. Several doors lined the hallway. I was half afraid that at any moment one of them would open and a man would ask us who we were looking for, but everything remained silent. Should we give up? That seemed too stupid. We tried another door and were luckier this time. A chubby man, dressed in officer's pants and a pyjama top, opened the door immediately. Behind him the unmade bed looked still warm. The smell coming from his room was decidedly unpleasant. The man had never heard of Buca R.

"But her parents own this house."

"Own ... own ... maybe. Try the end of the hall to the right."

The last door was the right one. Buca stood before us, surprised, dishevelled-looking, not quite awake. She must have wondered what had brought us here. But despite an uncertain smile, she looked like the same confident young woman who used to dance at our school balls. Finally she invited us into a room packed with furniture. She apologized for the mess, but the Billeting Office had requisitioned a large part of the villa for civil servants and officers. Her family could still be considered fortunate to have kept two rooms and a bathroom. We apologized profusely for having barged in so early and without warning. Milenko briefly explained the reasons for our visit. She listened carefully. Yes, she could give us Jelena Santic's address.

"And so you're leaving! A one-way trip, I imagine. So many people want to get away. Every week someone leaves. Pretty soon, there will be no real Belgraders left. You say you're planning to go to New York?" Buca's voice was tinged with sadness. Not long ago her world had looked so solid and permanent, and now it was falling apart. Our generation's future resembled ornamental plants: struck down by a spring frost. She gave us Jelena Santic's address: 300 Riverside Drive, New York City, New York. We had to memorize it. Should we be caught at the border, it was preferable not to have such information on us. We left immediately afterwards.

I came away feeling sad. We had opened yet another door on the distress of people recently impoverished. We were discovering our country's new reality. This villa, now inhabited by perfect strangers, confirmed the rumours: the new masters of the country were invading the formerly well-to-do neighbourhoods. Malicious gossip was calling it "the final attack of the first-hour fighters." Going down Marshal Voyageur Boulevard, I carried on thinking out loud, as usual, while Milenko listened absentmindedly. Was he thinking back to the summer of 1942 when he had courted this young girl?

The old bourgeois families were gradually being dispossessed of everything, sometimes brutally, like one old woman from this neighbourhood who found her furniture out in the street when she returned from shopping for food. Her apartment had just been requisitioned for a general. The new masters were very fond of luxurious houses and apartments. In the warehouses run by the Party, they could choose armchairs, pianos, sofas and household objects confiscated from the enemies of the people — or from Jews. To be fair, a few honest revolutionaries resisted this gold rush, but they were rare. How is it that the majority of the committed believers in the Master Design had succumbed so easily to the charms of bourgeois life? Whoever can come up with an answer is very clever.

The revolution didn't present its goal to be the simple exchange of property titles from the haves and the have-nots. The Party didn't actually distribute the goods; it merely allowed them to be enjoyed based on devotion to the Cause. And so came into being an original concept of property: the enjoyment of, but not the official possession of property. It was an ingenious ploy on the part of the new leaders. Despite their corrupt conduct, they still operated, so to speak, within the law. In short, everything evolved so that the instinct for possession could be indulged despite the professed ideal of equality for all men. Later, when some of the revolutionaries started to have doubts, the mechanism behind the enjoyment of all these possessions became brutally clear: those who lost faith lost their apartments, their cars, their privileges.

༄

I had three strange meetings within a short period of time. The first took place the morning of June 27 after my friends left town. I ran into my former classmate Theo P. opposite the School of Engineering. His membership in the Party was an open secret. Since the autumn, he had been involved in all kinds of student committees, but that didn't change our personal relationship which dated back to primary school. His commitment amused me. He seemed too intelligent not to discover, eventually, how deceptive and intransigent these men really were.

Theo regarded me silently, as if to consider the import of the moment: "It's lucky we meet. I have something serious to tell you. When are you going to stop acting like a clown?"

"What clown are you talking about?"

I had already guessed what this was all about.

"You don't get it? Do you take me for a fool? You know perfectly well what I'm driving at. Don't you care about having your name up on the bulletin board? Can't you read? You think you're smarter than everyone else, but you're in for a shock. Monsieur had to leave the lecture because Monsieur was feeling nauseous. Who do you think you are?"

"Now I see what you're getting at."

"It's about time. Listen to me. Do you want to know the truth? I'm going to give it to you straight, even though I shouldn't, but we've known each other for years. A number of students have been expelled already and you're going to be in the same boat. And it won't be long now, either. What will you do then? Your uncles, your aunts, friends of friends of your father ... influence no longer works ... you'll simply be expelled — as will I if they ever find out that I've spoken to you."

"Theo ... Thank you —"

"Don't thank me, just go and sign up for the People's Student Movement. That way you'll be taking a step in the right direction. And then volunteer for a youth work project. This summer we'll be rebuilding the railway between Brčko and Banović. It's not exactly a penal colony, you know. We only work in the mornings. In the afternoon, there are discussions and in the evening dancing with the girls around the bonfire. A month will pass quickly. You can't change anything. We are all in the same boat and there's no getting out of it."

What could I say? That this boat was nothing but a ship of fools and that Milenko and I were getting our raft ready to slip away discreetly? I would have put Theo on the spot had I told him. He would have faced a difficult choice. Either denounce us or become our accomplice. I couldn't put him in that position, so it was better to lie.

"Theo ... I've thought about it ... you're right, we're all in the same boat ... I promise, I'll sign up with the People's Youth Movement no later than tomorrow. And as for the youth work project ... yes, the country has to be rebuilt —"

"Finally, you're making sense."

I felt like bursting out laughing, despite my discomfort with lying to an old friend. Theo smiled, obviously happy that he had saved me from doing something stupid. He gave me a friendly pat on the back and wished me luck.

Flabbergasted, I looked around at the slow-moving crowd. This "we're all in the same boat" had struck me. How could such an intelligent young man speak that way? The times we were living through had anaesthetised our critical sense, although by giving away the game, Theo had proved friendship was stronger than the Party.

A strange idea came to me. Who knows if friendships and loves unauthorised by the Party would one day end up undermining this artificial justice just as rodents undermine dams?

Waiting around was slowly killing me. Milenko and Boris were already in Zagreb. My things — a knapsack and a raincoat — were ready. My last nights were consumed with anxiety. Waking up in the morning was like passing from one nightmare to another. After my meeting with Theo, I no longer had any illusions: escape was the only choice.

That same day, feeling at loose ends and unable to sit still, I decided to go and watch a tennis match to distract myself. The match was being played in the moat of Kalemegdan Fortress, which had been converted into tennis courts in the summer and skating rinks in the winter. Was it happenstance or fate? I never really understood the difference between the two. My second encounter involved a big wheel in the government. Number Two in the Party, to be exact. In the strange pyramid of power, he was right below the Grand Master of the Keys.

What a bizarre country to be living in. The principal leaders had numbers designating their position in the hierarchy. By carefully compiling the frequency of their appearances in the press, anyone could figure out the place each one occupied. Some claimed that the list consisted of two- or three-dozen names. The remainder were small fry unworthy of press attention, at least in Belgrade.

Number Three was thought to be a teacher who had become chief ideologue of the Master Design because he had read so many books. He published very abstruse articles in *Borba*, on theoretical issues that deterred even the most courageous readers. Some thought his articles were proof of his intelligence, but down-to-earth individuals were convinced they were simply gibberish.

My meeting with Number Two happened very simply. I arrived at Fort Kalmegdan and headed for the tennis court where Yugoslavia's two best tennis players at the time, Punčec and

Palada, were playing a friendly match. As I was crossing the median not far from the streetcar stop, a pre-War Packard zoomed up. Several gentlemen, wearing dark suits and wide-brimmed hats, got out. One of them came over to me. It was Number Two, in person. I had seen this thin face so many times on the front page of the newspapers. In the beginning, he was always photographed in a general's uniform, a sash crossing his chest. Later, he dressed in civilian clothes.

"Comrade, where is the Palada-Punčec match?"

"This way, Comrade."

"Thank you, Comrade."

From then on, I could boast about having spoken to Number Two, like the character in a novel I had read when I was young: *The Man Who Knew President Coolidge*. Our meeting was brief, to be sure, but it left me with the impression of a courteous and intelligent man.

It was difficult to imagine how such a seemingly civilised man could wield such power over life and death. In February of that year, Number Two had published a ground-breaking article. He was angry at the leniency of a tribunal in Sarajevo that had sentenced a dishonest cashier to only three years in prison. To a hard-line Communist, such a sentence was an insult to the working man. The Sarajevo judges, panic-stricken, passed a new sentence, which was contrary to the ancient principle of Roman law, *nec bis in idem* — what has been decided once should not be judged again. Three days later, the new sentence fell like a sword: death.

If Number Two had not read about the incident in the newspaper, the dishonest cashier would have served three years in prison, but in the land of Geometric Justice, a man's life might depend on a glance at a newspaper. The hard-line Communists will probably never know all the suffering they inflicted in the name of justice.

If a clairvoyant had told me in June 1946 that, eight years later, Number Two would lose faith in the Master Design, renounce his privileges and opt for a nine-year jail sentence, I would have laughed. Now I know anything is possible. Before becoming an Apostle, St. Paul was Saul, the Roman officer who persecuted Christians.

༄

The following morning, on June 28, 1946, I woke up to the disconcerting thought that this was indeed my last day in Belgrade. Yet, life would continue here as usual without me. The sun would shine on the chestnut tree, the noise of traffic and the cooing of pigeons would come through the open terrace door. In the hall, my aunt was making *café au lait*, as she did every morning. The alarm clock was ticking away the seconds. When I first came out of the army, the sound had filled me with peace, but since our preparations to leave, those metallic clicks resonated like harbingers of evil. Later, when I was wandering around a war-torn Europe, I would remember these mornings as islands of peace. Repeatedly I would ask myself: why do we recognise moments of happiness just as they are about to fade from memory?

On my last morning in Belgrade, I thought about why I had to leave my native city where I had spent most of my life. Who had forced us to live in a society that was unbearable and meaningless?

June 28 was also the anniversary of the battle of Kosovo in 1389, in which the Serbian army was defeated. More recently, on that same day in Sarajevo in 1914, Gavrilo Princip, a Serbian revolutionary and member of the secret organization Young Bosnia, had assassinated Archduke Ferdinand and his morganatic wife. Their murder had precipitated terrible events. Austria sent an ultimatum to Serbia. The little kingdom accepted all the conditions, except one. On July 28, World War I broke out. Later, some would accuse Serbia of triggering this terrible war, forgetting that the archduke and his wife were in a country that had been annexed by force. The young conspirators had considered it a terrible insult to see the Austrian army marching in their streets on the anniversary of the battle of Kosovo. Europe erupted into blood and flames, but the death of the princely couple was merely a pretext for a showdown between the great Powers.

In the past, history had mattered very little to me. June 28 meant the end of the academic year and the joyful release from boarding school. Was my departure on this date simple coincidence — or an evil omen?

Bored with thoughts that rarely reached a conclusion, I jumped out of bed. I decided to take a walk to Kalemegdan Park and the fortress, as much to revisit one of my favourite spots as to keep my mind from spinning out of control.

I walked to Galsworthy Street to borrow Milenko's bicycle. His mother, usually so friendly, received me ungraciously. Prematurely aged by the hard work necessary to survive and pay for Milenko's studies, she probably thought I had dragged her son into this adventure. I decided not to try explaining to her that our decision to leave was mutual. She wouldn't have believed me, anyway, this woman who, for years, rose every day at dawn to go to work, on foot, at the Government Printing Office. She would walk along deserted streets to save two dinars' streetcar fare. After working hard all day, she would walk back, but fatigue must have made the route seem much longer. Four dinars a day wasn't much, but after weeks and months, it grew into a tidy little sum earned by braving all kinds of weather — summer heat, November squalls, and winter snow. It is difficult to imagine the solitude of this woman who had moved from her native village to settle in a tough city. I pretended not to notice her bad mood.

Seeing the apartment brought back all those hours Milenko and I had spent together since last October drinking coffee, doing drawings for the faculty, imagining outrageous and absurd projects, and finally plotting our escape. An era was drawing to a close, and an uneasy emptiness permeated my being.

Milenko's room was unusually tidy. His books were piled on his shelf along with the mimeographs he would never use again for the differential calculus course. There was the great universal regulator he had started to build from scratch last autumn to test all types of radio tubes. We had spent long hours wiring it according to his plans — which were constantly being upgraded. He had conceived it as much for pure pleasure as to earn a living.

Little did we know that three months after our escape from Belgrade, this regulator, which looked pretty impressive in its black case bristling with measuring instruments, switches, and rheostats, would become an object of great curiosity to the secret police. Ozna discovered it when they searched the apartment, and were convinced that they had found a transmitter-receiver that had sent coded messages to capitalist countries. Its discovery was partially responsible for the arrest of Milenko's mother, who spent three long months in jail.

I leapt on his bicycle and headed for Terazije Square. Whenever I passed the big grey building housing the Engineering Faculty, I felt a twinge. Perhaps our friends were taking their exams at that very moment while we had abandoned the studies that we had dreamed about for so long. As I approached the square, I could hear a loudspeaker blaring. When I was a child, this is how circuses used to announce their arrival in the city and to invite the public to come to the big tent. The voice became clearer as I approached.

This was a circus of a different ilk. Radio-Belgrade was transmitting the trial of General Mihajlović directly from the ballroom of the Officers of the Guard. Powerful loudspeakers had been installed at specific crossroads, and the city was flooded with the voices of the judges, accusers, and lawyers for the defence. You couldn't escape the cacophony. In certain streets the voices were muffled, but you only had to turn a corner to hear them blaring forth. At the end of the day silence returned to the city like grace from heaven, but the following morning prosecutor Minić's metallic tones would return to haunt the city.

After ten minutes, I reached the entrance of Kalemegdan Park. Pushing my bike ahead of me, I did a quick round of the paths, almost deserted at this hour of the morning. In front of Serbia's monument of gratitude to France, red flowers were waving their heads in the breeze. On the white marble pedestal, the bronze woman depicting France was dashing forward to protect Serbia in times of distress. The inscription *Let us love France as she has loved us* seemed somewhat enigmatic to me. Who were we and why had France loved us? Why do small forsaken countries always need a big sister or brother?

Seated on the rim of the basin, children were dabbling in the water, trying to launch frail little boats with wet sails. In the middle of the pond, a muscular fisherman, cast in bronze, was wrestling with a sea serpent entangled in his net. The serpent was spitting out a powerful jet of water. The murmuring of the water meshed with the cries of the children.

I did a quick tour of the terrace overlooking the junction of the Save and the Danube Rivers. I wanted to have one last look at the mysterious line that demarcated the two powerful rivers. It had always fascinated me. As a child, I imagined this line as an evil whirlpool ready to suck up the passing paddle steamers. Further on, Great War Island and the steeples of Zemun were visible above the fog.

Suddenly realising how little time I had before my departure, I turned back and exited the park just in front of the French Embassy, still guarded by the Three Graces: Freedom, Equality, Fraternity. Pedalling back to Galsworthy Street, little did I know that another unexpected encounter awaited me.

I was suddenly cut off by a convertible, a Horche, emerging from Central Committee headquarters on Alexander I Boulevard, formerly the Madera Hotel. The car was moving slowly. I saw up close one of the faces that the press kept feeding us daily. Number Four — the big boss of Ozna, the secret police, was seated comfortably in the back. He looked at me with a bored expression as if I did not exist. Perhaps he noticed me in the way you see a stone lying by the side of the road. Had he looked closely, he might have detected a touch of insolence in my expression, brought on by the sight of men in power. His bodyguard, seated beside the driver, examined me for a moment and then decided I was harmless. I found it a strange coincidence to have run into Number Four on the day of my departure. Luckily, a machine for reading thoughts had not yet been invented.

Number Four's face was striking for its absence of particular traits. He could have been a storeowner, a stationmaster, just about anybody. A caricaturist trying to do his portrait would have found his physiognomy challenging. The only notable thing about him was that the collar of his uniform was so tight that the flesh around his neck formed a roll. In the evening, he must have been relieved to undo the buttons.

Later, happy to be out of reach of these thugs, I thought back to that moment. Did this man really personify evil, as some people claimed? I don't think so, although I say it at the risk of angering those who have suffered in the jails, or whose loved ones were executed by such butchers. That he was dangerous, in fact very dangerous, is undeniable. This man believed that he possessed the absolute truth, and he took for granted the right to make life-and-death decisions affecting thousands. Had he felt only an inkling of doubt, many lives might have been spared. Alas, he and his comrades were drunk on power. More and more I am convinced that doubt is a virtue.

Years later, I heard a story about Number Four that confirmed my opinion. After moving into a new villa, Number Four rang his new neighbours' doorbell, carrying a large basket heaped with delicious peaches. "I would like to offer you this fruit as a sign of friendship," he said.

As I pedalled back to Galsworthy Street, I mused over these chance encounters with the men who had shaped the recent history of my country. It had all begun one day in November 1941. That autumn the entire country was drenched in blood. The two resistance movements, the Partisans and the Nationalists, were fighting pitched battles against the German garrisons stationed in several Serbian cities. The German occupiers were so desperate they started shooting hundreds, even thousands, of citizen hostages. The fighting could not last as the Serbian resistance movements had overestimated their strength. A German armoured division of military vehicles and cannons, unstoppable and implacable, was advancing along Serbian roads. The vice was tightening on the insurgents.

On the last day of November, hiding in a farmhouse near Užice, I saw a man on a bay horse and an English officer ride by. Behind them marched a small detachment of men armed to the teeth. They were leaving Užice in a hurry. In a foreign accent, the man on the bay horse called out to the soldiers who were with them: "Hurry, comrades, hurry."

The man was none other than the Grand Master of the Keys. The irony of fate. The former *Feldwebel* (adjutant) of a Germanic empire, namely the Austro-Hungarian Empire, was escaping from a punitive German expedition. I learned this only later when I read his biography. Had I known it at the time, I could have said, like Hegel in 1812 when he saw Napoleon passing through Jena: "I saw History on the march." For us, it was a sinister premonition. A handful of armed men led by the Grand Master had emerged from their lair in the forest and successfully grabbed power. Supported by a powerful English ally, they did so with no regard for justice.

※

The final evening came as a relief. The unbearable waiting was drawing to a close. At last, I would be rid of my nightmare, the one in which a faceless guard leads me through an endless corridor on the way to the interrogation chamber. There would be no more nights in Belgrade when I would walk home late warily watching my own shadow. No more procrastination, hesitation, doubt. I was committed to action now and it would make me forget my fears.

June 28, 1946 was one of those hot summer nights perfect for relaxing in a park or having a drink on the terrace of a bistro. I spent my last evening with Aunt Lou and my cousin Dimitri who came over to say goodbye. The pigeons were already roosting in the trees. The city was slowly unwinding. The atmosphere in the apartment, however, reminded me of the last supper of a condemned person. We had German sausages for dinner. Our plates clinked discreetly. We talked in low voices since several judges from a people's tribunal lived on the same floor. Pitchers of beer soothed my angst.

We discussed what life might be like in France and Western Europe. The newspapers were predicting a popular uprising in Paris any time now, but we no longer gave credence to the radio or the press. Being naïve and optimistic, I believed that sooner or later Milenko and I would end up winning scholarships in France. My cousin probably thought I was foolishly optimistic.

By nine o'clock I was running out of patience. Everything that could be said between us had been said. This evening, which felt more and more like a wake, had to end. I bid Aunt Lou an abrupt goodbye to cut short any display of emotion. I repeated what I had said to my father: "We'll see each other sooner than you think." She didn't believe a word of it. Nor did I. My cousin wished me *bon voyage*.

As I made my way to the station, I thought back to the war years. I remembered that cold, grey morning in December 1943 when Aunt Elisabeth and I walked along the banks of the Djetinja. Mist had been hovering over the river and wisps of fog were snagged on the mountaintops. We were on our way to the station to give Dimitri warm clothes and a little food. The next morning he was to be taken to Zemun concentration camp. That night we found him looking pale and stressed on the steps of the station, closely guarded by German soldiers. They allowed my aunt to hand him the precious package and to hug him. When we left him, my aunt burst into tears. She was afraid she would never see him alive again. Many lost their lives in the camp across the river from Belgrade, but he came back, safe and sound. On his return Dimitri had some terrible stories to tell us, including one about the Jewish men, women, and children who marched to their death, led by an opera singer belting out a famous chorus from *Nebuchadnezzar*.

I walked down Ilija Street, torn between feelings of pride at having made the leap, and feelings of regret at leaving behind an unfinished life. There was the usual bustle around the station. The delicious smell of grilled meat and onions wafted out of the brasseries and the rotisseries. I made my way through the milling crowd in the great hall, and found a seat at the zinc counter. Sipping a soft drink, I watched the human tide swell and wane as the trains came and went. Men in need of a shave, exhausted women, and whining children were all hurrying towards new destinations and destinies. The suffering of a people who, in less than half a century, had undergone three wars and two occupations, was painfully visible in this station.

Just as my life was taking a decisive turn and my past was unravelling stitch by stitch, my thoughts kept returning to Aunt Lou — although there were parts of her life that I knew nothing about. Sensitive and discreet, she rarely talked about the past. I guessed from her silences that she, my mother, and my grandmother had lived for many years in abject poverty. If, by chance, she sometimes mentioned a detail, she would stop and change the subject, as if to imply: why stir up old memories?

I had read about my maternal grandfather's death in 1892 from an old newspaper clipping. He died in his sleep in a small Serbian town, only a few months after being named director of an agricultural school. The article mentioned my Grandmother Ana's precarious circumstances. She was left destitute, with three children: two small girls and a small boy who later died. My mother's and my aunt's childhood and teenage years may have been materially impoverished, but with pride and dignity. How did two girls, living in such deprivation, manage to continue their studies and learn French and German? It's true that my mother tutored wealthy numbskulls in the higher grades, but even so ...

Just before the First World War, the lives of the two sisters improved a little, thanks to their college diplomas. But in August 1914 the war broke out , and for almost a year the Austrian howitzers bombarded Belgrade mercilessly. The three women lived underground, in the cellars of the city, until September 1915 when the arrival of the Austrian troops seemed almost like a deliverance. During the Occupation, my aunt continued to work at the head office of the railway company while my mother, with a fresh degree in chemistry, found a job at Prendić Pharmacy opposite the new law faculty. An old photograph shows her behind the counter with her usual serious expression. Behind her the apothecary jars are lined up on the shelves. Another woman and an Austrian officer are also in the photograph. Who were they? Aunt Lou would probably know. These details, not very important in themselves, suddenly became precious as if by knowing them, I could bring my mother back. Had the rumours been true about my aunt, reportedly in love with an Italian from Dalmatia who died of tuberculosis?

Why hadn't I asked her all these questions, and many others? And now it was too late. The train was leaving in less than an hour, and it was highly unlikely that we would ever meet again. My Aunt Lou was probably also thinking of me right now. Not having children, she had lavished all her love on me, the son of her older sister.

Amid the confusion of people, it occurred to me that if nothing worked out in my studies or my new life, I could always become a French writer. An outlandish idea. Only my double, this strange being that followed me everywhere, could have concocted such a thought. I knew that I could never write in French, but my double wouldn't listen: "Don't you know the story of Jozef Korzeniowski who, late last century, vacillated between English and French before starting to write under the name of Joseph Conrad? What chance did he have of becoming an English writer when he left his native Poland?"

"He's a great writer. I could never compare myself to him."

"Nonsense, you have to aim high when you make up your mind to write. Remember how proud you felt when Kosta read your compositions in front of the class? You were torn between pride and humiliation."

"Stop. You're driving me crazy!"

"Ah! So that's it. You fear your own madness, but don't you know that writing means owning your madness, quietly and serenely? Literature could become your only pleasure. And if your life doesn't work out, remember that the memories of a loser are usually more interesting than those of a man who succeeds."

My double was teasing me, again.

It was hot in the concourse and yet I felt cold. When the minute hand of the clock indicated ten o'clock, I was happy to cut short this crazy conversation. The train for Zagreb was leaving in less than an hour. I hoisted my knapsack onto my shoulders and headed for the boarding platform.

There was an empty window seat in a third-class car. I stared out the window at the city lights. A few minutes before eleven, the train started to move. The platform slipped by almost imperceptibly, and then the train accelerated. People were waving goodbye. They would be reunited in a few days or a few weeks. Nobody bid farewell to me. I was leaving the capital for good. One life was ending, another beginning. It filled me with pride. I don't know why.

The train rounded a long curve and slowly rolled across the bridge over the Save River. The steel beams sliced up the reflections of the city lights in the water. The Orthodox cathedral loomed briefly against the starry sky, its dome lit up above the dark mass of the roofs. At the mouth of the Danube and the Save Rivers, opposite Great War Island, the ancient Kalemegdan Fortress had been guarding the waters for over two thousand years, ever since it was built by a Roman legion fifty years before the birth of the Nazarene.

Beyond the bridge were the dark huddled shapes of the pavilions of the Belgrade International Fair. During the Occupation, these buildings had been used as part of the sinister Zemun concentration camp. Ghostly creatures, gaunt and ragged, had languished there. Many died of starvation and the cold. Others succumbed to ss bullets or were beaten to death, like Andrej, a twelve-year old Jewish boy who was killed in the Hungarian Pavilion. While awaiting his execution he had time to write on the wall: "*Au revoir*, Mr. Mölters, soon you will follow me. Mother, they are about to bludgeon me to death ... Miki who loves you."

Leaning against the window, I gazed at the lights of the city, earthly constellations that would soon be left behind. Zemun Station, deserted and meanly lit, flew by and then the train started the arduous climb up to the Pannonian Plain. For a while, a halo of light hung above the city before fading completely. The locomotive was panting hard. The funnel spit clusters of sparks into the night. I felt condemned to ride on night trains for the rest of my life.

After the tension of the previous three days I was overcome by weariness. The self-confidence and pride I had felt only moments before crumbled. Old doubts resurfaced, aided and abetted by fatigue and the night. What does a man's brief life amount to? How does one escape the ephemeral and the ordinary? These questions had probably haunted members of my mother's family who had sought refuge in oblivion. Fortunately, a new day would dissipate these nocturnal shadows. My life was a constant oscillation between the darkening sky and daybreak.

Thirty thousand years ago, this plain lay under the restless waters of the Pannonian Sea. Schools of fish had moved silently over these fields of corn and wheat. Sea urchins, starfish, and strange flora and fauna had lived at the bottom, and now nothing remained except a few fossils. In thirty thousand years, would mankind still inhabit the planet? Would Belgrade still exist? The beds of the Danube and the Save Rivers might turn into cracked mud and then stony earth. Who will read the names engraved on the tombstones in the New Cemetery, overturned by the roots of a monstrous forest? Who will remember the two sisters, my mother and my Aunt Lou, buried in the same vault?

All across the sleeping plain, mysterious goblins were switching rare lights on and off. Today, men and women will get up at dawn to work that same land. Mankind must continue to sow and reap while awaiting the end of the world.

X

# The Border

*If death does not lie at the heart of life
like a hard core, is life not a soft,
soon overripe fruit?*

— PIERRE DRIEU LA ROCHELLE

THE DAYS SPENT in Celje will remain as the strangest in my life. While nothing extraordinary happened during this brief period, there was a haunting, unreal quality to it, as if we were living outside time. Leaving Belgrade, we closed the door on our past without opening one into the future. In short, we were suffocating, trapped in limbo between past and future. We had but one wish: to open the door as quickly as possible and gain access to our new life.

Being outside time, we were also outside the world. Behind us was the world of our youth: our parents, the years at boarding school, the streets of Belgrade, our brief loves, the Baths of the Seven Poplars on the Save, hikes in the mountains, the war years, the Occupation, our trip to the Black Sea with Kosta our head teacher, and a host of other memories. Ahead of us, on the far shore of the Mura, lay a world, a *terra incognita*, virtually within arm's reach, yet so far.

In Celje, Milenko and I hid out at the home of Boris's parents. His father, a retired schoolteacher, lived in a quiet neighbourhood.

From our room, on the first floor of an old house that looked very much like a building in a Franz Hals painting, we gazed out over flowerbeds hemmed in by the archways. We were bizarre recluses in this cloister-like setting, struggling to achieve a kind of inner peace before taking the great plunge.

Everything around us evoked Central Europe and a Germanic sense of order: the yellow stucco houses, the clean streets, the serious, hard-working men.

We thought it best to leave our hideaway as little as possible during the day. At nightfall, we would emerge like nocturnal predators. Two or three times, we ventured into a neighbourhood that a week later we would have been hard-pressed to find again. Images from our stay there are still with me: the deserted streets, the ochre houses, and the sharp shadows split by the sidewalk edges.

One evening, quite late, in a practically deserted brasserie, I uttered an imperious, "Jedan vrcek pive," which meant, "A glass of beer." My Slovenian accent left much to be desired because the owner answered me in Serbian. It was hopeless. They recognised immediately that we were strangers. The owner was busy behind the counter, filling tall, wide-rimmed glasses with draft beer, and speaking in a low voice to a young woman working quietly in the background. In our fugitives' imagination, we feared we had already been betrayed. We downed our beer and cleared out. We never could know who we were dealing with. On the other hand, the owner might have thought we were agents of the secret police, an idea that amused us greatly. General distrust and the fear of being denounced gnawed at people's consciousness and annihilated any desire to resist the system.

To kill time one evening, we left the moon-lit streets and crossed the railway yard, walked to the old fortress of Celje.

From its ruins, overrun with wild vegetation, we instinctively looked to the north. On the horizon we could just barely make out a mountain range. The Austro-Yugoslav border ran somewhere along those peaks. Further to the east, the border followed the raging Mura River. All around us insects were humming in the early July night. It reminded me of summer vacations in Užice, swimming in the shade of the old fortress, with the joyful clan of my cousins and Aurore, a girl with long black hair. Once we were beyond these blue peaks, all this would be a world forever lost.

Most of our days we spent anxiously awaiting Boris's return. Since leaving Belgrade, he had become the key man in our venture. A Slovenian, he could circulate everywhere without arousing suspicion. And his cousin, living in the border village of St. Ilj, knew the best way to reach the other side. As agreed upon our arrival in Celje, Boris left for his cousin's on a reconnaissance mission. He was supposed to return in three days, but at the end of a week, we still had not heard from him. It was as if he had faded into the landscape.

We could only conjecture. Perhaps he was having a fling with some beautiful Slovene, or else, he had been arrested and had remained silent to give us a chance to get away. But to where? Would we return sheepishly to Belgrade and await discovery, or make a dash for the border and try to get across come what may? At times, I felt we were trapped like rats. Indecisive, worried, we continued to linger, hoping that everything would work out. Each day we had the impression of becoming more and more of a burden to our hosts.

Fortunately, our man reappeared on the evening of July 6. We were enormously relieved. He was safe and sound. Our escape plans were finally underway. The next morning we would take the bus to Maribor. The same day, around four in the afternoon, a train would take us to St. Ilj, the border station. Boris's cousin would be waiting for us and would welcome us as if we were old friends. By passing ourselves off as locals coming home for a celebration, we hoped to mislead any watchful border guards.

There was also talk of a guard who, in exchange for a sum of money, would agree to take us into Austria. We were wary of this possibility. What if it were a trap? We had heard of so-called escape routes that led to the dungeons of the secret police. We decided to remain on our guard.

That night, which might have been our last in the country, I tossed and turned. In my recurrent nightmare I was being taken in for interrogation. Accompanied by a taciturn guard, I walked along an endless corridor. An olive-green stripe ran along the wall. Bare light bulbs hung from a wire stretched into infinity. I knew that long years of imprisonment awaited me.

When I awoke, I thought immediately of my father. I felt guilt for the pain and humiliation I would cause him should I be arrested. I could visualise the old man at the headquarters of the secret police, patiently waiting to be admitted into the office of Slobodan, head of the secret police, whose mood that day would decide our fate. I imagined my father begging him to take pity on us, as he had done in the past when he tried to get the death sentence of a high-school colleague commuted to life imprisonment. In the end, my father's actions were in vain. Pardon was denied.

Towards three in the morning, I awoke once more. I could make out the profile of someone standing by the window. Milenko was smoking, his elbows on the windowsill. The fragrance drifting in from the garden mingled with the acrid smell of tobacco.

"Milenko!"

The tip of his cigarette reddened. He inhaled deeply.

"Sleep. Everything will be alright. By this time tomorrow we might already be in Austria."

I turned over on my side. The night seemed endless. When daylight crept into the room, I felt somewhat relieved. Whatever happened, the next forty-eight hours would seal our fate.

Our trip could have ended before it even began due to some mishap, always a possibility in such an undertaking. Toward nine o'clock we arrived at the station to take the bus for Maribor. According to the pre-arranged plan, Boris had already bought our tickets, but from that moment on we had to travel as if we did not know each other. If one of us was arrested, the two others would escape and alert family and friends. I bought *Slovenski Porčevalec*, the mouthpiece of the Communist party in Slovenia, boarded the bus, and took a window seat. I pretended to be immersed in the newspaper although I couldn't understand a word. Inside the bus, people conversed in muffled voices. In Serbia, the voices would have been louder and more animated.

I had barely sat down when an old man with a large moustache and a farmer's hat sat down beside me. He immediately asked me in Slovenian if this was indeed the bus for Marburg. The old man must have spent the First World War in the Austrian army because he was still calling Maribor by its German name, as if nothing had happened in between. I continued to pretend to read my paper. He repeated the question, raising his voice. I didn't know what to do. This old man was making me nervous. If I answered him in Serbian, people around me would realise that I was not from the area. I could already see heads beginning to turn in my direction. Most of the travellers were probably decent enough people, but it would take only one informer among them for things to fall apart. All of this could not have lasted more than a few seconds, but to me they felt like an eternity. Luckily Boris, seated behind me, came to my rescue by answering him in Slovenian. I continued to pretend to be ensconced in the party newspaper. A few minutes later, the bus started up. The rumble of the highway reassured me somewhat.

During the trip, I admired, a tad enviously, the well-groomed countryside tamed by the hard labour of this people. I couldn't help thinking of Western Serbia with its houses perched on wooded mountainsides, its muddy roads and its high deserted plateau.

On Sunday morning, July 7, 1946, we arrived in Maribor at about ten-thirty, and were surprised to find ourselves in the midst of street celebrations. Slovenia was celebrating the first anniversary of the return of those who had been deported to concentration camps. Serendipity was working in our favour. Blending into the colourful crowds surging through the streets of the small town, we passed completely unnoticed.

The celebration seemed to me a strange hybrid — part fair, part ritual. Men in striped pyjamas headed a long procession of survivors from Mauthausen, Bergen-Belsen, Dachau, and other less-well-known camps. A jubilant crowd followed them. Had it not been for the banners proclaiming the triumph of the Master Design waving above people's heads, the procession could easily have been straight out of the Middle Ages — a trade association or guild taking part in a carnival parade. For most of the young people, though, this demonstration was just an excuse for having a good time.

We blended in with the joyous crowd that flowed like a river towards the courtyard of a large, old-fashioned brick building dating back to the Austro-Hungarian empire, no doubt an old military barracks or hospital for the insane. One party leader made a speech, the meaning of which escaped us, but to judge from the words that kept being repeated — workers, bourgeoisie, liberation front — it bore the stamp of officialese. Had we been able to speak Slovenian, likely we still would not have understood more of this jumble of words spewed out on these good people.

The crowd impressed me by its friendliness. People listened patiently and applauded without excess zeal. Being the first one to stop applauding the name of the Grand Master was not a crime in this part of the country. People were visibly anxious for the ceremony to end and for the popular celebrations to begin.

July 7 had a different significance here than in Serbia, where it commemorated the day in 1941 when, according to the official version, the Partisans began their struggle against the occupiers by assassinating two German policemen. In Slovenia, this date commemorated July 7, 1945, the day the deportees returned. This small distinction was no mere coincidence. It revealed the skill with which, for centuries, this small nation had resisted a power imposed against its will.

We listened half-heartedly to the orators' patter, anxiety gnawing at us as we thought of our four o'clock train and the hurdles facing us before we reached the other side of the border. But we were grateful for the festivities and for this crowd that allowed us to pass unnoticed. On another day of the week, an informer could have spotted us easily, as had happened to many people from Belgrade trying to escape through the small border towns.

At noon, Boris, Milenko and I lunched in a restaurant beneath the arcades of the main street. Boris gave our orders. We pretended to understand what he was saying to the waiter and quenched our thirst with beer. The other customers could easily have mistaken us for cheerful buddies, but our forced gaiety barely hid our nervousness. The decisive moment was upon us, and we felt that we had passed the point of no return.

For the *n*th time we discussed the best way to cross the

border. We had to choose between crossing over land or water. Near the border station of St. Ilj, there is a wide bend in the Mura as it flows out of Austria. It heads east, and for thirty kilometres or so it constitutes the actual border. If we chose to walk west from St. Ilj, we would cross the border via small wooded hills. If we walked east, we would have to swim across the Mura.

In opting for the western route, we could avoid the raging river, which was as wide in places as a soccer field. However, along this part of the border, armed guards patrolled more frequently than along the Mura. Going via the hills was practically impossible in the daytime. To catch those who tried to pass under cover of darkness, the border guards had invented a simple, ingenious, and fatal means of surveillance: empty food tins, filled with a few pebbles, were strung along wires on the busiest routes. A fugitive had only to brush up against one of the wires in the dark and the pebbles would jingle. The patrol would open fire in the general direction of the treacherous alarm.

After much discussion, we decided to risk the swim across the Mura. Having made that decision, we now faced a new dilemma: when? Would we do it during the day or at night? Milenko preferred daytime. I thought we would be safer at night. We each put forward our arguments. Milenko was afraid we would lose our way in the darkness. I imagined how easy it would be, in broad daylight, for soldiers to fire at two targets bobbing in the river. Finally, we concluded it made more sense to decide when we got there, taking into consideration what our Slovenian friends would tell us in St. Ilj.

Boris spoke again of bribing a border guard who, for an undisclosed amount, would agree to take us safely to the other side. The idea was both appealing and amusing: to cross the border illegally with the help of a man in charge of guarding it.

But we had to be careful. I remembered the false escape routes in Russia described by Archimandrite Théodosia. The Ozna secret police could very well be using similar methods. All of Belgrade knew the case of the two Ristić brothers, sons of a textile industrialist from Niš, who disappeared en route to Belgrade airport. No one ever heard from them again, almost as if they had been sucked into the void.

By two-thirty in the afternoon, the restaurant was emptying out and the waiters were clearing the tables. We were the last customers. Our train would not be leaving for over an hour. We had to kill time but remain invisible in the streets where the crowds were slowly breaking up. Boris suggested we go to a working-class neighbourhood to visit an old fortune-teller. I have never believed in soothsayers or psychics of any kind, and had always looked askance at the old women in Belgrade who peered at coffee grounds or looked at cards to predict the future, but I accepted his suggestion, hoping that it would help us pass the time and forget our anxiety. Besides, was this not the best way to remove ourselves from curious glances?

It felt as if the neighbourhood was at the other end of the world, and I worried whether we would get back in time for the four o'clock train, but Boris reassured me. In fact, the walk was pleasant: the comfortable houses, their windows bedecked with flowers, exuded a respectable prosperity, the girls we met were blonder and seemed prettier and gentler than those of my native Serbia.

Finally we arrived in a somewhat rundown neighbourhood. We climbed a long exterior staircase leading to a modest lodging. An old woman sat behind a small table, tarot cards spread out in front of her. She smiled slightly. I felt ill at ease in this room where every object betrayed thinly disguised poverty, and with this silent woman who did not give herself away by speaking any

Serbo-Croatian. Fortunately, Boris was there as our interpreter.

Milenko went first. The cards with the bizarre designs fell one by one and revealed my friend's destiny. Ah, there was the obligatory trip to another country mentioned by all fortune-tellers. The old woman also informed him he would marry a foreigner. Several times she repeated the word *tuikinja*. It remained etched in my memory among the few words of my Slovenian vocabulary. As for me, I would take an even longer journey that involved crossing a huge body of water. Was she reading this in her cards, or had she guessed the real goal of these two young Serbian men in a town a mere twenty kilometres from the border? It did not really matter, but I was nevertheless relieved to hear no talk of prison or unpleasant events. It was the first and last time I ever consulted a fortune-teller. We left her the dinars that soon we would no longer need. Now we had just enough time to hurry back and reach the station on time.

The crowds again helped us pass unnoticed, although not many travellers were headed for St. Ilj. As in the bus, we split up and I sat alone. The atmosphere in the coach reminded me of certain Daumier drawings: there were the same rugged faces, the same wooden benches. Milenko and Boris sat not far from me, on the other side of the aisle.

Such precautions may seem like a childish game, but unfortunately, earlier experience had proved that in a situation like ours, prudence was essential. Even today, I think these precautions helped us slip through the police nets.

Waiting for the train to leave, I opened my creased *Slovenski Porčevalec* and began reading the strange words that floated together in incomprehensible sentences. When finally, the three old railway cars started to lurch forward, I experienced a twinge of sorrow. This train was taking me away from a way of life, which, despite difficult times, had also moments of warmth and tranquillity. All my life I would be like the man who, not knowing how to swim, throws himself into the water, and once he is in the waves, curses his boldness.

The golden colours of that lovely summer afternoon have remained etched in my memory. The rolling sunny landscape, its gentle knolls dotted with clusters of trees, spun past the train window, a final exhortation to one opting for exile rather than remain in his native land. I thought sentimentally of all I was leaving behind while the old train snaked its way through the hills, puffing as it climbed. Wheat fields alternated with stubble, and the pastures were dotted with strange-looking *espaliers* topped with a little roof for drying the hay. On that Sunday only the harvesters were absent from this Breughel landscape. Everything breathed the tranquillity of a world far removed from vain ambition. In this country, death arrived as naturally as birth or winter, and old people peered at the sky, not imagining death, but to predict the next day's weather. The nagging question returned: how will I find the strength to go through with it, to remove myself from so much gentleness? Was this not also one of life's tragedies?

When the tracks curved, I watched the locomotive struggle up a track that kept climbing into the hills. The little train stopped respectfully at each station. Travellers got off, greeted the employee holding a small red flag and headed off towards their homes up in the hills; as the train gathered speed on departure, they could be seen walking along the country roads. At each stop, the carriage emptied out a little more and I exchanged furtive glances with Boris and Milenko. My anxiety increased as we approached the last station. In my mind, it had become a rite of passage, a mysterious door opening into another world.

We did not know much about this station except that, since the end of the war, it was the end of the line. Before the war, the train used to go as far as Graz, capital of Styria. Boris had spoken to us of a railway bridge across the Mura that linked Yugoslavia and Austria, but that was watched day and night by a sentinel who patrolled near the rusting tracks.

Finally the locomotive began to slow down. We were arriving in St. Ilj. Weeds sprouted on the tracks. Three or four border guards, rifles slung across their shoulders, peered into the cars.

On any other day of the week we might have been arrested getting off the train, but on this afternoon some of the party atmosphere remained in the air. About twenty travellers got out at the same time as we did. Boris went first. Milka, a brunette approaching forty, was waiting for us. She exchanged kisses with her cousin, and then embraced us quite naturally. We could easily be taken for people from St. Ilj returning from Maribor after the festivities.

Later, when we had reached the other side of the border, I would sometimes think of her, and try to pierce the mystery of her life. Why did she live alone in a house on the edge of the village? What tragedy was hidden behind her ingenuous air of sadness? Perhaps a man whom she had loved had disappeared in the torment of the war? Or were these conjectures merely the product of an overactive imagination?

I do not know who first suggested going to the train station restaurant to have a drink. The real reason we went was to look like people relaxing, with nothing else on their minds but quenching their thirst. Luckily, there were quite a few people in the little room. In the uproar, no one paid any attention to us.

We left the station restaurant. The moment we got up, my legs felt like lead. Was it the effect of the two or three beers? Or fear? We crossed the train tracks covered with weeds and headed for Milka's house. It was situated on a slope at the edge of a small pine forest. Neither too large nor too small, it seemed straight out of a children's story, with its white walls and contrasting green shutters. After dropping off our things, we took the road to the cellulose factory on the shore of the Mura where we were to meet the border guard who had agreed to take us out of the country. The factory workers' celebration was still going full tilt.

From Milka's house to the factory, we followed a dirt road that wound through the countryside. We passed two or three farms. Gazing into the courtyard of a house, I was struck by something unusual. Children were taking turns on a bicycle made entirely out of wood. I had never seen such a bicycle. Years later, I would think of it when I saw the first velocipedes in a museum. This bizarre machine was a good illustration of postwar scarcity and the genius of the Slovenian people.

Apple trees, laden with green fruit, bordered the road. The land, gently rolling, reminded me of the body of a woman, fallen asleep on the banks of the Mura. As we passed a square patch of fresh earth, Milka told us in an amazingly calm voice: "This is where they bury people caught at the border." Later Milenko and I asked ourselves why she would make such a terrifying remark to us. In hindsight, only one explanation is possible: she did not even entertain the thought that we could share the fate of these men and women.

Finally, we reached a knoll and saw the Mura, the churning river that originated in the Alps. It was muddy and flowed eastward across a vast plain on the Austrian side of the border. We also noticed the factory on the riverbank, an old-fashioned red brick building. On the Yugoslav side, cornfields alternated with vegetable fields. On the Austrian side of the river was a village that looked directly at the factory while downstream a skimpy forest grew on swampy land. A mountain range loomed in the distance.

When we arrived at the cellulose factory, the crowd was caught up in a whirlwind of folk dances. Beer was flowing freely. Apparently, this was where we would meet the mysterious smuggler.

As complete strangers in this closed world where everyone knew one another, we were immediately surrounded by friends of Boris and Milka, and were regarded with curiosity. To each one we had to repeat our far-fetched story, that as students of the School of Engineering in Belgrade, we had come to tour the cellulose factory.

Nothing about this tale was believable. How to explain our presence at the other end of the country when real students were taking their exams? A simple check at the School of Engineering in Belgrade would have revealed our hoax. By withdrawing our documents from the secretariat, we were no longer considered students. They could have asked us why we had chose that particular factory, probably the only one in the entire country located so close to the border. And what was the point in coming to see a factory on a Sunday, the one day it was closed?

Our explanation was so unlikely that the first policeman to come by would have found us out, especially if he'd searched us and discovered our Swiss francs and American dollars. But what other story could we have concocted? Later, when exchanging our experiences with other fugitives, we understood that in this type of undertaking, no matter how cautious one is, luck above all else plays a decisive role.

The extraordinary thing was that the Slovenians seemed to take our story seriously, unless they were feigning belief. One foreman even went so far as to try to find the key to the factory to take us on a tour. He was gone a long time. I was afraid that he was trying to turn us in, but he returned all apologetic because he had been unable to locate the watchman. He suggested a time to meet the next day. We promised to return without fail.

As we were waiting, my eyes strayed to the other shore of the Mura. It looked like a mirage floating on the choppy water. We could see half-timbered houses, a green meadow. Nothing moved. Our promised land seemed only a stone's throw away, yet I had the impression I was observing inhospitable shores through binoculars, and that at any instant, an imaginary enemy might open fire.

Milka had cousins on the other side, but since the end of the war, the people on the opposite sides of the river could no longer exchange cards or letters. For now at least, an unforgiving border imposed by the vagaries of history separated them.

One detail caught my attention. A steel cable stretched across the river four to five metres above the water line. We learned from our friends that it had been used to send logs from one side to the other. Since the end of the war, this abandoned cable was the ultimate impotent link between two worlds that shunned each other. I began fantasising about a basket and pulley that could spirit us over to the other side in a few minutes. The idea seemed relatively simple, but carrying it out was another story. Where to find the pulley and basket? Who would give us a hand? And how would the first one to arrive on the other side send back the basket? Besides, suspended above the river, we would make ideal targets for the border guards.

A girlfriend of Milka's showed up, then went off to look for the felonious border guard. Several times she returned. Arduous negotiations, the details of which escaped us, were going on. A plot was being concocted. I continued exchanging platitudes with strangers, smiling, and feeling as if I were walking on live coals. I had little strength left. Finally, the village girl reappeared, accompanied by a man in a grey uniform. An insignificant and shifty-looking character, he had nothing specific to tell us: neither the price he would charge, nor how he was going to get us across the border.

Once again, we were overwhelmed with doubt. How could we trust a border guard who agreed to be a mule? Why would he agree to help us? He must know that he risked the death penalty if we were all caught. Could we trust him? Or was he just bait put out to snare fools?

All the while the band played on — the brass reflected the sun's rays, the cheeks of the musicians inflated like frogs' with their effort, and the young people kicked up clouds of dust with their energetic dances. We could have been extras in a Smetana opera. We were not in a mood for rejoicing, and yet we had to keep on smiling, masquerading as students who had come there to learn and have fun.

Our lengthy discussions with the nondescript character amounted to nothing. Finally, he disappeared on the pretext of needing to speak with another guard before giving us a definite answer. We never saw him again, but to our relief he did not turn us in. Later, we concluded that the man was not an *agent provocateur*, but simply considered the affair too risky, especially given the amount of money we had to offer him.

Feeling it was a waste of time to stay on watching the party, we left the factory yard and headed back towards the house at the edge of the forest. The sun was setting, and the shadows of the willows along the river were lengthening. At a bend in the river, I glanced back at the red brick factory. The music was fading away in the balmy evening. The celebrations would soon be over.

On our way back, we continued our discussion. Now that we had eliminated the possibility of the border guard helping us, swimming across the river was the only recourse. By day or by night? I preferred the latter, remembering an October night in 1944 when, crawling like a lizard along the bottom of a ravine, I escaped from a city under siege. Naturally, total darkness held advantages and disadvantages. It would allow us to move without being seen but it also held the risk of finding ourselves face to face with a patrol waiting in ambush.

Finally, thanks to information provided by our Slovenian friends that the guards patrolled a narrow towpath every twenty minutes, we decided to cross the river the next day at about four o'clock in the afternoon. With the help of our friends, it would be possible to slip down to the shore between patrols.

The die was cast. Nothing remained to discuss save the details of our escape. Curiously, from that moment on, I felt less anxious, despite the endless waiting that unnerved me and made me want to go and throw myself in the river to get it over with.

It was already dusk by the time we passed by the plot of freshly turned earth. I had difficulty imagining that the bodies of strangers were resting there. Could the corpse of Danilo Marinković, my classmate at Alexander I High School be lying there? One fine day he had left Belgrade secretly to join his mother in France and no one had ever heard from him again. It was as if the earth had opened up and swallowed him.

Why? Why were these men killed? What Master Design, what imaginary human happiness could justify these mass graves that sprang up along the borders of my country? And why were there always men who valued freedom more than their lives? I didn't know the answer. The coolness of evening had settled over the countryside, and I continued to walk. A terrible will to reach the other shore was building inside me, as if such an act might resurrect all these dead buried in unmarked graves.

As we drew near the house, the rays of the setting sun flickered through the pine trees. This home breathed a mysterious tranquility. Were it not for the fact that we were fugitives, I would have felt engulfed by a profound feeling of peace.

The place rekindled an old dream that had long haunted my adolescence. Or was it the kind of reverie that appears on an evening when the mists start to rise in the valleys? In my fantasy, I am in a house at the edge of a pine forest. On my worktable, an opaline lamp casts a circle of light. The rest of the room is bathed in a soft half-light with greenish reflections. Seated in front of a window opening onto the night, I am writing a story or doing sums. Outside, a late summer rain whispers in the trees. The aroma of vegetation fills the room. Then the door opens noiselessly and a slender young woman approaches me on tiptoe. She gently takes my head in her arms. Her ash-blonde hair caresses my cheeks. Time has stopped. We are lovers drifting in eternity.

I was so ashamed of this dream. It made me blush. Yet, like an opium addict, I could not stop the secret pleasure it induced.

A threatening reality had long replaced this old dream, but it was revived by the house at the edge of the pine forest, as if my mind were making a final attempt to escape the anxiety at hand. I thought of how, in other circumstances, I could have felt happiness in this modest home that breathed order and cleanliness. If homes can have a soul, this one certainly did.

Over dinner, Milka told us the story of a student from Zagreb who, about a month earlier, had attempted to cross the border at night. A patrol had spotted him and opened fire. He was wounded, but in the darkness managed to find refuge in a house on the Yugoslavian side. He remained hidden there for a month, but someone denounced him. The house was surrounded, searched, and the fugitive arrested. They executed him with a bullet to the head and the matter was closed. I looked at the last clear streak of sky to the west. Somewhere in those hills, now slipping into night, a man's life had ended. I pictured his family, who would go on hoping to receive a card from Austria, or somewhere else: for them, this man continued to exist in the world of the living dead.

Before falling asleep, I had a curious vision of the world we hoped to escape. Every day it became more like the huge construction site of a new Tower of Babel. Everywhere, bare-chested ant-like workers were busily pulling thick ropes, hewing stones, laying bricks. Pulleys creaked and heavy blocks of granite slid on rollers. The tower rose higher and higher, with thousands of factories humming inside its walls. In the semi-darkness, long transmission belts distributed energy to the tower and to the drilling machines. On the site and throughout the immense tower, activist ants circulated tirelessly, preaching the slogans and enthusiasm of invisible leaders. The exhausted worker ants did not have enough to eat, but drove themselves to exhaustion knowing that finally, for the first time in history, they were working for themselves. They received small flags in reward. During this time, the soldier ants surveyed the workers and guarded the borders. And in the very heart of the tower lived an invisible foreman, who had given the order to pursue slackers and deserters ruthlessly. Finally, thousands of voices rose in a hymn to the glory of the Master Design, but no one knew whose singing was heartfelt and whose was just an act.

This society of supposedly implacable logic and subject to geometrical order was full of inexplicable flaws. Fugitives caught at the border were, as a general rule, shot on sight. Yet people intending to escape, caught twenty or thirty kilometres from the border or betrayed while planning their breakaway, could hope to get away with a few months in prison. The system lacked any coherence.

Another escape story had caught our attention, because it seemed so farfetched. One night a smuggler, probably on the lookout for a supply of lighter flints, left for Austria, lighting his way with a lantern. Of course this light moving along the sides of the hill was spotted by the border patrol and confused them. Only a fool or a drunkard would head for the border with a lantern. From afar, the patrol cried halt and immediately the stranger complied. The small light stopped moving. The soldiers then asked the man where he was going. He explained very innocently that he was heading home. The guards chuckled good-naturedly, then explained to him that he had lost his way and was headed toward the border. The man excused himself profusely and pretended to be lost. The head of the patrol then ordered him to approach, but the small light did not budge. They repeated the order with threats, but received no reply. The guards then advanced carefully. A few steps from the lamp, they had to face the facts: the lamp was hanging from a cane stuck in the ground. The man with the deceptive light had already reached Austria. Listening to these stories, I could not help but think that if all went well, this would be our last evening in the country, but if things went awry ...

Time weighed heavily. Waiting is what is hardest to bear in such situations, and my suggestion to cross the Mura that very night could have been due to a simple desire to get it over with. I also understood how fugitives who, once arrested, could feel almost happy to be relieved of the nervous tension.

We were still talking and finishing the meal when we heard a rap at the door. Everything happened so quickly that we did not have time to be frightened. Before Milka even got up to open the door, an officer clad in a grey raincoat appeared in the doorway, silhouetted by the darkness. For a split second I thought of the currency sewn into our jackets, irrefutable proof of our intentions. Then a miracle happened. As if in a dream, I saw Milka approach him with her gentle smile and kiss him. The man was alone.

Sometimes fate hovers for a single second between the tragic and the trivial, which is what happened that evening. The officer was not pursuing fugitives, but simply paying a friendly visit to the mistress of the house, his cousin. We were properly introduced to this intellectual-looking visitor. Smiling politely, he listened to Milka's explanations. For the *n*th time, we heard the improbable story of students of the School of Engineering in Belgrade come to tour the cellulose factory.

To this day, I doubt that he was taken in by this farfetched tale. I think he preferred to pretend to believe us. To avoid making trouble for his cousin? Perhaps. It is also possible that he was no zealous servant of the Master Design and that circumstances had dictated he wear this uniform. Since then I've had many opportunities to learn of men whose job or official affiliation forced them to serve Party interests, but who nevertheless betrayed the Party in the name of humanity. The young officer with the enigmatic smile was sensitive enough not to linger. A half-hour later, he disappeared into the night as suddenly as he had appeared.

Our arduous journey was almost over. When we left Celje that morning we had hoped, without really believing, that we would find ourselves in Austria by evening. At this late hour we were still in Yugoslavia, right up against the border, at the mercy of the slightest false move or untimely incident. The episode with the officer reminded us of this all too well. Perhaps another incident would not end so happily.

Although I was weary, I was reluctant to go to bed, fearing the nightmares that would haunt my dreams. Through the wide-open windows, I felt the coolness of the night and heard the sound of rain pattering on the trees. Milka's house, with its roughcast lime walls, rustic furniture, and stalks of corn hanging above the stove, breathed peace and tranquillity, and drew me back to the obsessive daydream of my adolescence. But this was no time for daydreaming. Somewhere in the darkness, the border guards, dressed in rain gear, were patrolling and watching. The nocturnal forest was full of mystery and fear.

Milenko, Boris and I slept on the main floor. Milka's room was upstairs. All night long I tossed and turned, constantly awakening only to fall back into a nightmare-ridden sleep. I would barely doze off and the kitchen door would suddenly open: in the doorway, the light-coloured uniform of the officer appeared from the darkness. No longer smiling, he was accompanied by a pack of dogs and soldiers. These men burst into the peaceful home and bound our hands with telephone cord.

I awoke with a start. In the forest, the rain was still whispering. The plant smells filtered into the room and I inhaled deeply. Then, after a moment, I fell back asleep. Immediately I was in my imaginary prison, walking down corridors lined with light bulbs that stretched into infinity.

With the first rays of dawn, I awoke for good. The rain had ceased. Soon I could see a little piece of a well-washed sun peeking through the trees. It was going to be a fine day. As always, dawn rekindled in me hope and the will to fight. With the escape plan settled and the irrevocable decision made, we spent the morning in the house. Time dragged by agonisingly. The moment of truth was approaching, and our outward joy thinly masked our exasperation. As if to take our minds off the subject, a girl, whose face would have enchanted Cézanne, appeared after lunch. She was to be our guide and would escort us to the river.

Because we were to swim across, with our clothes fastened to our heads, we had to leave anything superfluous behind. I gave Boris my raincoat which was too bulky. With a pang of nostalgia, I parted with my knapsack that had served me so faithfully during the war. Milenko also sacrificed a few objects that were not absolutely necessary. We were crazed with the desire for freedom and were ready to divest ourselves of anything just to stay afloat. I kept my black leather briefcase and stuffed it with a shirt and a few sausages. Milenko kept only his new Prince of Wales suit.

Towards two-thirty, we left our refuge. I was relieved; I was impatient to get it over with. Trying to resemble villagers going to work in the fields, we shouldered sickles and spades. We must have made a strange quartet: two young men in their Sunday best, equipped with farming tools and a briefcase, accompanied by two village women. We looked as if we'd stepped straight out of an operetta, but luckily we encountered no one on the road.

We retraced our steps of the previous day. I walked as if in a trance. The decisive hour was drawing near. At times, I felt as if I were motionless, while the apple trees, sagging beneath bunches of small green fruit, were filing past me. We passed the farm with the wooden bicycle, then the plot of yellow earth at the edge of a small ravine, the final warning for those setting off. I was no longer frightened. My dark thoughts had disappeared. A mysterious voice told me we would make it, the same voice that during the war had whispered to me: you won't die ... not you ... Oh, I knew that those who were going to die heard it too, but my voice ... my voice did not lie! I kept walking ... or else the dirt path was advancing beneath my feet. Keep moving, keep moving. I had no other thoughts, besides those that commanded action.

Then, reaching the crest of a low hill, we saw once again the impetuous Mura River rushing to the east. Rising from its muddy waters was a small island linked to the Yugoslavian shore by a frail wooden bridge. That spot provided a panoramic view of the entire area. To our left, a plume of smoke rose from the brick chimney of the cellulose factory. Straight ahead, on the small beach that ran alongside the river, were vegetable gardens and cornfields. According to Milka, a patrol sometimes targeted the island, but for the moment, all we could see were sheep grazing peacefully.

Our plan was to hide among the roots of the willows at the water's edge. There Milenko and I would wait for our young guide to cross the bridge and signal, by means of a discreet whistle, that the coast was clear. Then we would swim to the island, run across, and hurl ourselves into the current and cross the main branch of the Mura. Afterwards ... afterwards we could only count on ourselves and our lucky stars.

July 8, 1946 was a golden summer day. The hills, the river, the distant mountains in Austria all brought back thoughts of summer vacations long past. But this bucolic landscape concealed the face of death, like the children's pictures you have only to tilt at a certain angle to find the face of an old woman hidden among the leaves of a tree. Every twenty minutes an armed patrol would pass along the shore with orders to shoot anyone trying to escape the construction of their modern-day Tower of Babel. For the border guards, all that was required was a series of simple movements — pull back the bolt of the rifle, slip a cartridge into the barrel, aim as one would at a mountain goat on a rock, hold one's breath, and pull the trigger. Bang! Farewell to heedless youth, farewell to family, farewell to friends, farewell to life.

At about three o'clock we started walking toward the valley, leaving the factory behind. The young girl, who was our guide, went ahead to make sure the way was clear. She strode along with a supple step and our eyes never left her. At the slightest suspicious movement, she was supposed to signal to us to turn back. The forest thinned as we made our way down the hillside. By the time we reached the plain we were almost completely exposed. The few clumps of trees offered very little cover as we tramped in silence towards the cornfields. Fortunately, the cornstalks hid us from prying eyes. Relieved, we pushed our way into the first field. At least for a little distance, we were sheltered. Nevertheless, the tension mounted steadily. I felt as if I was being strangled and having my chest crushed at the same time. To give myself courage, I repeated over and over that all I had to do was to make it through the next thirty or forty minutes. Afterwards ... afterwards our fate would be sealed ... whatever happened. The worst of it was knowing that we were completely at the mercy of chance. Blind luck was about to show its hand.

Having pushed our way through the forest of cornstalks, we came to the dirt track between two fields that was used by the border patrol. Crossing it, we would be clearly visible for a distance of about ten metres but we couldn't turn back now.

I don't remember which of us was the first to step out onto the little path. I know for sure that Milenko was on my left. As I turned to look right, I saw three border guards some fifty metres away. Two were sitting on the ground with their rifles between their legs, while the third was standing facing them. He was busy tightening his belt. Or at least that's what I think I saw. All that any one of them had to do was simply turn his head and he would see us. It was a panic-blurred moment, but the image of those men in grey uniforms seared itself on my brain as if on a photographic plate. Our fate hung in the balance, to be decided by a chance movement from those men.

I froze with fear, and as if secretly hoping he'd tell me it wasn't true, I whispered to Milenko: "There are three guards on the road!"

"I know, I know!" he said. "Keep going ... keep going ... don't think about it!"

I turned my head away as if not looking at them would keep them from seeing us. That is exactly what children do when they put their hands over their faces and think they can't be seen.

Hardly had Milenko finished speaking when already we were slipping into the other cornfield. I still didn't feel very safe. How could I be sure that at the last moment one of the guards hadn't noticed us? I could hear them coming after us, guns at the ready. We kept going — and nothing happened. Chance, that cruel ogre, must have been splitting his sides laughing.

Through the cornstalks we now had glimpses of a field of cabbages and of the willows bordering the river. It was sunny and warm. A faint breeze rustled in the leaves. It could so easily have been one of those days during the long summer vacation when my cousins and I used to go into the fields and smoke corn silk. But I couldn't think about the past now. At any moment, we might hear our guide's whistle signalling that the coast was clear.

The moment had come at last to say goodbye to Milka. Our paths had crossed for just two short days, but it was a time of such intensity that later I would always feel, despite the aura of mystery surrounding her, that I had known her for a long time. Although I shall always be grateful to her for helping us cross the border, my conscience will never be easy. Boris, Milka, and the girl who guided us took great risks. Even today I still wonder whether those good friends paid dearly for their generosity when our escape became known.

We began our final preparations, but not without a certain embarrassment, because we had to strip down to our underpants in front of Milka. Like strange young forest gods preparing for some mysterious ritual, we took off our clothes and used our belts to tie them to our heads. For a moment I was tempted to abandon my black leather briefcase but upon reflection kept it, thinking of the precious sausages it contained. When we kissed Milka this time, it was the same conspirators' kiss that had identified us at the train station on the preceding day, but this time it was filled with affection. We were ready. Wearing our bundles on our heads, we must in fact have looked less like fauns and more like escapees from a lunatic asylum.

After a last *adieu* we rushed from the cornfield and raced across the field of cabbage. I looked back one last time. Through the cornstalks I thought I could see Milka's smiling face. A few seconds later we threw ourselves, literally, into the water and quickly hid among the thick roots of the old willows along the bank. For a moment the cold water took my breath away. I could see branches and stumps going past. The current was moving quickly and I realised for the first time that the river was in flood, but it was too late to worry about that now.

The island looked close and we were sure of being able to get there in a few strokes. The fear that had been gnawing at me for days had vanished. Now, in the heat of action, only one thing mattered — to start swimming and get across. All we could do was wait for the whistle. Crouched among those huge roots that clung to the crumbling riverbank like the tentacles of some giant octopus, we thought we were safe, but we were not alone ...

At one point, as I turned instinctively to make sure there was nothing behind us, I received a terrible shock. There, almost close enough to touch, was a man looking at me. A cry froze on my lips. The head, covered with a shapeless old black hat, was that of a peasant, a man of about fifty with features worn by wind and sun, a face with the sort of deep lines that inevitably remind one of the furrows of ploughed land. Silently and intently, this man stared at us. In his eyes, no emotion whatsoever could be detected. Endless seconds passed and we found nothing to say. Then, with a gesture as ancient as human history, the man bent and dipped his bucket into the river. He let it fill with muddy water and he vanished, taking with him the secrets of his impenetrable look.

Much later, in the long idleness of camps and prisons, I often thought of that man and of his face etched by toil and I would be irresistibly reminded of Brueghel's painting, *The Fall of Icarus*. Not that Milenko or I resembled Icarus or Daedalus or that either of us was about to plunge into the sea. But there was something ... and it occurred to me too that the world we were leaving in some ways resembled a labyrinth, a labyrinth in which the Master Design was rampaging like a Minotaur, likely to loom up at any turn in our path, ready to crush and trample us, and all the more terrible for being beyond Good or Evil. What I saw in that *tableau vivant* on the riverbank was the image of the labourer in the painting who is turning away from the fallen Icarus or the still airborne Daedelus. Clearly, the old man felt neither contempt nor admiration for us. He was simply doing his chores and was utterly devoid of any capacity for understanding, or for taking any part in our adventure.

That old Slovenian peasant was not so very different from the Serbian ploughman I had seen one day in April 1941. He was tramping steadily along behind his plough while a battle against German tanks was being fought in the nearby valley. Our soldiers, in panic and disorder, fled back towards the mountains and as they went, threw away their weapons and uniforms in the fields. The old man just kept on ploughing unperturbed. Whether peace reigns or war rages, someone has to feed the people.

The old Slovenian's face had just disappeared when we heard two short whistle calls from the island. Milenko was the first to push off from the bank and immediately the current carried him a dozen metres to the right. I had enough time to reflect on what that meant. Glad the suspense of the last few days was over, I plunged in eagerly after him. We swam with all our strength and almost immediately were climbing up through the bushes on the bank. The island was nothing but a green meadow with lush grass. Not a tree. There were a few sheep which stampeded at the sight of two naked men rising from the water with strange turbans on their heads. I glanced toward the wooden bridge and saw for a split second the girl who had been our guide. She was waving goodbye. I raised my left arm without breaking stride. Naked, we raced across the island, crouching like soldiers under fire. All it took to get over the border, or so it seemed, was a little daring. But I had congratulated myself too soon. On the other side of the island, there was little reason to rejoice.

The Mura was flowing very fast. What we had just crossed was only a side channel, hardly more than a brook compared to the heavy, threatening waves rolling past us now. The mill and the trees on the Austrian side suddenly seemed very far away. But now we were pumped for action and nothing could stop us.

Milenko was the first to jump in and was literally snatched away by the current like a piece of straw, and again I followed him without giving myself time to think. That was how we said farewell to the shores of our native land.

The power of the current was astounding. It sucked us violently towards the middle, pulling us downstream. On the other side the stunted poplars, willows, bushes were madly rushing past. The shores we longed for leapt towards us and those low and muddy fields, so often dreamed of behind closed curtains in Galsworthy Street in Belgrade, actually seemed within reach. Did destiny always repay adventure like this, and the madness of the brave? In barely thirty seconds we were in the middle of the river, in the centre of a current that was braiding long, strong ropes of muddy water. Was this crossing in fact going to be easier than we had dared hope?

Unfortunately not. Those twisting muddy cables, which had yanked us so enthusiastically into their midst, refused to release us. It was as if the river was hungry for our living flesh. In strict accordance with the laws of hydraulics, the forces that had pulled us so quickly into the middle of the river now held us imprisoned there. Caught, we began a life-and-death struggle with the Mura. No matter how hard we swam toward the other shore, if our strokes weakened for only a moment, all our efforts were immediately lost as the current dragged us back to the middle. Each time we had to begin the fight all over again.

I continued hurtling downstream, swept along with the dead branches churning around us in the racing waters. On the Yugoslav side a larger hill had now appeared, while the Austrian forest was thinning out. Some twenty metres ahead of me Milenko was struggling as desperately as I was. Although my brain was working fast, I saw no way out but exhaustion and drowning. As I fought the river the belt under my chin was strangling me like a garrotte. Soon I only had one thought — to breathe deep down into the bottom of my lungs. To do that, I'd have to get rid of the stupid bundle on my head. I shouted to Milenko to throw away the package of clothes. Like an echo mingled with the rushing of the Mura, his voice came back to me: "Let it go ... let it go ... let it all go ..." I saw Milenko's bundle come off his head and be carried away, far ahead of him. So we were going to emerge completely naked from these muddy waters. But I couldn't ... no, at least not yet ... not with a five-hundred Swiss franc banknote sewn into the lining of my jacket ... it was all we had now.

The border patrol could easily have heard us, could have opened fire on two moving targets just for the challenge of a good mark on a beautiful summer afternoon. But that no longer mattered to me. I was too busy struggling against this bottomless liquid mass that was ferrying us into a dark country ... and my strength was failing. Several times already I had swallowed and vomited the dirty water. Now for the first time, a thin black veil covered my eyes, followed by the thought of death. With what remained of consciousness, I went back in a flash over my whole life, my peaceful childhood and the death of my mother — whose shadow had hovered long afterwards over my father's life and my own — the careless years of boarding school, the war with its procession of comrades killed, the silly love affairs of my youth ... and finally my own death in this river on a July day in 1946, the last page of a useless life. Weirdly, I felt no regret except perhaps at leaving my father to grow old alone. At the end of my diminishing consciousness, like the sputtering flame of a candle stump, there was the thought that death was not as terrible as I had so often pictured it. I would just drink a little more of this dirty yellow water and after that the black veil would come down and blot out all thought. I was leaving for the next world or maybe for nothing at all, and the question didn't seem important.

But if what was left of my consciousness had already accepted death, my body, with its billions of cells, was still resisting. Against all odds, it was determined to survive. The truth is that I shall never know exactly what really happened. Did the wild river take pity on our youth — or was it out of indifference to our fate that it threw us up onto the bank in exactly the same way it was tossing up the cadavers of drowned ewes? I only know that I made a final effort and turned over onto my back in the hope of getting a few good breaths of air for my oxygen-starved brain. When I did that, the package of clothes on my head was suddenly transformed into a cushion that held my head above water. At last, greedily, I could breathe. My strength came back and with it, the desire to fight. On my back, I began to swim for the other shore and after only a few strokes I felt the grip of the current loosen. Each movement brought me closer to that forest of stunted trees. Then a few seconds later I felt soft muck under my feet and my legs sank into it up to my calves. Long ago on summer swimming trips, I'd had a horror of the muddy bottom, fearing the teeth of some nasty swamp creature, but now I welcomed the silt like the softest of Persian carpets. I turned over and walked. With each step I rose a little farther out of the muddy water. I was breathing, I felt drunk. Never would I have thought that the simple act of filling one's lungs with air could be so exhilarating. I looked with unbelieving eyes at the tufts of grass overhanging the clay banks and at the scrubby trees that were leaning over to meet me. Was it in this world that I was seeing all this? Or was I taking my first steps into the afterlife?

I staggered out of the river. The soles of my feet squelched in the mud and the last of the Mura ran between my toes. Downstream, I saw through a mist that Milenko was also coming out on the bank. The two of us were like mythic beings, born of clay and water. At last I took off my weird turban and walked towards Milenko. He came to meet me. Without a word, we hugged each other and collapsed into the weeds.

That was the sudden end of a long dream, shot through with hope and nightmares. We had touched the other shore, slipped beyond the clutches of the uniformed ruffians, past the informers and all those gutless beings who, in the building of their enormous Tower of Babel, vied with each other to prove their loyalty to the Master Design, hoping to improve whatever pittance they received for their efforts. Whether the Tower was built or whether it collapsed, we had nothing further to do with it.

I don't know how long we lay there, semi-conscious. I only remember vomiting more yellow Mura water as, little by little, with my returning consciousness, I became aware of a burning sensation over most of my body. We were lying in a patch of nettles. Then and only then did I get up. First I scratched, then I started to put my clothes on. Milenko also recovered, and together we succumbed to a fit of hysterical laughter, pounding each other on the back.

All the while, at our feet, the indifferent Mura flowed on, as it has since time immemorial, unaware of the men who had made it their boundary. The landscape on the Yugoslav side looked different. The red brick factory and the cornfields had been replaced by wooded hills — but beyond the screen of trees the patrols were surely still making their rounds. What we had to do right away was to get into the patch of stunted trees. Against the green of the vegetation our naked bodies would offer a tempting target for an over-zealous border guard. So we went farther into the sparse woods and sat down on stumps to assess our situation. Milenko had nothing left but his soaking wet underpants. Along with his Prince of Wales suit, he'd also lost about fifteen dollars. I had salvaged my brown suit, my shoes and my black briefcase, along with a shirt and a kilo of sausage. We also had the five hundred Swiss francs, quite a fortune, still sewn into the lining of my jacket. And there was some chocolate left, plus a few cigarettes, a box of matches and three watches.

We were, on that July afternoon, literally drunk with our freshly won freedom, and too happy at having thumbed our noses at the Grand Master and his pack of thugs to worry much about what to do next. Naturally, he would never learn of the disappearance of two students from the engineering faculty but still, it was the Grand Master and his acolytes who had invented the hateful tribunals that had been set up on university campuses. Shortly after our escape they began to condemn and expel confused and helpless students whose only crime, usually, was that they were born into bourgeois families.

Once we had eaten some chocolate and pulled ourselves together, we took our first steps into *terra incognita*. We had to walk back up along the river to where we would once again be seen across from the factory. It had been agreed that the girl who had guided us was to wait there in order to transmit the news back to Belgrade that we had made it safely into Austria. We had no illusions about finding her there. It had been at least an hour since she had whistled to let us know we could leave our hiding-place in the willow roots. By now she must have tired of waiting.

We'd been walking only a few minutes when we met the first living being on this side of the river, an old woman who was gathering dry branches and tying them into bundles. In her rags, with a toothless mouth and her weather-beaten, toil-worn expression, she might have stepped straight out of the Middle Ages. She could just as easily have been the wife of the peasant on the other shore. The woman looked at us as the natives of distant countries must have looked at the first explorers. No surprise. Were we not beings from another world? Our clothing bore witness to that.

Milenko, barefoot, in his underwear and a shirt that was visibly too big for him; me in a wet brown suit, with a black leather briefcase and gold-rimmed glasses — we looked like caricatures. The woman must have thought we were the Devil and his apprentice, climbing out of the troubled waters of the Mura to haunt her scrubby woods. My slim knowledge of German, just barely improved by my discussions with Joseph Tapeiner had given me enough confidence to try to talk to the old woman.

"*Guten Tag, entschuldigen Sie bitte, wo ist die Polizeistelle?*" But all we got for an answer was "*Grüss Gott! Ich voas net.*"

Our attempts to get information out of her were met with a blank stare. Then the ragged old woman, representative of the endless struggle of humanity, walked away bent under her bundle of firewood. Like the labourer in *The Fall of Icarus*, she too preferred to turn away from two adventurers. So there was nothing for us to do but keep on walking. My pocket watch indicated five o'clock when the cellulose factory on the Yugoslav side finally came into view. All was motionless on the opposite bank. Only a little plume of smoke drifted from the tall chimney into a blue sky. As arranged, we showed ourselves beside the steel cable that still ran between the two shores. But on the other side there was no living soul. Our young guide must have tired of waiting for us, or else she simply thought that we had drowned for she'd seen us battling the currents of the Mura. At any rate, she must have had serious doubts as to the success of our crossing. In fact, the first news to reach our friends in Belgrade offered nothing but uncertainty as to our fate.

We tore ourselves away from the banks of the Mura. I cast a last glance back at the willows which masked the border patrols. I looked back at the peaceful hills hiding Milka's house at the edge of the forest. Farther along, though we couldn't see it, was the little railroad station with its rails overgrown by weeds, and downstream towards the plain, Maribor with its arcaded streets, and Celje, where for eight days we had lived outside of time and space. Still farther away there was Belgrade itself, the ancient town of Singuidunum, a fortress built by the fifth Roman Legion at the confluence of two swift-flowing rivers. So many memories, so much sadness and so much joy tied me to that city. Better not to think about it. It was too late for regrets and too early for nostalgic reminiscences. Besides, a voice deep inside me whispered that I had not left my country to betray it, but only so I could remain loyal to it. Ever since, that voice has never ceased repeat the same thing.

We started walking again. A path soon turned into a road and we came to a tiny hamlet beside an ancient half-timbered mill that looked exactly like the mills I was later to see in the paintings of the old Flemish masters. There were the same weathered beams organised in rectangles and diagonals against a stucco of uncertain colour. Farther along was the beginning of a street which we would have preferred to avoid; however, between the river and the forest, we hadn't much choice. And anyway, we were looking for a distant cousin of Milka's, a certain Franz J., who might give us supper and a bed on our first night in Austria. We had no choice but to walk along that street in our grotesque garb, unwilling actors in a play that I shall never forget.

We strode along the middle of the road like a couple of luckless *hidalgos* returning in defeat from some obscure skirmish. Saying nothing, we made our way down the row of medieval houses and, as if by magic, the children stopped playing, doors and windows opened, and old and young put down their tasks for a moment to stare at us in silence. They couldn't have been in much doubt about where we were coming from, but who did they think we were? Did they think we were spies or homeless tramps arriving from some mysterious elsewhere to trouble their peaceful existence? We kept on walking, not sure whether we should laugh or just hold our heads high and look straight ahead. Our pride at having conquered the raging Mura was mingled with a sense of the ridiculousness of our situation, so we assumed an air of bravado like Rodrigo and his companions after fighting the Moors.

*Just to see us stride with such a face*
*The worst affrighted took heart apace.*

I must admit that no Moor was threatening us and no battlefield lay ahead, but nevertheless a long and bitter struggle for life was just beginning. We had asked for it and we were ready to take up the challenge. This was our pride and the price we must pay to be free.

At the end of that seemingly endless street, I screwed up my courage and spoke to one of several men squinting distrustfully at us from the doorsteps of their homes.

"Do you know where Franz J. lives?"

In as few words as possible, the man gave us directions.

We turned off to the right, into a maze of sordid alleyways. Here the houses had tiny windows and the high walls around their yards, evidence of a suspicious, inward-turning attitude. We found the house, pushed open a heavy portiere and stepped into Franz J.'s yard. The man himself was the reflection of his village. Short, paunchy and shifty-eyed, he made me think of some wild rodent — half-man and half-beast — the kind you might meet in fairy tales. With his storehouse filled to bursting, he would die worrying about not being able to make it through to the next harvest. He questioned us at length. He had to know everything: where we were coming from, who we were, where we were going, and who had given us his address. He also wanted to know how we had got across the Mura when it was in full flood and had caused so much harm in the neighbouring town of Leibnitz. The river's raging waters had been sweeping away livestock. Clearly extremely distrustful of us, the man was afraid of getting mixed up in some dirty business, all the more because he was Slovenian and didn't want any trouble with the Austrian authorities.

At last greed won out and persuaded him to take us in. It was urgent that Milenko find himself a pair of trousers and some sort of shoes so that we could continue the next day towards Graz. We offered the man a swap — trousers and shoes for a watch. This swap was the source of the first disagreement between Milenko and I. From the moment we had left Belgrade there had been a tacit understanding that we would hold everything we owned in common. We owned three watches: a Doxa pocket watch that my father had given me as a gift for Orthodox Christmas in 1937, and which I had always carried, a silver Omega we'd brought along as currency for hard times, and lastly Milenko's Certina, to which he was attached because he'd bought it with his own money. Milenko wanted to keep his Certina and exchange the Omega for the trousers and shoes, but I disagreed because the silver Omega was worth more than his Certina. At last, unwillingly, he agreed to relinquish his wristwatch. Even today I feel remorse for having forced him to give up his Certina. I think he held it against me a little for the rest of his life. The worst of it was that the trousers he got in exchange were like something out of a museum of medieval poverty. They would have been perfect as a theatrical costume for a tramp. Never before or since have I seen anything like them. They were so patched that it was impossible to discover what material they had originally been made from. And the sandals matched them perfectly. When he tried on his new clothing, Milenko didn't know whether to laugh or cry. He looked like a Harlequin who'd lost his jacket. The little rodent man came out the winner in our swap. In 1946, the war was barely over and a Swiss wristwatch had considerable value, but our backs were to the wall and we had no choice. Milenko couldn't go into Graz barefoot and in his underpants. As a bonus, we were given a supper of fried potatoes and head cheese. Heartened by this country fare, I began, for the first time since leaving Belgrade, to take an interest in food.

After dinner the peasant showed us into the hayloft over the stable. With the cows busy chewing their cuds below, our beds beneath the rafters loaded with hay, and the whole wall open to the northwest, the scene reminded me of the Nativity.

If I live a hundred years I shall never forget that first night on the other side, the fragrance of the dry hay, the calm of the countryside, the warm summer air, and the enormous sky sparkling above us. All that and the drunken dizziness of our newfound liberty combined to overwhelm me with a sweet peacefulness and unspeakable happiness. Were I to die the following day, I would have told myself that at least I had known one moment which had given meaning to the whole of life. In spite of my weariness, I couldn't sleep. My mind, suddenly freed from long anxiety, went bounding forward. The world was opening before me like a new and fascinating book to be read and pondered.

Not far from the barn, the Mura was still rolling tree trunks downstream, and maybe animal carcasses as well. I tried to imagine what it would have been like if we had tried to cross under cover of darkness. Milenko had been right about that. We probably would have died in the attempt.

My thoughts turned to the vast building project for the new Tower of Babel. What did it all mean? Was it really a tower, a palace of crystal — the most fabulous enterprise that humanity had ever embarked upon — or was it all an illusion? What was the meaning of that Titanic enterprise? Was it the kingdom of lies and cruelty or the hope of mankind?

In the name of the Master Design, so many thousands had been walled up in its foundations, so many great minds, artists, scientists, and philosophers among them. These were men who could have contributed to the advent of a more just, fraternal society. Instead, the Master Design behaved like an ogre, devouring its own children as if its people were a never-ending source of life, as if the dead of the war had not satisfied its hunger and it wanted still greater destruction. Yet the Master Design had absolved itself of all those crimes and transformed them into just punishment. What had really changed? In the factories and in the mines the workers still toiled, helpless and smiling timidly when, in fiery speeches, they were promised control of their fate. How could they rise up against themselves?

Yet I could find no capacity in myself for hatred, as usual. The oppressed and the oppressors, the victims and their executioners seemed to me to be part of the same tragic mechanism, which would crush and mangle them all eventually, the former immediately and irrevocably, the latter more slowly but just as inescapably.

Sometime later in the night I awoke. Around me, nothing had moved. The night was as calm as ever. In the stable below,

I could hear the cows still chewing their cuds. Milenko was sleeping. The brilliance of the firmament overhead promised another golden summer day. But the constellations had shifted in their movement around the invisible axis of the starry vault above — only the North Star was still on course.

I had just been born into a new life. Strangely, I was not worried about our new status as vagabonds or pilgrims. I felt sure that our mysterious star would guide us towards the intangible sanctuary of freedom. I fell asleep, at peace at last.